# tell me no lies

Also by Adele Griffin

*Where I Want to Be*
*Picture the Dead*
*Tighter*
*The Unfinished Life of Addison Stone*
*Be True to Me*

# ADELE GRIFFIN

ALGONQUIN 2018

Published by Algonquin Young Readers
an imprint of Algonquin Books of Chapel Hill
Post Office Box 2225
Chapel Hill, North Carolina 27515-2225

a division of Workman Publishing
225 Varick Street
New York, New York 10014

Library of Congress Cataloging-in-Publication Data
Names: Griffin, Adele, author.
Title: Tell me no lies / Adele Griffin.
Description: First edition. | Chapel Hill, North Carolina : Algonquin
Young Readers, 2018. | Summary: In 1980s Philadelphia, Lizzy,
a studious high school senior, befriends a new girl in her class and is
introduced to a life of clubs, street life and art scene, and a new life
filled with doubts and deceptions.
Identifiers: LCCN 2017055474 | ISBN 9781616206765
(hardcover : alk. paper)
Subjects: | CYAC: Friendship—Fiction. | Philadelphia (Pa.)—History—
20th century—Fiction.
Classification: LCC PZ7.G881325 Te 2018 | DDC [Fic]—dc23
LC record available at https://lccn.loc.gov/2017055474

10 9 8 7 6 5 4 3 2 1
First Edition

*For Erich*

# tell me no lies

# my first one

I'M SHORT, SO I'M standing in the front row of chorus class.

We're all singing "Cupid" by Sam Cooke.

*"Nobody but meeee,"* I sing, and then my left eye sputters into darkness.

I look down at my Top-Siders, blink blink blink.

The eye flicks back and forth like a burned-out strobe.

Now there's a tingling in my fingers and the back of my skull, a rush of heat.

"Something's wrong," I say. "Help." But I'm quiet. I don't want to be the one to ruin the one fun number in our eighth-grade program of corny folk songs and creaky lullabies.

My right eye blacks out next. I'm blind, my brain floods with panic as my bones bend, my feet give out, I slip and fall backward to the floor. My head slamming against the bottom riser, hot pain cresting up in waves.

"Lizzy! Lizzy Swift is choking!"

Lizzy *Swift*, so as not to confuse me with Lizzy *DeBatista*, who's a foot taller than me and standing in the back, troublemakers' row.

Girls are shrieking and repeating my name, "Lizzy, Lizzy, Lizzy! Lizzy, talk to us! Is this some kind of a game?"

Wendy Palmer's voice cuts in lower, amused. *Oh my God, she's spazzing out.*

My friends are with me—Mimi's hand is on my twitching shoulder, while Gage comes at me sidelong. "Lizzy, stop!" she hisses. "Why are you being so weird? Everyone's looking!" But I'm drowning, I'm a plane plummeting to Earth, I'm lost to the sheer horror that this is how I die.

Another planet away, the piano stops.

"Get back, get back. Give her room, girls!" Then Mr. Hock tells Mimi to run to the nurse's office as he rolls me on my side and unbuttons the top button of my collar.

"Lizzy, I know you're scared," he says. "You're having a seizure, and it'll pass, I promise, it will pass and you'll be fine." Later on in the week he'd tell me about his college roommate, who also had epilepsy. But now it's this morning, and I barely know that word.

*She doesn't look fine.*

*Shut* up, *Wendy.*

The billowing panic that I'm not fine.

And then I black out.

My mom's in the infirmary when I come to. I'm crying and she's nothing but a comfort—but this gets wrapped up in the awfulness of that day, when I learned the words *grand mal*, and began to fear the possibility of another one.

I know girls still whisper about it. How crazy I looked. How freaky I seemed. The word *spaz* is a permanent haze around me, especially in those moments when Wendy catches my eye. I've heard she does a dead-on imitation of my seizure, though I've never caught her outright.

Gage and Mimi promised it was hardly anything, but best friends are supposed to lie. As it is, I'm on guard forever. Imagining the next time, dreading it, trying not to think about it. Failing.

part one
fall

# one

THE NEW GIRL ARRIVED at Argyll on the Tuesday after Columbus Day weekend, a month late for the start of school. Not that anyone was expecting her, late or ever. I'd slumped into the art room after lunch, my brain burned out on physics and history but reorienting for the one subject where I could lose myself.

We all saw her right away, an elegant stork over by the stereo system, painting her nails with a bottle of Wite-Out.

*Who's that?* I mouthed to Gage and Mimi, who shrugged in sync.

*But seriously, who was that?* None of us knew. Could you be a new girl *and* a senior? The two facts scraped against each other.

She had on a navy school kilt, too new and baggy on her hips—upper schoolers wore our kilts short, faded, and (if you looked close) doodled on with Sharpie pen. But the rest of her style was a middle finger to the uniforms section of the Argyll handbook, from the pair of men's boxer shorts that drooped below her hemline to her conspicuously wrinkled, untucked button-down to her beat-up pink espadrilles that she wore with heels crushed like bedroom slippers.

We shuffled around her, retrieving our projects from the flat files, watching as she jiggered a cassette tape with one hand while blowing the nails of the other. She held herself in that alert, pose-y way of someone used to compliments. I couldn't see her face full-on, but her hair was black and glossy as a doll's. Tendrils fell soft to brush the pale nape of her neck.

What was her story?

AP Art was taught Tuesdays and Thursdays by the Custis-Browns, our husband-and-wife art teachers. The rumor was that lurid nudie pictures of her by him hung in galleries in Philadelphia—Maggie Farthington had sworn she'd seen one last fall, and it was a complete and total gross-out. But at least it wasn't *him* naked, we all agreed, with his woolly beard and woodchuck's overbite.

For the first few minutes of class, Mrs. Custis-Brown made long-distance calls in her office. She'd fling herself into the main room eventually.

Once the new girl had snapped in her cassette, she slid nearer to one of the long metal tables where Mimi, Gage, and I had spread out. My quick, shy glance proved my hunch that she was pretty, with dark eyes and delicate bones. She moved in a sort of purposeful trance, her fingers trailing the edges of easels and shelves.

Last week, Mimi, Gage, and I had chosen our "concentration" to submit for AP portfolio credit. We'd had the summer to think about it. Mimi, who liked designs, had decided to focus on "Patterns." Gage, the maverick, had gone with "Water." I'd picked "Hands," which had seemed like a clever challenge—or at least, Mrs. Custis-Brown had been pleased.

"Hands are technical, but expressive," she told me. "I think you could do something interesting there."

So far, I hadn't.

The new girl dropped at our table, resting her chin on its surface, her heavy-lidded gaze fixed on nothing, clicking her jaw and singing lyrics she knew by heart. The song was in French— an old man's pervert voice, sometimes joined by a whispery girl-woman. It sounded nothing like what we loved, the British techno bands fronted by guys who sounded like they'd drive Vespas, make out with you in nightclubs, and know all the slang words for drugs.

Mimi plunged in. "Are you new?" she asked. "Are you a senior? Are you in AP Art?"

Without lifting her chin, the girl nodded a yes that answered all the questions.

"Mrs. C-B will be out soon. Or I can go get her." I sounded too helpful, which girls said about me. Teacher's pet. Kiss-up. But it just came naturally, like preferring mint chip or being a good babysitter.

"No, thanks."

"I don't mind."

"No." The girl lifted her head, then raised herself higher, arcing her back and stretching her arms. As she glanced at me, I stared. Popcorn-pale skin dusted in freckles. A beaky nose balanced by her wide, kohl-smudged eyes. Knobby cheekbones, lips on the thin side. She had looks people got in arguments about, where some called her beautiful and others said no, too racehorse, too freakish, too harsh—a haunted face that was closed to me, to everyone, and yet I couldn't shrug off the sense that any moment she might cry.

"I can get you some sketch paper," I said, "while you wait?"

"Lizzy . . ." Mimi didn't like when I got too eager-beaver.

But the girl just shrugged. "Sure."

I jumped to tear a piece of butcher paper from a roll on the other side of the room, then slid it in front of her like a waitress providing a place mat.

With a suggestion of thanks in her nod, the girl took a pencil from the coffee can of chalks and pencils I set down. She pulled a mirrored compact from her sling bag, opened it, propped her chin in her hand, and began to draw herself.

Right away, the sketch captured an enhanced, Hollywood version of her, with a pouty mouth and swooping eyelashes. It was almost comic—if she'd been a friend of ours, we'd have laid right in:

*Hey, in love with yourself much?*

*Oh, I didn't know you were secretly Isabella Rossellini!*

Mimi, Gage, and I were now trading so many disbelieving looks around the table that we couldn't even concentrate on our own work.

When Mrs. Custis-Brown finally appeared, I could tell she didn't think much of the sketch, either.

"A portrait!" she said, and nothing else. "Are you Claire? Claire Reynolds?"

"That's me." *Claire Reynolds.* As she stood, we all buttoned her into her name.

A normal name. Almost plain, but pretty.

Claire made a sophisticated contrast to Mrs. Custis-Brown, who—in her bright, shapeless smocks and clogs—looked like someone who worked at a Swedish day care. But Mrs. Custis-Brown was smiling, her blue eyes crinkling. More delighted by Claire's artsy style than with her actual art.

"Great! I've just read your transcript. Welcome to Advanced Placement Art. I teach the first semester and my husband takes over in January."

Claire was half listening, the way you hear a stewardess do the safety talk.

"I don't know if the girls filled you in that we submit AP portfolios come spring?" Mrs. Custis-Brown chirped on. "The panel judges between twelve and fifteen pieces on breadth, quality, and concentration. Technically it's called a 'sustained investigation,' but that sounds so detective show, right? You don't have to decide—" Mrs. Custis-Brown broke off, startled by the music, the woman's voice saturating the room with gasps and animal breathing.

"My mixtape," said Claire.

"Okay!" said Mrs. Custis-Brown. "I'm not familiar! And I'm from New York, originally—but we never get in to see the new acts anymore."

"But this song is old," said Claire. "I'd have thought by now Serge Gainsbourg's got zero shock value."

"Oh, *Gainsbourg*!" Mrs. Custis-Brown batted a hand. "It's been so long since I heard him. Fine by me. It's everybody's art room." She threw out a nervous laugh.

Under the table, Mimi pushed her leg against mine. Gage rolled in her lips. I looked down—to start laughing would be to make the worst noise possible.

"And I already know my art concentration," Claire said.

"Oh? Wonderful! What is it?"

"Myself."

"Okay, right on!"

The song had melted into liquid sighs and squeals.

Gage was visibly shaking, in the throes of a silent laugh-attack.

"The art room is also open after school, and you'll want those extra hours," Mrs. Custis-Brown continued loudly over the sex music. "As for someone taking you through the nuts and bolts of where we keep art supplies, I nominate Lizzy Swift." She looked at me, knowing I'd be happy to.

"Sure," I managed to wheeze through a laugh-breath. "I'd be happy to."

With a nod, Mrs. Custis-Brown left us, her hands clasped behind her back as she moved to another table. We all exhaled relief.

"My parents play this repulsive guy," said someone at one of the other tables.

I sketched my right hand with my left, watching my fingers shape into a pile of kindling. Nerves clenched in hope that Claire would ask me for the art room tour.

Claire didn't ask me for anything.

# two

"What's the story with Claire Reynolds?" I asked my mom that afternoon on the drive home. Mom worked at Argyll in the alumnae relations office, and she was my ride whenever I couldn't bum from Mimi or Gage.

"Jane Sleighmaker is Claire's aunt, and she called in a favor to Barbara," said Mom. Barbara Birmingham was our school head-mistress. "Jane has given a *fortune* to the school over the years. So Barbara found Jane's niece a place."

"Mom, that's not an answer."

"I don't know *why* she's here." Mom waved off the intrigue. "My guess is that something bad happened. Death, divorce. Coming in new as a senior isn't anyone's first choice. Oh!" Her mind was already hurtling toward the usual afternoon obstacles. "Before we pick up Peter, we need to hit the Stop and Shop. Your brothers went through an *entire* family-sized bag of tortellini last night."

Between a full-time job and three kids—me, Peter, and Owen—Mom was always running late for something and worrying about something else at the same time. Once we got to the Stop & Shop, she was worrying that we were late to pick up my brother Peter from the orthodontist. And by the time we retrieved Peter, late, she was worrying that she and Dad both had forgotten to take out chicken parts this morning to defrost for dinner.

She was done with the mystery of Jane Sleighmaker's niece, but her "something bad" stuck in my head.

Except for Tuesday and Thursday art, Claire wasn't in any of my classes, but Wednesday afternoon when I saw her in the hall, she'd layered her black bra with a white T-shirt, and had paired her ripped black tights with biker boots. The only evidence of a school uniform was the kilt. It was a frankly impressive amount of rule breaking.

When I started waving, she raised a hand, but maybe just to get me to stop.

She was alone again the next day, when I saw her in the library lounge after school, reading *Paris Match* magazine. I hadn't changed from my dorky modern dance sweatshirt and jazz pants—not a "real" sport by Argyll standards, but the only option for nonjocks like me—so I hid a little deeper behind the potted plastic fern as I watched her. Claire had the air of a popular girl, and I wondered why she hadn't jumped right in with Maggie and Wendy and other Nectarines—Gage's name for the "It" girls, based on their collective obsession with frying their skin to radioactive-bright "tans" over at the Bronze Age tanning salon at the mall.

"What do you think of the new girl?" I asked Gage and Mimi on Friday at lunch.

"She dresses like a punk," said Mimi. "She's got on these storm trooper boots today. And she's always slightly condescending in my French class. She thinks she's smarter than she is, but French is her only honors class besides art."

"I dunno." Gage shrugged. "She plays field hockey like a guy. She swears on the field, too. Boarding school manners, but it keeps everyone on their toes."

"Speaking of sports, do either of you want to stop by Lincoln?" I asked. "I'll go if anyone's up for it." We were out early today, because it was Lincoln Academy's homecoming weekend. Most seniors had cut out already to watch the football.

Mimi sighed. "I wish. Dr. Rodriguez's first big calc test is Monday. I need to start studying for that, like, right now."

"Count me out, too, but on the grounds of No Interest." Gage looked annoyed. "Once I graduate, I refuse to waste another precious second of my life running up and down some stupid field—or watching anyone else do it."

"Watching the game isn't really the point," I said.

Gage frowned. "Come hang out at my house if you're itchy."

I'd been over at the Hornblows' last weekend. Videos and pizza. Television and ice cream.

"I just mean for a change. I just mean"—I took a breath and went for it—"that you have a *jeep*, Gage." She'd gotten a brand-new red Cherokee for her birthday this past June, which she used almost exclusively to pick up pizza or to ferry her little sister, Helena, to tuba practice. "We could pile in it right now and drive by Lincoln. People were saying Matt Ashley's parents are out of town and he's having a party. Maybe we could stop by later tonight?"

"*Nooo!*" Mimi was laughing as she put her hands to her ears. "Even imagining that is so embarrassing. Just showing up at Matt Ashley's house! I'd die before I'd let him see me out on his doorstep, asking if I can come in and party! I'd just die!"

"Who's *people* anyway?" Unlike Mimi, who was always crisp and smooth in her headbands and button earrings, Gage could look a little untamed, ink stains on her fingers and dried food clinging to her sweater, but she carried herself with an athlete's ease. "I'm the friend who can open all the jars," she liked to joke, but when she wanted to intimidate me, she could. Now she folded her arms and squared me off in her stare. "Who was talking about Matt Ashley's party? Nectarines?"

"Yes, in the senior lounge." I turned to Mimi. "And Matt wouldn't have forgotten me. He'd let us in."

Mimi shook her head. "I'm really sorry, Lizzy, but Noah and I have a phone date later tonight." Noah was Mimi's longtime boyfriend, a freshman at Bowdoin.

"And I need to be up early for fencing tomorrow," added Gage. "The tournament's in Trenton." Fencing was Gage's weekend passion, though she acted like she needed it for her college transcript—as if three varsity sports weren't enough.

"Even if we skip the party, homecoming is not an insane suggestion." My face was hot. I wasn't used to sticking up for my point.

Mimi flicked her fingers. "Okay, okay, then go do what you want, Lizzy Swift. You don't have to drag us into it." But she knew this wasn't true. Without a car, I did have to drag them into it.

Senior year was the summit of my Argyll journey that had started as a kindergartner in the main campus colonial house: *"once a historic inn where General Washington himself had stayed!"* according to our school brochure. As I graduated to middle and upper school, my glimpses of senior life—their mysterious snack pit, their VIP corner of the parking lot, their exclusive senior lounge with its saggy couch and bunny-ears television—just made me more hungry for it.

Seniors got everything. There was no bigger prize than the last year of Argyll.

But now here I was, a senior, and all I felt was tricked. In a yearbook meeting yesterday, while I was choosing photos for a spread called "The Year in Moments," I actually felt kind of sick about it. Why hadn't I ever gone to a Pumpkin Patch mixer or Winter Sugarplum? Why hadn't I shown up for the Valentine's Dance with DJ Howard? Why hadn't I stuck around for a single Spirit Day rally?

Of course, Mimi, Gage, and I always had our shy excuses for not going. Somebody was either babysitting, or had a cold, or needed to cram. When the reality was that Mimi Kim, Gage Hornblow, and I were the class grinds, the brains, the eggheads. We made the honor roll, sang in chorus, went to bed early for Saturday matches, and used any extra hours in the art studio. We weren't the giddy girls who jumped around to "Rock Lobster" unless it was with each other, up in Mimi's room with her light-up mirror set to "evening." We'd never paint our faces the blue and gold school colors. We never felt free enough to cruise Lincoln Academy's homecoming, hooting at guys while waving blue-raspberry Slurpees.

It had been years since that fall freshman mixer at Lincoln, when I'd slow-danced to "Forever Young" with Matt Ashley. I couldn't even hear that song without remembering Matt's hunter-green wool sweater rough against my cheek.

After the dance, he'd kissed me good-bye—in the dark, on the mouth, with a relaxed confidence, a molten memory that burned me up every time I replayed it. But he'd never used the scrap paper he'd stuck in his pocket after scrawling my phone number while we'd stood shivering outside the school, waiting for parent pickups.

*Would it be* strange to arrive at Matt's party? I knew so much about him already, from all he'd told me that night. Like where he lived and that he was one of four Ashley kids, with a married older sister and another, younger sister, plus a brother in elementary school. I imagined myself at the Ashleys' front door, politely invited in by the older sister even though Matt had said she lived in Boston. Of course parties weren't tame like that, but my palms went clammy to imagine the wild reality of Matt's bash, starring a bunch of rowdy Lincoln guys getting wasted with Nectarines.

I often wished Argyll were coed. Mimi, Gage, and I were more of a clump than a clique, but if we'd had some boys in the mix, then Lincoln guys probably wouldn't seem so scary. We'd given up on their dances after that first one, too, where the girls had hunkered all night by the snack table munching graham crackers. My second chance with Matt Ashley wasn't any incentive for them to return.

While I waited in line to dump my lunch tray, my head was noisy, trying to persuade Mimi and Gage all over again.

And then I went numb. Pins and needles in my fingers that quickly sparked up my arms and down my spine. I could feel the seconds unwind in slow motion as I fell, my tray and plate clattering to the floor, my leftover chili con carne landing in a splat like warm vomit beside me. I was pitching and jerking, a fish on a line, as the Nectarine table flash-focused its attention on me.

Blink blink blink.

No. Nothing had happened.

Only the terror of it.

Slowly and with care, I used my knife to scrape my leftover food and I dropped my utensils into the large metal tub, my hands shaking.

A hard slap, a bucket of ice water.

I had close friends. I was a straight-A student. My early-action application to Princeton, halfway complete and due in two weeks, was spread out on my desk at home, ready for another round of thought and care.

It was just a dumb homecoming game. I'd probably hate to be there anyway.

I walked back to the table. I knew Gage and Mimi felt slightly uneasy with how I'd reminded them what so many other seniors were doing today. I could sense it by the way they gathered up their trays and murmured about being busy.

"Call me if you change your mind about tonight—I'll come get you," said Gage as they left.

"Okay, thanks." I was shamefaced by her easy kindness.

It was only afterward, walking the glassed-in hallway with its view of the nearly empty student parking lot, that everything resparked.

It was Friday! Homecoming weekend! Senior year! I wasn't crazy to want to be part of it. Was I? I wasn't!

Mom worked till six. There was nothing to do for the rest of this afternoon but head to the Arts Center and draw my right hand until my left hand ached.

On the way, I stopped in the bathroom, and there she was. Claire Reynolds. Staring at herself in the mirror with tears in her eyes.

# three

"It's fine." Claire's gaze was hard on me. "The best trick to stop crying is to watch yourself cry. Right?"

I was nodding, like *Obviously*, though I'd never done this.

Claire now used her thumb pads to wipe away the wavy gray traces beneath her eyes. She yanked out her elastic and I itched for a sketchbook to capture the moment, the fall of her hair, the tilt of her chin, the plant of her boots. Instead I went to a stall to pee and when I came out, Claire was holding a stick of dark eyeliner between her teeth like a cigarette, with the pointy end in her mouth.

"What are you doing?" I asked as I went to wash my hands.

She waited a few seconds before she removed it. "Heating it up. It goes on smoother if it's warm." Then she leaned into the mirror and black-bordered one entire eye. She liked me watching, so I kept watching. It looked edgy and dangerous but not fake. She used her finger to resmudge. Then she moved to the next eye.

"Stay away from me, right?" she said when she was done. "I'm trouble."

My heart leaped—but no, she was joking, just delivering a line like an actress. I'd been watching her too long. I dried my hands. "Fair enough."

"Want me to do your eyes? I'm not uptight about germs."

"Oh." When I turned, she stepped close, wielding the eye pencil. I could smell fruity gum on her breath. I nodded permission.

"You're so short." She leaned over me as her fingers *Clockwork Orange*d my eyes apart to apply the liner. "What's the deal with this boy haircut?"

My heels lifted; I was five feet two and not quite okay about it. "It's longer than my brothers' hair."

"Ah, so you all go to the barbershop together?"

Yes, actually. Mr. Al on North Wayne Avenue. We were a package deal: me and Peter at full price and Owen's haircut for half. It had made sense for years, but now with my face offered up for Claire's makeover, it sort of didn't. "I like my hair."

"I don't. Grow out the top." She laughed. "You're like a surfer dude with boobs."

It was a mean laugh, and a mean thing to say, and I knew from that moment, and that comment, that Claire Reynolds could hurt me too easy. It should have been a warning. I could never argue I wasn't warned.

Claire took me by the shoulders and turned me to the mirror. "Face the strange. I think we found the real you."

"Oh!" My eyes, a standard-issue maple brown that matched my hair, were now bracketed in kohl. I looked older—knowing and jaded by things that hadn't yet happened to me. Could makeup really do that?

The mirror and I both knew my milestones. Braces. One dead grandparent. Two dead hamsters. Epilepsy. Not much had happened to me at all.

In fairy tales, mirror images sometimes speak and tell your fortune.

The girl who stared into my eyes seemed to be someone from my future. I saw things in her that I didn't know about myself.

"Do I really look that different, or do I just think I do?"

"Aw, that's cute." Claire laughed again, but this time not unkindly. "You look good. Let's go somewhere."

# four

Cars at Argyll were divided into three groups: new, not bad, and crap. Half the girls in the senior class had been given brand-new cars last year along with their driver's licenses. Favorite models: Jeep Cherokees, Volkswagen Cabriolets, BMW convertibles. Favorite colors: red, black, or white.

Not-bad cars, likely parent pass-downs, were secondhand gray or navy Volvos or Saab station wagons, with the occasional Mercedes nudging in. "It's not bad," a girl might say. "It's not what I wanted, but it's not bad."

Crap was the third- and fourth-hand Toyotas, Buicks, and Caddies bought from uncles or dealerships, with dings and broken cigarette lighters and patch jobs and stains and rust. But crap was a step up from nothing, crap would be mine if Mom ever got a new car and I inherited her six-year-old Corolla.

Claire drove something totally different: a circus-orange VW Beetle, tucked in the lower school faculty parking lot. However she came to drive this car—as a pass-down or lender—it seemed like a decision she'd made about herself, another way she seemed older than the rest of us. I decided not to tell her she wasn't allowed to park here, or that she appeared too tall for this car, the way she had to scoop her spine and fold her legs into the shape of it.

I'd never been in a Beetle myself, and while I was sized better for it, buzzing down Conestoga Avenue in a car this small felt surprisingly dangerous—the herky-jerky manual gearshift, the putt-putt engine, the fact that we were six inches from the road below. I had to fight a nerdish impulse to put on my seat belt as my feet nudged for room in the messy heap of cassette tapes and plastic cases.

Meantime, Claire rummaged intently in the cassette-packed glove compartment. She relaxed only after she got the first track going.

The sound was dark, slow punk.

"The lead singer of this group is dead," she said. "Ian Curtis. He hanged himself."

"Oh."

"Joy Division. Do you know them?"

I wanted to lie so badly. "No."

"They're New Order now."

"Well, duh. I've heard of *them*."

"He was only twenty-three. Just a kid."

"Twenty-three seems kind of old to me," I said. "He was an adult, actually."

Claire looked troubled, like I'd come to an unexpected

conclusion about Ian Curtis, though it seemed obvious to me. "Well, just think of all that music we'll never have, because he's not around anymore," she said.

At the next light, Claire turned onto Lancaster Avenue. "My aunt Jane told me this funny thing the other day. If you follow Lancaster all the way to the end and then you make a right, it takes you smack into West Philly. Aunt Jane said it used to be called Lancaster Road, and it's the oldest long-distance paved road in the United States. I've been meaning to try it."

"No no no no. You don't want to do that," I said. "I'm positive your aunt didn't mean you should actually drive it. Lancaster Avenue gets totally sketchy after Overbrook." We were coming into Haverford. The next light would take us to Lincoln Academy. "Hey—let's cruise by Lincoln and see the football game? It's homecoming today, I don't know if you knew—you turn here."

"We're taking this all the way down the Line."

"You mean drive into Philadelphia—*now*?"

"Sure."

"Why?"

"Give me one good reason why not."

I didn't have an answer. I'd figured when Claire said "Let's go somewhere," she meant somewhere normal. Lincoln. Friendly's. The King of Prussia Mall. I hardly ever went into Philadelphia unless it was for a school trip or to spend a birthday dinner with my parents.

"Theoretically, I'm cool to go into Philly," I said. "But."

"*But?*" We'd stopped at the red.

"But I'm wearing my school uniform."

"Um, so am I? More important, I'm craving sushi. I hear

there's a place on Chestnut Street. There's no good sushi around here, haven't you noticed?"

I'd never even tried sushi, barely could picture it. "My mom will have a cow if I'm home late."

"I've got a quarter. Call her when we get there. You can tell her you're at my house doing homework." She cruised straight through the green. "And I'll have you home by six thirty. Does that work?"

"I guess."

We were zipping into Ardmore. Claire was singing along with the song.

I settled back in my seat and held my breath to slow my speeding heart. There was really nothing else I could do. I was along for the ride. I was along for the ride! Even if it felt like we were entering a stranger's house by the back window. Joy Division was a grim soundtrack to my smoking nerves. The bass line vibrated under my feet as if the songs were seeping into me.

After a few minutes, Lancaster Avenue had narrowed by half. But in the golden autumn afternoon, the dive bars, barred windows, and blighted stretches of row houses didn't match the dangerous ghetto I'd always heard about. What I saw was plain old depressing. I used my elbow to lock my door anyway—Claire gave a snort when she heard the sound. "You need to get out more."

Ten minutes later, Lancaster ended in a right-hand turn onto 34th Street.

"Holy moly, we're at *Drexel*?" I sat up. "It's like this road is a portal into the middle of the city."

"Holy moly," said Claire, wryly emphasizing each syllable.

But seriously! We'd swung in with the traffic, the Beetle

weaving in and out like a clown car among the cabs and buses. We putted past churches and storefronts and glass-windowed office towers, hugging the middle of 34th as it intersected Walnut Street and then Sanson Street before we turned onto Chestnut.

"It's like a magic trick."

"You're a nerd, right?" Claire quirked an eyebrow. "Confess."

My cheeks heated. "No. Not even at all, really."

"It's fine," said Claire. "I'm done with fake people. Nerds are for real. Authentic."

I didn't like being called a nerd, especially an authentic nerd—but I didn't know how to deny it more forcefully, or if I even had the right.

"I skipped third grade," I told her. "I'm the youngest in the class. I won't be seventeen until July."

"You baby! I was eighteen this past June, I'm over a year older than you."

"But I have the second-highest average in the class, after Gage."

"You're such a nerd to say that. A nerd baby. Okay, Hinata," she said. "Watch for signs. We can park on the street." She cranked down her window. "I'm so in the mood."

"Same!" I didn't know what Claire's mood was, and did it even matter? In my whole history of dipping into Philly for chaperoned class trips or dressed-up family outings, it had never even remotely belonged to me. Now, in a single car ride, a new idea of the city had jiggered loose. Suddenly all I wanted was to stuff this afternoon with as many sights and sounds and tastes as could fit. I was up for anything.

I tried and failed not to bounce a little in my seat.

# five

THERE WAS A PAY phone up front at Hinata.

"*Who?*" asked Peter.

"The new girl. Mom will know. Claire Reynolds." I held my breath against the bleat of a fire truck. "We're doing homework at her house, will you tell her?"

"Yeah . . ." My brother was already hanging up.

Back at our booth in the empty restaurant, Claire had ordered for us, and the waiter returned to set down a pot of green tea along with two mugs.

Claire poured. She didn't ask for sugar, so I didn't. The tea was too hot and tasted like grass, but Claire cupped it under her chin and sipped like it was the best thing she'd had in days.

"I knew this guy at Strickland," she said, her eyes gleaming through the steam, "and one weekend last fall, we left campus and came down here. We saw South Street, mostly. And Old

City." Something about the way she spoke—too casually, throwing down her words like she was playing cards as her body held so still—alerted me that something was up. The way you just *know* things about people with hardly any evidence other than a bone-deep hunch that "this guy" was somehow important.

"Are you still going out?"

"We never went out, we just hung out for a while."

"What was your old school like?"

"Strickland? Eh, all those days blend together into oatmeal."

"The guy, too?"

She hesitated. "No. Not the guy. Jay was very French. As in he could speak French fluently, not the lame way you learn it at school. His dad worked for the UN, and his mom was from Toulouse, so Jay was really into arts and culture. A progressive, he liked to call himself."

That sounded slightly snotty, which also reminded me of French people. "Why'd you two break up?"

"I told you, it wasn't like that. He was—he turned out to be . . ." Claire frowned into her teacup. "It's better for me to remember the good stuff." When she glanced at me, her face was unguarded in pain. "Do you have anyone you think about? Someone your mind can't get rid of?"

I tried to look wistful. "I guess maybe that's a story for another day." In the heartbreak department, I had only Matt Ashley, and he was no story at all.

She nodded, and I wished I could give Claire something realer.

The waiter appeared and set down a wooden serving board that startled me almost as much as the gaudy, candy-colored objects arranged on top of it.

"I thought you said it was fish."

"Haven't you ever seen sushi?"

I shrugged, like maybe I just didn't recall. Each piece of food looked like some weird sculpture for an arty dollhouse.

"Okay. Sushi lesson. Watch me."

She unwrapped her chopsticks, split them, and rubbed them together as if to start a tiny fire. She used one chopstick to daub at a bamboo-green lump on the edge of the board, delivering the dollop to a saucer, adding a splash of soy sauce, and mixing it to a paste.

"What is that?"

"Wasabi. It's like a horseradish-y mustard, for kick. Now pick up your chopsticks and think of it this way. Rest a pencil on your ring finger, hold a pencil on top." She snapped the chopsticks as if to bite my nose, then swooped and pinched something off the board that looked like a piece of chewed Wrigley's. "Eel," she said, and popped it neatly in her mouth.

After a couple of minutes of trying to work my own chopsticks, I gave up. Why had I always reached for a fork at Mimi's house whenever we ate kimchi?

In the end, I used my fork and knife to cut up a black-bordered rice wheel that was center-packed with green and pink slivers of crabstick and avocado.

"You don't like it."

"It's bland."

"California rolls are beginner's sushi. That's why I ordered one for you."

I took another stab with my chopsticks, accidentally sending an entire disk Frisbee-ing across the room.

Claire winced. "Oh my God. I don't even want to know you right now."

"Hang on, I'll get it." I stood.

She held up a palm. "Don't."

I sat. I could see the California roll under a far table. Introduction to Claire Reynolds was a class I was flunking in spite of my very best efforts. Claire would never be friends with me after this afternoon. No doubt she regretted doing my eye makeup and letting me be her hop-along. A crawling, prickling behind my eyes startled me. Now I was shaking. Now I was shaking too hard. Was it happening?

"Try the eel." Claire pointed.

No. I hadn't been shaking. I took a breath. When I picked up my fork, she frowned, so I put it down.

"So, are you an Argyll lifer?"

I nodded. "Since kindergarten."

"Aunt Jane was a lifer. She's all rah-rah Argyll, but honestly I don't see why."

"It's pretty small potatoes compared with boarding school." I decided to brave it. "Why aren't you graduating from Strickland? Why are you here at all?"

Claire was quick with her answer. "My dad lost his money in the crash last year, and he couldn't pay alimony anymore. He and my stepmom moved to Florida, and I had to leave school, so Mom and I came here to live with her sister, my aunt Jane. She's a crazy cat lady, but we were out of options."

"Oh." My mom had been right—*something bad happened*. In a hazy way, I knew about that stock market crash, but it hadn't affected us. My dad was the senior accountant for Lupini's Valves,

Pipes & Fittings. Everyone needed plumbing, no matter what happened on Wall Street.

"Your aunt wouldn't even pay for your last year at Strickland?"

Claire looked evasive. "No, just Argyll."

"That seems unfair."

"It is, it really is! Aunt Jane lives for those horrible cats!" Claire spoke in a burst, as if she'd been waiting to commiserate with someone. "There's sixteen of them, and there's no place they aren't allowed and the fridge is crammed with opened tins of liver-flavored cat food, so the kitchen is, like, disgusting. I do takeout whenever I can—canned soup if I'm desperate." She speared another piece of sushi. "It's been weeks since I had anything decent."

"Sixteen cats?" My nose scrunched. "That's fifteen too many."

"Right!" Claire laughed. "Exactly!"

She told me the cats had the run of the house and could do anything they wanted, plundering like pirates, knocking over vases, scratching curtains and portraits, sleeping anywhere. Picturing those cats was so creepily enthralling that the waiter's interruption with the check startled me.

"Nineteen dollars and fifty-six cents," I said, glancing oh-so-casually at the bill. "But we each put in eleven, that covers the tip." Whew, since I had only fourteen dollars.

"I forgot to hit an ATM." Claire frowned out the window. "Who even knows where the nearest bank machine might be. Dammit."

"It's okay, I have a card." Strictly for emergencies—I couldn't even remember the last time I'd used my Mastercard, so fresh that its raised numbers resisted from the imprint they'd worn onto my wallet's plastic insert when I tugged the card free.

"Next time, it's on me," she said. "And I'm not just saying that."

The rosy idea of a *next time* buried my worry about using the card. I tipped twenty percent and signed with a flourish.

Outside, the low sun cast long shadows onto the street. "It's not even five," said Claire. "When Jay and I came here, we planned to go to the Mütter Museum, but we never did." She looked at me. "You're cold."

"Not really."

"Here. I'm in two layers." In one fluid motion, she'd shrugged off her army jacket, and then her cardigan, which she tossed to me. It instantly shot to the front of the line as the nicest thing I'd ever worn.

"Thanks."

"You can keep it. Want to go?" As she slid back into her jacket.

It wasn't really a question. We jumped in the car and found a parking place on the street, just a few blocks down from the museum. As we walked over, I kept stealing glances at Claire. She moved—chin up, shoulders back—as if she knew she was being observed.

"Do you and Jay still talk?" I asked as we waited for the light to change. My finger traced up and down the black silk placket—did she really mean I could *keep* the cardigan forever?

"No. He graduated."

"What's he doing now? Is he dating anyone else?"

Claire turned on me. "You need to grow this out." She yanked at my bangs like she was crushing a dead leaf.

"Hey!"

"And then bleach some of it, maybe. That'd look cool. If you kept the rest short, it'd be a style, at least. Think about it."

"Um . . . okay." So Claire didn't want to discuss Jay. Her leggy stride left me winded as I struggled to keep pace. She looked quietly pleased when we wheeled up on a brick, colonnaded building enclosed by an iron gate.

"I never forget an address. And it's open."

Our student IDs let us in for free, and from the foyer we entered a grand room of Victorian portraits, garnet-red velvet carpet, and brass-railed stairs. In my history of school field trips—the Betsy Ross House, the Liberty Bell—I'd always moved in a herd. This felt like a special private viewing.

"Remind me, what is this museum about?"

"Medical curiosities from the College of Physicians."

"Medical *what*?"

"Like fetuses and organs. I think Einstein's brain is somewhere."

Claire veered off into one room, but I stayed where I was. This museum was awful, like we'd stumbled into someone's personal freak show, a depressing display of disfigurement. The glass-fronted cabinets showed me nothing but horrors: plaster casts of death masks, misshapen skulls, and wet ugly things in jars.

"I wish I could unsee all this," I told Claire when I found her on the second floor. She had stopped to stare at a life-sized plaster cast.

"Chang and Eng Bunker," she read off the placard. "The original Siamese twins—it says here they're actually from Thailand." She lifted her eyebrows. "Mrs. Birmingham told me each of us has to do a senior assembly. Mine's not till sometime in February. I could talk about this place, right?"

"You can talk about anything. Mine's in January, sometime after we get back to school." I hadn't decided what topic I'd pick—I hated even thinking about speaking in public. But I'd never choose anything as tragic as Chang and Eng Bunker. I felt unhappy just looking at their death cast, the chest-to-chest artery pipeline that forced them to spend their whole lives facing each other.

Claire walked to the car so fast, I struggled to keep up. Her head was down, her body hemmed in with private thoughts. She was still preoccupied as we drove down 22nd Street. "Which one of those twins had it worse, do you think?" she asked abruptly, like she'd just remembered I was in the car with her.

"Stuck together forever is an equal problem for both of them."

Claire shrugged. "Maybe one of them didn't mind the closeness as much."

I wondered if she wasn't thinking about Chang and Eng, but herself and Jay. Whatever was on her mind, Claire missed our next turn, burrowing us deep and then deeper into a residential neighborhood. "Okay, detour. We'll take Ben Franklin Parkway." I envied her easy grasp of the city, piecing it together, mapping it out.

But I was the one who saw the mural first. "Look at that!"

She slowed down and we stared. It covered the whole side of a building, a bold, bright dance scene of interlocking figures, and red and yellow and blue bodies on a clean white background. I felt like I was seeing two things at once, the fun and the dare of graffiti but also real art. Each body was composed with such perfect balance that it turned the whole wall into a perfect harmony of motion. I could feel the joy in it, too, and loved its splash, a blast of fun at the end of this tired old street.

"That's a Keith Haring," said Claire. "He does those murals all over. Last summer, some of my friends and I went to his Pop Shop down in SoHo. I bought a radiant baby button. I don't really know what Keith Haring looks like, but I swear he sold it to me himself. Little nerdy guy with glasses. That's how I like to tell the story anyway. I mean, wouldn't you?"

I didn't know who Keith Haring was, or what radiant baby meant, or what a Pop Shop was, and while I'd heard about SoHo, I'd never been there, either—New York for me was the sixth-grade class trip to the Statue of Liberty. The whole story seemed so glamorous, yet another glittering example of Claire Reynolds as someone who knew all things I didn't, and who had done all things I hadn't.

"Totally," I answered.

# six

"How was your study group?" Mom asked at family dinner that night.

I shot Peter a look, as in: *Thanks for taking down my message—NOT!*

"Peter said you were in a study group at the library?" Now it was Mom who shot Peter a look.

"I *told* Peter I was at Claire Reynolds's house." I felt indignant. Somehow Peter's carelessness with my message canceled out my lie.

Peter looked surly. "I thought you were at the *library* because you sounded weird and you were whispering."

"I was never at the library. I never said that."

"Then why were you whispering?"

"I wasn't!"

"The message pads aren't just decorative," Dad said mildly.

Peter reached for his glass of milk and took a swig to show he was finished talking with all of us about it.

"Claire's aunt, Jane Sleighmaker, lives at that enormous property off Merion Square Road, is that right?" asked Mom. "Laven—no, *Lilac* House."

"I didn't meet her. She's a crazy cat lady, according to Claire."

"She's been very reliable for Annual Giving. The house is supposed to be stunning, one of the great old properties. She used to host fund-raisers for Argyll. I did hear that she took her husband's death very hard."

I shrugged. It seemed like a betrayal to confirm anything.

"So is it enormous? More ridiculous than Gretchen Drinker's house?"

I nodded and hoped Mom would stop. Peter went to Radnor High, where Owen would go, too, after he finished at our local middle school in Wayne. But I'd learned to read at age three, could recite all the state capitals in pre-K, and as a result, my parents scraped to send me to a school that felt like a country club. We were always aware of Argyll's lofty connections, too, like my friend Gretchen Drinker, who'd transferred to Choate for high school, and whose family lived in a mansion complete with its original ballroom.

Meantime, I was stunned that my lie kept working so well. I couldn't think of the last time I'd told my parents I was doing one thing while I went off and did another; it was as if Claire Reynolds had put a spell on me. But I didn't call Mimi or Gage after dinner to give them the scoop about Philadelphia. I felt protective of my afternoon. It wasn't a thing to gossip about. I'd have to let it come up naturally.

I'd saved a matchbook from Hinata and a business card from the Mütter Museum. In my room, I arranged them in my sock drawer with last fall's U2 ticket stub and this past summer's James Taylor ticket stub—two of my favorite nights.

In one day, I'd doubled my secret brag display.

After homework, I took my sketchbook to the living room, switched on MTV, and tried not to care that homecoming parties, including Matt's, were happening from Paoli to Ardmore. Matt Ashley's best friends were Tommy Powers and Jonesy Sweet. Jonesy was dating Kristina Roe—"Kreo" to her Nectarine friends—and last spring, Matt, Jonesy, and Tommy had stopped by Argyll to watch Kreo's lacrosse game. When I'd caught sight of Matt in the upper school breezeway, dropping quarters into our soda machine, I felt ill: clammy palms, light-headed, the works.

*Go, walk up to him, say something.*

But I'd backed away. And spent this whole past summer regretting my decision.

I flipped a page of my sketchbook. Matt was probably hooking up with a Nectarine right now. Maybe they were in his room, listening to *Forever Young*.

My mind flipped through things Claire had told me earlier, details of her boarding school friends and stuff about Mr. Français, Jay. The afternoon already felt like a dream. Claire was probably somewhere fun tonight, too.

I ached with missing out. Why couldn't Mimi and Gage live a little?

Later Peter and Owen joined me on the couch, overruling my channel choice with an Indiana Jones marathon and plowing through bowls of cereal as if they hadn't just eaten dinner a couple of hours ago.

It was midnight before the boys went to bed. I switched back to MTV.

Martha Quinn was veejaying. Late-night videos were outdated, obscure, and mostly lame. Usually someone had filmed the band standing around playing their music and added in some random visual effects. But the music itself was good, and reminded me of Claire's taste. Martha kicked off the hour with Tom Tom Club's "Genius of Love." The video made it easy to watch, sketch my hand, watch some more. When the song changed, I wouldn't have known to look up if I hadn't heard the next band earlier that same day. But I instantly recognized the bass-heavy chords, and the proof was printed at the bottom of the screen: Joy Division, *She's Lost Control*/Factory Records.

Ian Curtis was singing in a close-up. My heart jolted. When I'd first heard his deadpan alto, I hadn't expected someone so boyish, so good-looking—in a choirboy way, the kind of guy who'd have made Mimi and me nudge elbows and raise eyebrows if we'd jostled past him in Suburban Square. Knowing Ian Curtis had killed himself made him seem otherworldly. There was a hypnotic quality to his glassy eyes, like he was an alien caught between one world and another.

And his dancing! His arms and legs moved so crazily, like a man trying to catch a train. Moves that seemed barely contained by his willpower, but also purely connected to his music. An alien—or a *spaz*, Wendy Palmer might call him—but he was in control of it, too.

By the time the video was over, my nose was nearly touching the TV set. I felt like the whole song was his attempt to explain a journey to a dark, familiar place where I'd also been, and when Joy Division was gone, replaced by the Psychedelic Furs, for a while I just sat there, listening to the pound of my heart, flooded with that awful memory of my first seizure, when I'd been an alien, too.

# seven

Gage called me Saturday—she'd won her fencing match at Trenton and she wanted to celebrate. She picked up Mimi and me in her jeep that night for a movie. The only one worth seeing was *Pumpkinhead*, which was so terrifying I kept my eyes closed through most of it while Mimi and Gage, on either side of me, pinched my arms in attempts to force me to watch.

"Lizzy, your screaming is scarier than the movie," teased Mimi as we raced back to the jeep. "And you hardly even cracked open your eyes for five minutes!"

"Are we hitting Chili's or Boston Chicken for dinner?" asked Gage. "Yeesh, I hate walking around in the dark! Pumpkinheads are everywhere!"

"I vote Boston Chicken," I said. "You guys, that movie was stupid. A murderous ghost with a pumpkin for a head? Give me a break!"

Gage laughed. "You can't give a review if you hardly even watched it! Maybe you should just stick to PG movies until your birthday."

"Hey, did you know Claire Reynolds is the new oldest?" I asked. Finally here was a semi-easy way to talk about her. "She's even older than Katie Fox. I didn't tell you guys, but the two of us went to Philadelphia yesterday."

"What? Claire? How? *Why*?" asked Mimi. She and Gage traded glances as I climbed into the back of the jeep.

"I don't know." I stayed nonchalant. "One minute we were in the art room, the next minute we were driving into town for sushi."

"Bizarre," said Mimi. "Claire Reynolds seems so standoffish. Did you get any scoop? I just figured she got kicked out of boarding school for drugs or something, and her family pulled some strings for Argyll."

"I think her mom needed a change." As much as I wanted Mimi and Gage to ask me about Claire, I also didn't want to betray Claire with the personal juicy details of her life.

"Her aunt lives in a mansion," said Gage. "I heard some girls on the team talking about it—how she used to have big parties there but now she's an old hermit."

"Ooh, maybe it's a cursed house like the demon in *Pumpkinhead*!" Mimi squealed. "Don't go in there, Lizzy. You'll never come out!" Then Mimi began telling Gage about how Noah and some of his Bowdoin friends were seeing a campus band later that night.

The dynamic never really changed. Gage and Mimi in front and in charge, me in the back, mostly listening. But tonight, it had shifted slightly.

At Boston Chicken, a den of plastic chairs and ugly fluorescent lights that bounced off the tabletop laminate, we ordered the usual—herb-roasted chicken, creamed spinach, buttered corn, and biscuits with honey butter.

Gage was staring at me. She blinked a long, deliberate blink.

"Happy Halloween to you, too, Lizzy."

"Sorry?"

"What's up with the eye makeup? You look like Elvira, Mistress of the Dark."

"Oh!" I laughed, feeling slightly stupid. "Yeah, I probably didn't do as good a job as Claire. She showed me how."

"I like it," said Mimi. "It's kind of dramatic, but yeah."

Gage shook her head. "My vote's no."

"Don't listen to Home Perm." This was Mimi's favorite tease, since the summer between ninth and tenth grade, Gage's short, wavy chestnut hair inexplicably had changed to frizzled ringlets.

"You keep using that term *home perm*. I do not think it means what you think it means," said Gage. But she looked upset. "Meems, it's been years. Let it die. I've never gotten a home perm in my life."

"One day you'll admit it. I know you." Mimi shifted her full attention to me. "Lizzy, do you still need a ride to the library tomorrow? I was planning to study there all day. If you stay over with me tonight, you can borrow some clothes, and we'll go in together."

"Yeah, thanks."

It was rare that Gage was on the outs, and I was in. As if to underscore her point, Mimi passed me the rest of her apple pie.

"Fair warning, the great returning Theo is home from Yale this weekend."

She meant it as a joke, but Mimi's older brother, Theo, *was* kind of heroic. As senior tennis captain, Theo had taken Lincoln all the way to the state championships. He was also a globally ranked chess player, and had traveled to Russia and Iceland for matches. As if that wasn't enough, he occasionally worked as a model, so you never knew when you'd see Theo staring back at you from the pages of *Philadelphia* magazine or newspaper ads. Right this minute, there was a poster of him in golf gear in the window of the Tog Shop in Berwyn.

While Mimi jokingly called him "the Korean James Bond," Theo's trophies and jawline had been tough on her. The one time, his junior year, when he got an ugly buzz cut was near the happiest couple of months in Mimi's life.

After Gage dropped us off, we found Theo in the Kims' kitchen, leaning back against the counter and using a soupspoon to excavate Ben & Jerry's Rainforest Crunch straight from the carton.

"Blizzard, how's it going?" Theo was the only person who called me that.

"Not bad." I was always a little more on alert when Theo was around, even if I could remember him from elementary school days, when he walked around in a Darth Vader cape.

He looked up, and it was as close to a double take as Theo had ever given me. His attention shot through my body.

"What?"

"What?"

"What?" I stuck out my tongue at him.

He laughed and gave a shrug, then went back to his digging. "Nothing, goober. Just look who's growing up."

"You're such a dog, Theo," said Mimi. "One month in college and now you think you can perv on all my friends."

"Calm down, Meems."

Later that night, tucked up in one of the two ice-blue-quilted twin beds where I'd spent my very first sleepover back in first grade, I replayed the moment of Theo's stare. Relishing that little jolt of surprise in his face.

Mimi had acted as if Theo had been the one who'd changed, but I knew it wasn't true. My eye makeup. My black cardigan. My trip into Philly. All the changes were mine. Theo had noticed the difference in *me*.

# eight

I'D SNAGGED THE JOB at Ludington Public Library after I'd helped Lenora Blitz pass Organic Chemistry. My tutoring skills had hoisted her grade from a D to a C, and so this summer, before she'd taken off for college, Lenora had bequeathed her position to me.

At Ludington, I earned $3.35 an hour, working nine hours on Sunday and six hours on Monday. Twice a month I collected a check (after taxes) of $76.30. My parents referred to this money as my "allowance."

As in, *Lizzy, please pay for new jeans out of your allowance?*

My allowance money also bought my lunch tickets, school supplies, and extras like leotards and tights for dance squad.

But it was a pretty cushy job. Dealing with the actual books didn't eat up that much time, leaving me hours to study at the circulation desk. Mimi liked studying at Ludington, too, which was always nice for work breaks, when I wanted to feel more like a kid and less like a librarian—especially since Mrs. Binswanger often sent me out to tell people to lower their voices or put away their snacks. Today, though, Mimi had disappeared to the periodicals section to look up some old articles on microfiche. Scanning the main room, I saw Wendy and Kreo, along with a few core Nectarine hangers-on, all holding court at a round center table. The small, private back tables were crowded mostly with whispering couples, and the stacks were thick with loner freshmen.

I spent my first hours on the floor, reshelving, and then on the dot of three, I replaced Mrs. Binswanger at the desk so that she could punch out. This was my key study time, broken only if someone needed a book stamped.

Soon I'd sunk into my favorite subject after art, Ancient Civ. I was strolling around the city of Ur when an exaggerated male cough interrupted me. I looked up.

"Oh!"

The solid block of Tommy Powers loomed over the desk, a pile of books in his arms. Right behind him was Matt Ashley.

Matt's smile was as warm as afternoon sunshine. "Stripes?"

*Stripes?* What did that mean? My body was melting into jelly.

"Freshman mixer," Matt clarified, his eyes like twin dark blue torches. "You wore that striped jacket. We talked about cheese fries versus . . . something else. Then it was last song. Remember?"

"Oh. Yes. Uh-huh. I do." Of course I remembered our conversation about cheese fries. I'd actually been wearing Theo's windbreaker, which I'd found in the back seat of the Kims' car and put on last minute. Black with electric-green stripes at the elbows, and obviously too big, but with the sleeves pushed up, I'd thought it looked the right kind of different.

I could feel myself blankly staring at Matt. I couldn't think of any words. I was just so shocked that he remembered that night, a night I'd thought about thousands of times, every detail magnified by my overplayed memory.

Tommy made an impatient gesture. Quickly I reached for his books and stamped them. Then I took Matt's. Could Matt see my hands shaking? I needed to say something, right? All those years and we'd never crossed paths, never had reason to speak to each other again. Until now.

Matt broke the silence. "Hey, were you at my party the other night?"

I nodded. "Yeah." Such a stupid lie—but I didn't want to be the one single senior at Ludington Library who hadn't been at Matt's house Friday night.

"Really? I didn't see you."

"I didn't see you, either."

"It was a mob scene."

"We left early, too," I said. "My friend Claire wanted to go to Hinata." This was my one card to play—the only glamorous, glittery thing I'd done since school started.

Matt looked interested. "What's that?"

"A sushi restaurant in West Philly. Since there's nothing good around here. You have to go to the city for it."

"Ah." His laugh was low in his throat—like the rest of him, it had become older since freshman year. "You missed a hot party. I heard Matt Ashley was there." He winked.

I laughed. The very first time I'd seen Matt Ashley under the dim lights of the Lincoln gym mixer, he'd reminded me of Glynnorin, a favorite character Gage invented from her brief but passionate sixth-grade fixation with Dungeons & Dragons. She'd stopped playing D&D years ago, and in that time, Matt Ashley also had aged out of that boyish elf self. But his long-lashed navy-blues still had a touch of the wild, as if he might just as easily be peering out at me from the depths of some dark fantastical woods.

I couldn't stop staring at him, the ways he was familiar and the ways he seemed so much older. All my same Matt Ashley feelings were churning inside me with a giddy new force.

"Next time I come to your house, I'll say hi," I told him. "I didn't mean to be rude."

"Deal." He tipped his head back and looked around as if assessing the library's space for the very first time. "So you work here?"

"Of course she works here, dumbass," growled Tommy in his sleepy baritone. "You think she just likes to sit at the teacher's desk?"

"It's a librarian's desk, dumbass," said Matt.

"Shaduppah ya face, ya fag." Tommy gave me a smile and Matt a push. "We're out."

"In a sec." Was Matt having a hard time looking away from me? I'd done my eyes smoky Claire-style, and styled my hair the way Claire had suggested, using some of Mimi's mousse, a quick puff like scented whipped cream to add some texture to these bangs I was now, officially, growing out.

My new look, I'd decided this morning in Mimi's bathroom mirror. I felt defiant but also shy about it as Matt's gaze frankly sized me up. "I'm glad I ran into you, Stripes. We should . . . I dunno . . . hang out or something."

"You know where to find me." And I rolled my eyes to show I was stuck in this job (which was feeling like just about the most fantastic employment opportunity ever handed to me).

His eyes were holding the moment.

From the second I'd met Matt Ashley, I'd sensed such a zing of connection, and when it turned out he hadn't felt the same, my disappointment had been an ache that never really healed. Our time together that night had been the closest I'd ever come to believing in something as mystic or ridiculous as "love at first sight," and even when he didn't call, I'd never imagined myself as the girl who spent years pining for the boy who didn't want her. No, I wasn't that girl. In my fantasies, Matt and I always connected again in some sophisticated future, at a summer music festival or on a European backpacking trip.

But was the story of Matt and me actually restarting on a Sunday afternoon at Ludington Library? I'd dreamed of rekindling us for so long—was it really happening?

Waving, watching him go, my heart felt like it might cartwheel straight out of my chest.

# nine

MONDAY MORNING, I WAITED for Claire's judgment. Were we friends now? Sorta kinda? But she wasn't in homeroom in time for senior assembly—a school tradition, twice a week from September to May, when each senior took a turn delivering a speech to the upper schoolers in the theater on any topic she wanted.

This morning, Pepper McDonald was talking about Amish people.

Five minutes in, I saw Claire push through the theater door, slipping like smoke up the darkened aisle. After assembly, I never ran into her—was she avoiding me?

The school day came and went. I wondered if she'd cut out early.

That afternoon, I caught the Paoli local from school to Ludington. My nerves were jittery for Matt Ashley—only this time, hopefully, without Tommy Powers.

But no. No Matt or Tommy.

Shelving books from the cart, I eavesdropped on a couple of Argyll juniors talking about a party planned for this Saturday at Liz DeBatista's house. At some point, Lizzy DeBatista had become *Liz* while I'd stayed *Lizzy*. Liz was captain of our varsity field hockey team, and you could hear her earsplitting, two-fingered whistle anywhere on the campus. She was also our school mascot, with no fears about pulling on the floppy-pawed Argyll lion costume and running around the field to pump up the bleachers before games.

"Hey, I hear Liz is having a keg and some people over this weekend," I said to Gage and Mimi at lunch the next day.

"Yep," said Gage. "She already invited the team for pregame. We play Beekman Hill this Saturday, so we'll be near her house already."

"Oh, maybe we should all go? Not pregame, but to the party after?"

"Not me," said Mimi. "Noah's coming home Halloween weekend. So this weekend I'm staying in and studying."

Gage swallowed the last bite of her toaster-oven pizza before she answered me. "Has your Hard Rock Café eyeliner leaked into your brain? Do you know how much I *don't* want to hang out with girls on the team, after I've spent the whole entire week practicing with them? It's the *last* thing I want to do. Wendy and Kreo and Liz and your so-called new pal, Claire, are *not* my friends—they're my teammates, because I have no choice. I don't party with them, and they are perfectly happy not to party with me."

"Gage, you've got it wrong. I forgot to say this, but Matt Ashley came by the library on Sunday, and we kind of reconnected, and Matt would be there most likely, and he'd be someone we—"

"Hold up." Mimi put up a palm. "I don't remember seeing Matt Ashley."

"It was when you went down to the microfiche files."

"Then *Matt Ashley* can pick you up and give you a ride to the party." Gage crumpled her napkin and dropped it onto her food tray. "Since that's what you *really* need from Mimi and me. The ride."

"It's not about a ride. I'll borrow my mom's car." I couldn't even make a mental picture of me pulling up to Liz DeBatista's house in Mom's brown Corolla. "It's about us having a good time together."

A frustrated silence held the table.

"Lizzy, do you know what you are lately?" Gage said at last. She narrowed her eyes and sealed her lips tight for a moment, as if she was sneaking up on her answer. "You're a claimer."

"A what?"

"As in, you keep *claiming* that all this stuff is true—you and Claire Reynolds in Philly, and you and Matt at Ludington. But in the real world, from what Mimi and I see, Claire Reynolds barely knows you're breathing. And now you're claiming that the big romance you've been fantasizing about with Matt Ashley is true? There's positive thinking—and then there's *claims*."

Mimi laughed. "*Claimer*," she repeated.

I said nothing. We all teased one another from time to time, but it was embarrassing to think I was so dopey that I couldn't even tell reality from wishful thinking.

That afternoon in AP Art, I could feel Mimi and Gage hugely enjoying the fact that Claire ignored me, simply for the *claimer* joke of it. She was just in one of her preoccupied moods, but I felt too shy to approach her directly.

And while I hadn't expected a call from Matt, I hadn't been *not* expecting the one that didn't come all week.

Maybe I really *was* a claimer. Maybe I was misreading situations, bending vague facts into the pretty shapes of my desires.

Claire was absent from school the next couple of days, and by the time the phone rang Friday night, I figured it was one of my aunts hoping to tie up the line with Mom on family gossip. I hardly registered the sound.

But the call was for me.

# ten

"Hey, what's going on?"

"Claire! Hi! Nothing!"

"I can hardly hear you."

I'd come down to the kitchen on Owen's yell, loud enough so I could have heard it in any room of the house. A choice I immediately regretted. Owen and Peter were using the table to play paperclip hockey. Peter had a sports radio station on too loud, and the scorched haze in the air from whatever they were broiling in the oven stung my nose and was in danger of setting off the smoke detector.

"Let me go in another room."

"No, I don't want to stay on that long, I've been sick—"

"I know! Are you okay? Did you get your homework assignments or should I—"

"I got them. I wanted to do something tomorrow night, and there's a party—"

"Yes! I know, at Liz's!"

"—and since that sounds really beat, I wondered if you'd be into hearing the Painted Bandits over at the Troc."

"Oh." I'd grown up hearing radio DJs talk about the Trocadero, which sounded like some sketchy dive in Center City. Of course, a night out with Claire made all other details unimportant.

"I could come get you and we'd drive in—you could stay over."

"Except I have to work at the library on Sunday."

"I'd give you a lift. How's your ID?"

"It's okay." I swallowed. "Not great."

"It doesn't have to be great. It just has to get you in. I'll pick you up tomorrow around three."

After I'd hung up, I wandered all around the house, feeling like a grenade waiting for someone to pull the pin.

The problem wasn't that I had a bad fake ID. I didn't have *any* ID.

I chewed my bottom lip, staring out my bedroom window to the view of our dark lawn. The streetlamp at the corner glowed over a chunk of sidewalk. I couldn't quite see the Schrempf house, but my parents were over there, having dinner. Next weekend, on Friday or Saturday night, my parents and the Schrempfs would stroll the three blocks over to Chestnut Street, where the Midges lived. ("Are you eating with the Shrimps or the Midgets?" was Peter's standard joke.) Were my parents partly to blame for my own habits? Their lives were boring. My brothers' lives were boring. My friends' lives were boring. When I got to Princeton next fall, how would I stop myself from defaulting straight to boring?

Boring was my training! How would I ever find fun and excitement if I didn't even know where to look?

My eyes had gone very dry, and I saw sparks when I resurfaced. The light from the streetlamp was painful. I'd been staring into it for too long. My fingers had curled stiff on each side.

Slowly I unclenched my fists.

Absence seizures, which I got from time to time, weren't too scary. They weren't the same as what had happened in the music room back in eighth grade. Absences—"staring spells," my parents called them when I was little—were glitches in my brain patterns. I thought of them as blanking out, and they never lasted for more than thirty seconds or a minute.

But after an absence, I usually felt numb and flattened out. Other times, I felt a fresh spring of clarity: that's how I felt now.

I'd figure out a fake ID. Somehow.

The important thing was that tomorrow night, I was getting out of this house. The Troc would be something totally new, exciting, out of bounds, maybe even dangerous. Whatever happened, however it happened, was beside the point. The point was the experience. The point was change.

# eleven

I SAT ON THE front stoop, guarding against Claire meeting any member of my family: Dad puttering around the toolshed in his terrible acid-wash jeans, Peter and Owen grinding their skateboards up and down the driveway.

She was almost an hour late. "Sorry. First the game, then I was at the doctor's. His office is right in Devon."

"Are you sick?" I swung my straw bag into the back of her VW. It was actually Mom's beach bag, and only slightly better than the teal-and-purple duffel that I'd rejected as too babyish.

"My shrink. Didn't you tell me you see one, too?"

"No!" I stiffened. Why did she say that? Why was she looking at me like that? How could she know about my Tuesdays with Dr. Neumann, with her orangish lipstick and her browning spider plants and her questions and her Rx pad?

Claire shrugged. "My mom makes me go. But it's fine. I use most of the time to talk about my crazy aunt. I'm not ashamed to see a shrink," she added. "Mine is mellow and helpful. It's not like I've got all the answers."

I made a noise of agreement. Today something about Claire's effortless cool stabbed at me harder. This week, I'd bought a colored mousse foam-in at the drugstore, which had done nothing to my hair but stained my nail beds a dark, radioactive copper. Claire's look couldn't be found at a drugstore. You couldn't buy her long, dark denim legs or her perfectly threadbare T-shirt. There was no price tag on her knotty cheekbones or the casual wisps of hair that escaped her uptwist.

"You have a tattoo?" I saw it on her forearm through her cotton shirtsleeve, about an inch long, with a design like a star but narrower. I'd seen tattoos only on muscled-up guys who served beer or pumped gas. "What is it?"

"Ace of Swords. Part of a tarot reading I got last birthday."

"What does it mean?"

Her lips pressed together. "It means I was drunk."

"Ha."

Soon we were driving down tree-lined Merion Square Road. The B side of REM's *Document* was on, more boppy than Claire's usual taste. She smirked as I gave her the key death scenes of *Pumpkinhead*, and then she recapped highlights of the day's hockey game.

"Your friend Gage is like an ancient Highlander. When she pulls off her goalie mask to bully the ref, she is *the* scariest person on the field."

"She's been like that since we were kids!" Claire had Gage exactly right, and I cracked up to imagine her as a raging Scotswoman yanking off her mask in fury at some tough call.

Eventually Claire slowed, and we turned through the iron gates that protected her aunt's estate.

"Whoa." I was used to the money overspill of Argyll, but I didn't know any kids who lived in a place like this. "These trees must be hundreds of years old." I stared. "And the land alone—it's like a college campus."

"Or a mental institute."

"And you have peacocks!"

"Yeah . . . somehow peacocks make it worse."

Really? How? The half dozen peacocks that strolled the lawn of Lilac House were as dazzling as Mardi Gras. Their dipping tails were sapphire plumes that brushed the autumn lawn as they paraded slowly past us.

"It doesn't even matter where you end up," I said, "with a driveway like this. It could be a mud hut at the top, and the whole thing would still be amazing."

"I'll remind you that you told me that, once you see what Aunt Jane's done with the place."

Of course there was no hut, but a Tudor-style mansion at the end of the drive. It was immense and rich with Gothic flourishes—leaded-glass windows, multiple chimneys, stone gargoyles spouting from a high turret. It wasn't until we were out of the car and walking up to the front door that I began to notice how the pebbled walkway was choked with weeds, and that the silver linden trees were gnarled, their roots untended and their branches entangled with bittersweet.

"It kind of looks like a castle cast under a spell, to keep the world away." I was probably idealizing it, but I wasn't lying, either.

"Since my uncle died, Aunt Jane is all about the cats." Claire had her head up. "Mr. Mack—her gardener—can't come near the house. I mean, lord forbid he startles them with his leaf blower or his mower. He keeps his distance—thirty feet. That's the rule."

We stopped at the large, peaked front door. Claire fished a key from her bag. "Jump in. If any of these cats escape outside, there'll be hell to pay."

"Got it."

She turned the key, and no sooner were we scooting sideways into the house than cats charged us from all directions. I gasped. I'd never, ever seen cats like these. Huge and sleek and brightly marked, with long necks and large ears, they were like a pack of tigers, all making a run for freedom as Claire slammed us in.

I wanted to hold my nose. The front hall reeked.

"Are these cats . . . all from one family?"

"I have no idea." A few cats were pushing past my calves to claw at the oak door—already chopped and sliced with vertical marks, some so deep they looked like the work of an axe.

"Are they like a mix of cat and—I don't know—lynx or something?"

"No, just some creepy rare breed my aunt loves. And they're allowed to piss and shit everywhere, as you can tell."

The biting smell of cat pee was so intense my eyes smarted. I blinked and stared around. The hall was mostly empty. I saw a marble-topped table heaped with mail, a litter box that looked like it might have once been a lasagna pan, and a couple of carpet-covered scratching posts worn bald. The cat stuff contrasted with the beauty of the hall itself. There were paneled walls and a crystal chandelier that was squared above the center staircase, as well as beautiful wooden scrollwork of carved flowers, trailing vines, and fruit.

I looked up the stairs. I could imagine a ghost bride on the landing. "Is anyone home?"

"Aunt Jane is in her bedroom watching old movies. Mom works weekends at Galway Dress—she'll be back later. I'd offer you food, but I'm never in the kitchen."

"No problem." I was following her down the long, dark hallway. "A suit of armor? Stone floors? It's like King Arthur lives here."

"Yeah, or Scooby-Doo."

"Ha." Now I noticed all the damage. The carpet runners were discolored with cat pee, and floor moldings had been clawed to trauma.

At the end of the hall, two mean-eyed felines nestled on a tattered chaise lounge. Its brocade upholstery was shredded. Claire opened the last door into a cold draft and a dark, vertical library, another room with the soul of the Renaissance. A faded hanging tapestry cloaked one wall, while the opposite was dominated by a huge bay window heaped with cushions and quilts. A stone fireplace with a mantel display of German beer steins banked the far end of the room.

The room's high-backed sofas and easy chairs were upholstered in blue-and-mustard-striped fabric—silk, I guessed. It looked like Claire must have pulled them close together to make the space cozier. *Paris Match* magazines, McDonald's soda cups, and Argyll textbooks were stacked on the tables, while Claire's field hockey equipment was piled in a corner.

"This is your room? This library?" Bookshelves had been cleared for stacks of Claire's clothing, and she was using the desk as a personal dressing table, her vanity mirror set up alongside her makeup bag and hair dryer.

"I had to. The cat smell is worse upstairs. But this room is No Cats Allowed."

"You sleep in the window?" I shivered involuntarily.

"Yeah. It's comfortable. Sorry about the cold, but I swear I can smell the cats everywhere. So I've always got the air conditioner going." Claire bit at her thumbnail. She looked so alone that if she'd been closer to me—a cousin, maybe—I might have even hugged her.

"I'm really sorry, but I don't have a fake ID," I blurted instead.

"Well, that's that." Claire blinked, but her face offered no path on what she was thinking.

"So you can drive me back home."

"Okay, if you want."

I didn't know what to say. It was only the vision of Claire ejecting me from her car into one more Saturday night of watching MTV and drawing my hand that screwed up my courage. I took a breath. "There's also that party at Liz DeBatista's?"

"Sure, yeah." She shrugged. "We'll just go to Liz's."

"Well, great. That'll be fun." I tried to sound relaxed. I shivered again, I couldn't help it.

"Too cold, I know." Claire made a face. "But we've got an indoor pool, and in there it doesn't smell—not like cat pee anyway.

It's warm. We could eat dinner there before we get ready to go. I'll do your makeup. We'll leave around nine. Okay?"

My smile was so big I could have been in the chorus of a middle school musical again—*Oliver!* or *The Jungle Book*—as Mr. Hock was telling me that I had to "telegraph joy to the back of the house."

Only this time, I wasn't telegraphing. This time was real life.

# twelve

IN THE KITCHEN WERE more clawing posts, plus metal bowls lined up in rows on the floor, like for a cat orphanage. Litter boxes were parked in the corners. If the front hall was all pee smell, the kitchen stank with the liverish odor of cat food.

Slit-eyed cats, draped on chairs and slung out in windowsills, stared at us from all sides like bored predators. "I guess this is their main hangout zone, huh?"

"The whole house is their hangout zone. It's finding the people-only zones that's the challenge."

Claire's quiet embarrassment embarrassed me. Her face was an aloof mask as she opened and shut random cupboards. I could tell by her general confusion about where things were stored that she didn't spend any time here, but I made myself not do my usual eager-beaver help thing.

"Don't sit," she snapped when I tried to upend a cat from a high stool. "We'll be out of here in three minutes."

It was a relief to us both when she found the can opener that wrenched the lids from two cans of Chef Boyardee beef ravioli. The smell of microwave tomato sauce plus cat food made me queasy, but it seemed important to act like I wasn't grossed out, and at last, dinners ladled, we carried spoons and bowls through the kitchen's swinging door and down a pantry hall, through a dutch door that led to a sun-washed solarium of marble statues and potted ferns.

"Oh, wow—it looks like a hotel." I was whispering, awed, even though we were alone. "With a skylight and everything."

"This house is kind of like playing rock-paper-scissors," said Claire. "Air conditioner covers the smell of cat ass. Chlorine cuts the smell of cat ass. With most other rooms, unfortunately, cat ass is the rock that crushes everything."

"I don't mind the smell of chlorine." Especially after the kitchen. I was trying to fix things with words, but nothing about Lilac House was normal. Parts of it were sad and decrepit, but anyone could see that this pool was built with no expenses spared. The tiles winked like black and silver diamonds, an Egyptian-style mural unfolded along every wall, and the lounge chairs were upholstered in a creamy fabric untouched by the drag of cat claws. A long bank of windows gave a sweeping view of the strutting peacocks and the woods beyond.

One of the lounges had been pulled up against the windows, and here Claire plunked herself down, pasta bowl in her lap. I dragged up another lounge next to hers. The space around us was littered with blue-glass bottles of Clearly Canadian, along with crumpled bags of Cool Ranch Doritos and Pepperidge Farm Milano cookies.

"I do my homework here," Claire explained. "It's warm from the sun and it doesn't depress me as much as the rest of the house. I'll be bummed when it's winter."

Today had been sunny and heat lingered in the stone floor. "I feel like a first-class passenger on a cruise ship." I stretched out and dipped my spoon for a bite of ravioli.

"You sure can spin it."

"What's the expression, when life gives you cat pee, make lemonade?"

"Eww!" At least that got Claire laughing, and the ravioli was surprisingly delicious, living up to my nostalgic grade-school memories.

We finished eating in silence and when I was done, I set my bowl on the floor and walked over to the pool's edge, clenched my toes around the coping, and braced myself on one foot as I dunked for temperature with the other. The water reflected dark from the tiles, but you could see all the way to the bottom. "Do you ever swim in it?"

"I tried once, but it felt slimy. Aunt Jane says it gets cleaned and refilled every summer, but I don't trust a word out of her mouth."

"Do you know how far—oh!"

It had sunk to the deepest part, near the drain. You could hardly tell what it was. Hairs lifted on my arms as a sour taste of ravioli notched up in the back of my throat.

"What?" Claire jumped up and ran over. When I glanced at her, she seemed spellbound by the vision of the matted, lifeless body.

"Um, okay. Who deals with that?" I had my hand at my heart, as if I could slow down its beating. "Us? Your mom?"

She didn't answer.

"Your aunt Jane?"

"Now even *this* room is ruined. There's nowhere to go that's clean. Everything's so . . . tainted. And she thinks *I'm* the problem."

"I'm sorry, Claire." I paused. "And also, practically speaking, someone needs to remove the body."

"I know, I know." Her voice dropped. "Listen, I'm not telling Aunt Jane just yet, or she'll unravel, and—I can't deal with her tonight."

Against a wall, I saw a couple of aluminum poles, the nets and brushes of pool cleaning equipment. "So should *we* fish it out?"

"No, no. I'll tell Mr. Mack when I see him."

"I think I need to throw up."

"The bathroom's through that door."

I skittered away. I didn't need to vomit, exactly, but I could feel something coming on. Inside, I locked the door and sat on the closed toilet, rocking forward.

Someone was speaking.

A tap. "You okay?" Claire repeated.

Time had passed. I'd had a lapse—where was I? I exhaled, remembering. I hadn't worn my watch, I didn't know if I'd been in here for one minute or three or six.

"Yeah." When I felt stronger, I stood. My reflection looked unfocused and sleepy. I ran some faucet water, flicked it in my face, stepped out.

Claire peered at me as if she were trying to hear the thoughts inside my head. I felt myself flush—what if I'd had a worse seizure right here, in her house? Had anyone at school told her anything?

"You sure you're okay?"

"Perfect!"

"I feel bad, inviting anyone over. It's so weird and disgusting here."

"No, it's not."

"I mean, these cats, the living ones—and now the dead one."

"Little brothers are grosser, I promise."

"Let's get ready. I'll do your makeup."

I swallowed. "Sure."

"Unless you want to go home."

"No," I said. "No way."

Back in her room, Claire put on some weird French music like what she'd played last week in the art room. None of us had much liked it, but nobody dared to tell her that, since right from day one, she'd seemed to have elected herself in charge of art room tunes. She changed into a black T-shirt and jeans, also black but tighter than her day jeans.

After she'd finished with herself, Claire sat me at her desk-dressing table and gave me an identical makeover—smoky charcoal makeup and mascara. She vetoed my lightly shoulder-padded paisley blouse in favor of her own ribbed white tank top, the black cardigan she'd given me, and a pair of her biker boots one size too big but with a chunky heel I liked.

The total effect made me feel like I was in costume, a punk-rock paper doll anchored to an extremely heavy stand, but exhilarated by her overhaul.

"It's Jay's birthday today," said Claire as we shot quickly out the front door into the crisp October evening. "I really wanted someone around with me tonight. Last year, he and I were hanging out—in a good way, I guess. At least, I thought it was good." She dipped her head to rummage for her car keys. "I despise that I remember those kinds of dates." Her voice was thick.

"Right," I said. "I totally get it." I got so little of it. But what I did know: Claire had picked me. Claire thought I was the right one to hang out with her tonight—even as she was missing her old love, the mysterious Jay. The guy had unwound her so completely, and was still so hard for her to talk about. Besides, Claire would be right by my side if I saw Matt tonight—and she was as cool as any Nectarine.

In the car, she sniffed the air. "I'm starting to think I can smell cats all the time."

"Party crushes cats," I announced.

She laughed and snapped in a 10,000 Maniacs tape. Soon we were rattling down the drive, into the night and all of its promise.

# thirteen

A HAPHAZARD LINE OF cars and jeeps popped up as soon as we turned onto Ravenscliff, the development where the DeBatistas lived in one of a circle of stucco homes overlooking a golf course.

"She's four-three-six." I read the address that Claire had scribbled out of the student directory.

"I'm pulling into a driveway a little farther down," said Claire. "Remember this house with the window boxes. If the cops come, meet me back here."

My heart went higgledy-piggledy, as my grandmother would say—I'd never made an "if the cops come" plan before.

We shortcut backyards. The lights were bright through the DeBatistas' downstairs windows. Liz had been varsity in three sports all the way back to freshman year, and her postgame parties were well known. This was my first one. At the door, I quaked while Claire pressed the bell as bold as FedEx.

It yanked open into Bob Marley music and Liz, fiercely smiling.

"Middie!" She whooped as she slapped Claire with a high five. "Nice surprise. I don't mean to suck, but it's five bucks a head for the keg, even girls. Oh, hey, Lizzy."

Did I imagine she looked surprised to see me, a shy shadow behind Claire?

Earlier, I'd stuck a ten-dollar bill in my sock, and when I took it out, Claire gave me a nod, so I was paying her way, too. But she had bought the gas and was my ride.

"There's a card game in the kitchen, but everything's happening in the basement." Liz thumbed the right direction.

As I followed Claire downstairs, her teammates cheered her on sight. Even Gage had a measure of power hinged to her excellence in varsity sports. I was probably the only modern-dance-squad girl in the room, a fact I would not be broadcasting.

And then, there he was.

Matt Ashley, his wheat-blond hair casually mussed, in a rugby shirt and jeans and an *Aha!* smile that made me know he'd been looking for me, hoping for me. He began moving in so quickly that I wanted to run upstairs and take a breath and come down again.

It was happening too fast! I wasn't ready!

"Stripes," he said loud over the music as soon as I reached the bottom of the stairs. "You showed up. I didn't know if you'd be at some downtown rave with your buddy."

"We're both here, actually."

As he guided me off, Matt glanced over at Claire, who was talking with some teammates. "Oh, *her*. She's the boarding school transfer, right?"

"Yeah, from Strickland."

"I've heard some crazy stories about her."

I tried not to look startled. "Seriously? From who? About what?"

"Just, from other guys. I mean, she's cute and plays hockey— so she's on the radar."

"What have you heard?"

He lowered his voice. "Troublemaker, kicked out, bad news."

"I don't know who your sources are, but no way." My mother saw all of the Argyll transcripts, and while Mom would never break a privacy clause outright, she wouldn't have been able to resist warning me about the dangers of hanging around with "a bad influence."

"It's just when a girl's good-looking and new on the scene, guys want to discuss. But that's your friend, so I don't mean to talk shit." He thought I was covering for Claire—which I didn't mind.

"Didn't you have soccer today?" I knew Lincoln had played Fieldstone, and soon Matt was talking all about it, his face bright as we slowly inched our way to a private section of the room behind the Ping-Pong table, away from the Jell-O shots and drinking games.

Matt had grown since freshman year. Even in my borrowed boots, he had six inches on me. Tiptoe perfect.

"Want a beer?" he asked.

"I'm good." I did want a beer, but what if Matt left me, became distracted by other party people, and never returned?

He'd abandoned me once before, after all.

"You know," he said, his deep blue eyes suddenly serious, "in the library the other day, you didn't see me, but I was watching you for so long. I didn't believe it was you, the same Lizzy Swift. I haven't seen you in years. Not since the freshman mixer. Or maybe I *have* seen you, and I didn't realize it? Where've you been hiding?"

"I don't know. Let me know when you find me." My smile froze on my face as it hit me that I'd just quoted an extremely stupid joke from one of Owen's *Mad* magazines that had been lying around the bathroom for weeks.

Matt didn't seem to know or care. "What are you up to these days? Are you always in the city, like a secret club rat?"

Is that what I looked like? What exactly was a *club rat*? The whole night felt like playacting, with my makeup and costume compliments of Claire. "I do like to go out, to dance and, yeah, I love going into the city." All technically true.

Matt was nodding. "There's a place I went in New York this summer called Palladium—we've got nothing like it in Philly. It's a huge dance space and the whole back wall is graffiti. It's pretty radical."

"So *you're* a club rat."

"When I'm not at the library."

"Liar. I never see you there."

"Ludington's too social. I like Greenfield Public. I think I might have read every single thing by Madeleine L'Engle and Ray Bradbury in the stacks of that library." Matt grinned. "But now obviously I'm switching my library alliance."

In the other corner of the room, some of the jocks were hoisting beefy linebacker Stephen Clancy into a keg stand while others cheered. Matt shook his head. "My friends are idiots." He looked at me thoughtfully. "So are you still into fantasy and science-fiction stuff?"

I flushed. I could remember tons about what Matt said to me at that long-ago mixer, but hardly anything about what I'd said to him. Had I really exposed myself as such a die-hard sci-fi fan?

"Cops in a paddy wagon, front door! Time to bolt!" Jonesy Sweet sprang into the room with news that instantly saved me from having to admit that Isaac Asimov's *I, Robot* was on my nightstand, three-quarters of the way finished.

"Aw, come on." Matt rolled his eyes as everyone else began barreling up the stairs in a rush hour stampede. "What's the plan, Sweet?"

"Follow me is the plan. I know this house like the back of my hand."

Jonesy used to date Liz, and now he signaled Kreo, who was with Claire, and we all gathered close behind him. He split us from the crowd, pushing toward the kitchen's back-door exit, and veered us down a short hall into the DeBatistas' powder room. Jonesy went first, a flash of coppery flattop and black overcoat, his yellow Timberland boot leaving a mark on the wallpaper as he hoisted up and wriggled through the tiny high window.

His hand stretched to help Kreo, Claire, me. Matt would be last to escape.

I fell with a soft scream into a hedge. I could hear kids scuffling and scampering in all directions. In the next instant, Matt toppled over me. The sudden crush of his weight was a head-and-body rush—*Matt Ashley is on top of me and it feels so good.*

"Sorry," he whispered, rolling off to a stand but then gripping my hand to help me up.

"My car's that way!" Claire pointed as we all sidled from around the hedge.

When I looked over my shoulder, flashing blue and red lights in front of Liz's lawn sent a hiccup of terror through me. What would my parents say if they had to pick me up at a police station?

Head down, I ran.

It wasn't until the Beetle came into sight that I slowed to a jog. Nobody was following us. Matt suddenly tugged my jacket. "We parked on another street and my boys are waiting for me. I'll call you, okay?" And then in the next second's surprise, Matt Ashley's mouth found mine. I held my breath and closed my eyes. Could everything be felt and known and said in a kiss? So much seemed to be happening for me in this one. The pressure of his lips was so sudden, his tongue a warm brush gone too quick. But it was all the contact I needed to lose my mind, an instant injection that put me in a stupor as my eyes opened to stare at him.

"Bye," I whispered.

Matt was already turned away, his back to me, running to catch up with his boys.

# fourteen

"Waxing. Gibbous," I murmured. "Why does the moon have such weird words?"

We were lying together tops-to-tails in Claire's window-seat bed, propped up by pillows. The cloud-shredded moon stippled soft light over our quilt. The window seat was long enough to fit us, but we were both on our sides to adjust for the width.

Gage probably would have gone into a whole thing about the moon or word origins, but Claire didn't answer.

Now I felt stupid, talking about the moon like a nerd, and I rushed to change the subject.

"Why were you a month late starting Argyll anyway?"

Claire sighed and took a minute to answer. "I wasn't ready."

Jay! Heartbreak! Eating disorder! Flunked out! Attempted suicide—Jay! Attempted suicide—Claire! Stories of tragedy and drama crashed around in my brain as I nodded. "Tell me more about Jay. You miss him, don't you? At a party like tonight, when he's not around, I figured you were thinking about him."

She tapped her fingers to her lips. Maybe she was remembering Jay's lips? Or maybe she was guarding herself against confessing all that she wanted to say about him? "I don't miss him," she said. "But I do think about him. I do."

"Where is he at college?"

"He's not."

"Why not?"

"Because he's away, he's abroad . . . Paris. Far away."

"Is that why you listen to all those French songs? Does he ever write you?"

She bristled. "I liked French music before Jay. And no, he doesn't write. Not anymore."

"Do you wish he would?"

"Yeah, maybe. Sometimes." I knew she wanted to answer me for real. "Just because, it was the letters that started it. He'd slip them into my mailbox. They'd be about nothing—what he'd had for lunch, or a bird on a branch outside his window. Jay could make music out of anything around him. His letters . . . they were why . . ." She inhaled deeply, unresolved. "That was his talent."

She turned her head, her eyes holding a middle distance. "It's stupid to keep his letters, but they remind me of all the best parts of him. And then maybe the worst parts, too. But I guess every-thing's the worst parts now."

"Why?"

"I really don't want to get into a whole soap opera right now, okay?" Her voice clipped me, even if it made me more curious.

"It's strange how in the beginning, a guy doesn't seem to have any worst parts," I said. The truth was I could talk only about beginnings. I'd never been to the end of anything with a guy.

Claire refocused me. "You're thinking about Matt." By the light of the moon, the drift of her freckles stood out against her parchment skin, and she looked so luminous that I felt like I could see backward through time into her seventh grader's face. "He's a pretty good beginning, right? Cute, funny, soccer stud."

"I'm amazed that I like a jock. It seems like such a cliché, a guy who needs his teammates around him at all times. Like a pack."

"Sometimes a pack is a nice place to disappear. That's why I like hockey."

"Matt seems like he wouldn't want a pack."

"It's obviously where he feels comfortable."

"Do you think we make a strange couple?"

"Kind of, maybe. I mean, you're not a glamorous Wendy Palmer type, right? I'm not saying that to be a bitch. Just as an observation. But if you both like each other . . . that's cool." She yawned and stretched long, then settled into sleep, leaving me more awake than ever. Was Claire possibly jealous because Matt preferred me to her? Maybe this was her way of flexing her power, by unsettling me? Then again, Claire didn't sugarcoat her opinions.

When I woke up into the sunshine of next morning, alone in the window bed and cramped from my unnatural position— funny how the only creatures that usually slept on windowsills were cats, which is exactly what we were hiding from—I felt tired. It was like my brain had been working subconsciously on overtime to untangle Claire's mysteries.

I dressed and left the room quickly. A couple of cats met me on the other side of the door and followed me down the hall like slinky security guards. I heard voices in the opposite direction of the kitchen. I trailed the sound through a high-ceilinged living room where white bedsheets had been thrown over the furniture, and I stepped through a side door onto a covered porch.

Claire and an older woman sat opposite each other at a small table, drinking take-out coffee, a box of Dunkin' Donuts open between them.

"Good morning! I made a breakfast run." Claire handed me a coffee to-go cup. "There's also packets of cream and sugar. Lizzy, this is my mom, Suze."

"Nice to meet you, Lizzy."

"Same, thanks."

Suze was built shorter and a couple of sizes wider than her daughter, and she looked all ready for work in a brass-buttoned red suit and matching brass earrings. She seemed tense and watchful as her gaze darted around the fields.

"Tosca!" The voice was shrill, lost somewhere out in the woods.

"She's been looking for that cat all morning," Suze murmured. Her slick red nails drummed the table.

*Aunt Jane*, Claire mouthed at me, then made a face.

"Tosca!" Down where the lawn met the fields of long grasses, a woman emerged, striding toward us. How long had she been out there? As she approached, she reminded me of a ghost, maybe because of her wild gray hair, or maybe because she was wearing a filmy white nightgown that was so sheer I could see through to her high-waisted underpants and her bony chicken legs. "Is he up there? Did I chase him out?"

"No!" called Suze. "I've been watching."

Aunt Jane stopped at the bottom porch step. Up close, she looked less ghostly and more flat-out pissed off. "Maybe after you finish breakfast, you can all help me look for him," she said. Her tone implied that it would be the right thing to do.

"Aunt Jane, this is my friend Lizzy," said Claire.

"Have you seen my cat?" Aunt Jane's gaze pounced to me. "Black-and-silver coat, twenty-one pounds, highly intelligent."

And I knew, even before Claire shot a warning look my direction, that Tosca was the dead cat at the bottom of the pool.

"No," I said. "Sorry."

"Did any of you let any of my cats out? It would be a great help to me if you just admitted it, and I could adjust my search."

"We know better than that, Jane! Goodness me!" Suze blinked nervously as she reached forward and swiped for another doughnut. I resisted my urge to smooth things over by helping Aunt Jane go hunt for a dead cat.

"Claire?" prompted Aunt Jane. "When was the last time you saw him?"

Claire shrugged. "The cats don't check in with me. But you need a bathrobe, Aunt Jane. We're getting a free show here." Her voice neutral, but now her aunt looked as if she'd been slapped.

"*You're* a fine one to talk." Aunt Jane bit back so sharply that it raised all the hairs on the back of my neck.

But Claire barely reacted. She sprang up from her seat, as if she'd expected the challenge, and she flexed a finger for me to stand, too. I did. "Okay, well, good luck. Lizzy needs a lift to work. Lizzy, will you grab my bag and keys along with your stuff?"

Not a suggestion, a command.

I raced back to the library, where I collected my bag. I took a minute to calm down. Usually I didn't start my mornings with doughnuts, and I knew the sugar injection was partly responsible for the wild patter of my heart. Both Claire's bag and her keys were on her desk, and scooping them up, I noticed a couple of framed pictures I hadn't seen before. One of Claire and her dad, who was obviously the genes behind her self-possessed good looks. Another of an older couple, possibly grandparents. There was a pretty carved wooden box, too, which I opened absently—it didn't have a lock.

Letters. It was full of letters, high as a stack of pancakes, some in envelopes, others loose on lined white notebook paper or folded yellow legal paper, and all with the same distinct slant of penmanship. Later, when I agonized about the stupidity of my decision, I couldn't recall any more initial thought in my head than curiosity. Jay's letters! Was that what I'd found?!

"Lizzy? Are you coming?" Claire was somewhere in the front hall.

"Yes!" *Don't.* But I'd already crushed the envelope I was holding to the bottom of my bag—"Yes, coming!"—and now I was darting out of the room.

*Put it back put it back this instant this is not what friends do.*

Out in the hall, I was already a sweat of guilt as I smiled at Claire and thrust her bag and keys at her, terrified that something in my face or action would give me away. *What am I doing?* But it was too late to undo it.

Claire was quiet for most of the trip. Joy Division blew out of the speakers. The stolen envelope felt like a tiny bonfire in my bag.

"Aunt Jane's such a crazy old bitch," she said eventually. "Do you have any relatives you're scared you might become? Do you ever worry about how you'll end up?"

My condition was the thing in me I worried about most. Once, I'd seen a documentary about epileptics who lived in the back bedrooms and front porches of their parents' homes. I could be one or two grand mals away from that nonfuture. There were no rules to seizures. At any moment, they could snatch you up and carry you off into a prison of confusion and darkness. You couldn't predict them. You couldn't prevent them. And a really bad one could change your life in an instant. "No," I said, pushing out my voice for strength. "Never."

"Me, either. I'll never be her. Ever. But the other day, I dug up her Argyll yearbook. Varsity lacrosse, class vice president, shit-eating grin in every picture like she was ready to own the world. Now look at her. A madwoman searching for her dead cat."

"What did she mean by—that you were 'a fine one to talk'?"

Claire frowned. Her hands were gripping the wheel. "Basically, Aunt Jane thought my mom was dumb and easy because she was pregnant when she ran off with my dad. So I guess she thinks I've got that slutty DNA, too. I mean, whatever. I hardly listen to her. Who can pay attention to a freak like her?"

"My mom says she used to throw big parties at Lilac House. But after your uncle died, she got all reclusive."

"Yeah, that's ancient history. I barely knew Aunt Jane before we moved here." Claire shrugged. "I get it that she misses him, but she forces everyone to be part of her great tragedy, because she pays the bills."

"Paying the bills is something," I ventured.

"Well, yeah, and that's why I'd never drown her cat, although she thinks I did, and I understand that things could suck much harder for me. But still, I'm counting the months until I graduate and escape from here."

"Where do you want to go?"

"Doesn't matter." Claire smiled wryly. "I didn't even believe in monsters till last year. But now I know better. Just because I couldn't see them, didn't mean they weren't right in front of me. But they are, Lizzy. And no matter where I live, no matter what I do, I'll always be on the lookout for them."

# fifteen

10/2

Dear Claire,

You'll laugh to read this but it's midnight and I'm in bed and wearing the hat you knit me. Seriously, I love it—and it's the opposite of "dorky," okay? And you must be some kind of angel to have spent all that time knitting it for me. I don't think I've ever had such a kickass homemade present since—okay, since those lemon squares you baked me. Even if I've got no idea how you can make anything delicious happen in the Strick Kitch, is that place a dungeon, or what? Those were great lemon squares but let me tell you—this is an excellent hat.

I wish I'd met your grandma. She sounds like a righteous dame. And she taught you a hell of a lot, besides knitting.

Aright it's late and I've got so much work to get through
but thought I'd procrastinate on a note to you. Gorgeous night
if you can get out in it for a minute. I'm still thinking about
you calling me "Ace" in French—ya minx. I'll bring my cards
and read your fortune tomorrow sometime, as promised, but we
gotta go somewhere so I don't have to do everyone else's, too.
J.

10/15
Dear C,

So it looks like Hutch is on the warpath again—I swear the
Strickland Charter is a throwback to the Reformation. Also
I'm catching heat from Mike and the guys, so maybe we should
ipskay ourway ecretsay eetingmay in Lothrop tonight, okay by
you? My bet is that Friday is better when it's emptied out.

But tell me if you're thinking about what I'm thinking:
weekend field trip? Permission notes to get outta this town,
get to another town? Philly, Beantown, Baltimore? (A vote for
Philly means I can show off my excellent knowledge of where
to get the best cheesesteak. There's like a bazillion things I
want to show you there.)

And we gotta keep it quiet—no tagalongs, though I think
it'll be easier over Parents Weekend, since most everyone's got
parent plans. Just a thought, so tell me your thoughts. Nights
like this I can't sleep, can't eat, can't work, can't hang out.
I've been having too many of these days and Jesus Christ I
sometimes wonder what's wrong with me. It's like all I think
about is getting out of here. That time last week when we were

in Robertson's and we were all sitting around shooting the shit, talking about old movies, I wanted to stand up and grab your hand and just—jump into one. Literally escape into the black and white, trade reality for a kiss and fade out to The End. Sheer desperation, but I know it comes out of the total lockdown stupidity of this place.

X J.


10/23

You,

It's late and I'm awake again, with you on my mind. I was thinking how many nights I've spent thinking about you, how when this all started it was fall and now we're in these dark, cold months where it could be any month, all gray and brown and melting snow—like maybe it's October or March, it's all the same, doesn't matter, since you've been on my brain for what feels like an eternity.

Have you put some kind of spell on me?

Sometimes I feel this kind of bad, sick, worried thing in my gut that I'm gonna lose something before I've even gotten a chance to have it, you know? It's totally irrational, but the thing is, if you want to do something to get what you want most, you need to take a risk that you don't even know you have in you. Being in school or sitting at my desk and especially in those long, goddamn empty hours lying in bed seems like all the worst, dumbest, most inane ways to handle the intensity of what I'm dealing with. Most of the time I feel like I'm going to do this thing, go forward in this way that breaks everything apart between us and messes us up forever. How do I know that we're salvageable? It's what I keep asking myself.

X J.

I FOLDED THE LETTERS, returned them to their single envelope, and lay back in my bed. I'd read them over and over, searching for meaning and hints about how and why it had ended, and when I closed my eyes, I could still see Jay's handwriting, his words trailing inky scrawls of barbed wire across the page.

In every note, the clearest thing was the *J.* that was his signature, dark and heavy, like an ancient symbol.

Claire had mentioned they'd ended things this spring, when he'd left for Paris. Maybe that's why I'd imagined Jay as a guy who would send a note sprinkled in cheesy French phrases and brimming with poems and references to Voltaire and the Marquis de Sade. But these letters seemed different. They were thoughtful and frank and not so Frenchish, not so intellectual or airy-fairy.

I mentally removed Jay's sulk, along with his beret and baguette, and revised him with new touches of quirkiness. Like maybe he had some Mom-bought polka-dot socks, a beat-up leather backpack, a charming need of a haircut. I saw him striding to class, kicking his way through New England snowdrifts in his boots and a heavy overcoat. I even sketched him in my notebook, though I had zero idea what he looked like. I gave him Bambi dark eyes and Claire's cute homemade wool hat yanked over his head.

What I couldn't find in his words was a guy who'd coldly decided to break Claire's heart. In fact, Jay seemed a lot like

Matt—almost *too* well liked, to the point where he had to find ways not to be hounded by others. Lots of Jay's thoughts were about desperately trying to be alone with Claire without getting crowded.

Why didn't a funny, sweet guy like Jay even write or speak to Claire anymore? If I could see clearer to the end of Claire and Jay, and the mistakes they made, I might be better equipped for the beginning of me and Matt.

Of course, it was horrible that I took these letters, and worse that I'd read them. I felt hot with shame for even having touched Claire's property.

I needed to figure out how to return them, although imagining myself slithering around Claire's room and fumbling with her personal items made me feel like such a creep. In the end, I tucked the envelope into my retired-since-sixth-grade Holly Hobbie purse that hung on a hook in my closet, where it would have to stay until I could get myself back to Lilac House and put everything right.

# sixteen

OVER THE WEEKEND, GAGE tied for third place at a fencing tournament in Pottstown, while Mimi had been lucky caller number eight to Hot-94 radio and won two tickets to see the Hooters on tour next summer. So Monday's lunch was upbeat, and when the talk finally did roll around to me, I was surprised by my reluctance to share. Liz's party and Matt's kiss both felt secret—and so did Lilac House, the cats, Suze, Aunt Jane, and most especially Claire.

"I made turtle brownies last night," I volunteered instead, "and I brought extra." I took them out of my book bag to pass around.

After school, toward the end of my Monday shift at the library, Matt dropped by Ludington. He looked princely in a long dove-gray overcoat that probably cost more than everything in my closet.

"I like your coat."

He rolled his eyes. "It's too preppy. Mom wants the entire family to look exactly like we fell out of some flaming Ralph Lauren ad."

"Oh, poor baby. How totally awful to be dressed in all that cheap, sucky Ralph Lauren."

He frowned. "I know I sound like a spoiled brat. It's just I'm eighteen and I never get a say in what I wear."

"I get to choose all my own clothes, but I also have to pay for them," I said.

Now Matt looked shamefaced. "Stripes, this is why I'll be working for you one day. You're already the boss." And even if it would have taken me all year to save up for his Ralph Lauren coat, I wondered if he really thought I had the better deal.

We wheeled a cart to a far end of the stacks, where we pretended to shelve books as we traded stories about the crazy end of Saturday's party. Liz had been fined a hundred dollars and her parents had been called.

"Nobody told you?"

"I'm not friends with Liz and that group," I admitted.

"Who'd you hang out with before Claire?"

"Gage and Mimi. Those same two girls I was with at the mixer when you . . ."

"When I kissed you the first time?" he finished teasingly.

I shrugged, as if I barely recalled it, let alone spent three years pining over it. "They're my oldest friends."

Matt nodded. "Jonesy and Tommy and I go back to kindergarten. It's cool but—"

"But sometimes I feel like my oldest friends know me too well."

"Yeah, and at the same time, don't know me at all."

I nodded agreement, consumed by the sweetness in Matt's smile, and remembering last weekend's surprise electricity of his mouth on mine. Maybe I knew him better than his jock friends already.

"So," he began slowly, "what are your plans for Halloween? Technically it's next Monday, but this weekend's some parties. You and Claire hitting clubs in Philly?"

"Maybe." I flushed. I'd been playing up my connection to Philadelphia, unspooling that one trip I'd made with Claire to make it sound like a few different adventures. "The thing is, I need a good fake ID. The one I've got isn't letting me into anywhere. I feel like bouncers have really cracked down lately."

Matt snapped his fingers. "Okay, you're talking to the right person—Tommy's older brother Walt's home on fall break this week. He's a junior at NYU, he's a great guy, and the ID he made me is how I got into Palladium. Walt told me that last weekend he got himself and some of his friends into Limelight, no problem."

"Wow, nice."

"So here's a plan." Matt touched my wrist lightly. I'd never been so conscious of the tap of fingers on my skin. "Thursday, a few of us are coming to Argyll to watch Kreo play, and after the game, I'll give you a ride over to Tommy's and you can get yours made? I know Kreo and Jonesy want in. Walt won't charge much, but don't forget to bring cash."

"Yeah, sure. This is so great."

His smile pierced me. "Then Claire can hook us up with finding a scene downtown. Something different than basement beer pong."

"Absolutely, we can just move the party to Philly."

He hesitated. "Nah. Just you, me, and Claire. We can make our own party."

So maybe Matt really was sick of the jock herd. And Claire was wrong, he didn't crave a social butterfly, Wendy Palmer connection. Whatever else we talked about, Thursday became the new blood-beat in my brain. My wild fantasy that Matt Ashley would stroll back into my life was the real thing, and I could hardly sleep at night.

Later that week, when I found time with Claire in the art room, I told her about Walt Powers. She was working on a charcoal, intently sketching her face onto a wrinkled brown paper bag.

"So . . ."—I stumbled to the finish—"if you want a really good ID . . . and with Halloween coming up . . . and going to the clubs and all . . ."

Now Claire looked up, her black-smudged gaze refocusing from a distance deep inside herself. I thought of those guys from KISS, how a few years ago they started performing without makeup, and it was like they'd turned into a whole different band from those scary clowns of my childhood. Makeup could really hide a person if you wanted it to.

"My ID works great, and I'm not that big on Halloween." She cupped her chin in one hand, her eyebrows arched, her face a shield to protect her thoughts. "But thanks for inviting me. For thinking about me. Maybe your friends Winnie and Gage need them?"

"Mimi and Gage."

"Right." If Claire asked, I'd admit I'd taken the envelope. It would be a relief, in a way. I never stole things, and even though

I was planning to return the letters as soon as humanly possible, the guilt hammered at me.

But then Claire went back to her paper-bag portrait, calmly dismissing me. It seemed like that was the end of that. And so I was surprised when she called me that night, and the urgency in her voice made me exchange the kitchen phone for the more private one in my parents' bedroom.

"What's up?" I asked. "What's wrong?"

"Aunt Jane has lost her mind." Claire was speaking in a furtive whisper, like a hostage. "She made me go to Tosca's funeral."

"Wait—a cat funeral?"

"Yes. Outside. In the rain."

"Tell me everything." I kicked off my shoes. Whatever else Claire thought about me, I was the one she'd wanted to talk to. Me. As she described the whole insane ordeal, I climbed onto my parents' waterbed, settling in, the receiver cradled against the side of my face.

"We all had to wear black. There's a chapel on the property, and Aunt Jane was carrying a CD player, and she was playing Mozart's Requiem."

"In fairness, cats love Mozart."

Claire snorted. "And of course the whole time, Aunt Jane is giving me dirty looks. You saw how she was, and you know how she blames me for it. Like I've got it out for her stupid cats."

"Hey, you can confess anything to me. I wouldn't be judgmental if it was an act of self-defense. Those cats are humungous—I wouldn't want to be alone in a room with one."

Now Claire laughed outright. "Then Aunt Jane did the eulogy and Mom read a poem and Mr. Mack dug a little cat grave."

"For many reasons, I'm so glad I wasn't there," I said. "But mostly because I think it would have been too hard for me to stop laughing."

"Believe me, Mr. Mack and I almost lost it. But considering he needs his job, and Mom and I need a roof over our heads, we sobered up quick. It was ridiculous to see everyone trying so hard to be dignified."

"You know, Claire, I might as well tell you—the first time I met you, I suspected you were plotting a cat assassination."

Claire laughed, and we kept up that joke for a while, and we stayed on the phone until my parents came upstairs and demanded their room back.

But Thursday morning, when we passed each other in the hall, Claire smiled at me closemouthed, but didn't stop walking.

Did she know how much it hurt, when she changed her mood on a coin toss? Did she care?

"I'M EXHAUSTED," MIMI SAID at lunch on Thursday. "Between my AP workload and these college essays, I'm totally wired and disconnected at the same time."

"Me, too," agreed Gage. "Anyone want to take a break Saturday night? We can order Domino's pizzas, eat cookie dough, watch movies, the works."

"Fun," said Mimi. "I'll need something to look forward to."

"Not me. I'm too behind." I cleared my throat, then delivered my lie. "I think I'll just stay home and finish my Princeton application."

Gage looked skeptical. "With all those hours at Ludington, how are you behind?"

"It's not like it's always study hall for me at the library. Monday I couldn't do any homework because I needed to reshelve books while the Roto-Rooter guys worked on a plumbing leak. But I'm going to come catch your game this afternoon," I added.

"For real?" Gage brightened. "That's a surprise."

The three of us saw one another so often throughout the school day—and usually weekends, too—that our unwritten rule was nobody needed to attend the extras: my lame modern dance recitals, Mimi's junior varsity tennis matches, or even Gage's varsity field hockey games.

But Gage was smiling now. "We're playing Saint Hubert and they're not very good, so it should be a nice easy victory—I expect to hear lots of cheering."

"Definitely."

It was unsettling for me to see Gage so happy at the prospect of my coming to watch her. I hadn't banked on that. She didn't think I'd be there for any other reason than to cheer her on.

I couldn't bring myself to give another.

# seventeen

PARENTS, SIBLINGS, AND BOYFRIENDS were already on the field when I walked over after my last class. The Saint Hubert girls, jumpy with pregame tension but not comfortable enough to scatter all over another school's playing field, did calisthenics in place. My eyes picked out Gage on the bench and Claire stretching.

Jonesy, Tommy, and Matt were third row up on the bleachers. Jonesy Sweet was like the electric version of Tommy Powers. Or maybe Tommy Powers was the acoustic version of Jonesy Sweet. Both guys were good-looking, but Jonesy was wiry and reactive, a contrast to Tommy the mellow brick.

Matt wasn't like either of them, though from a distance you could see he was also their leader. As soon as Matt saw me, the guys looked in my direction, too. And when I came closer, Matt shoved Jonesy over so that I could tuck into the tight space between them.

None of my daydreams had prepared me for sitting between two of Lincoln Academy's most popular seniors. My inside voice said, *Act Normal*—which felt like hopelessly inadequate instructions.

At the center pass that started the game, it was strange to clap for Kreo's attack, but the guys were cheering so hard for her—and for Wendy, too, that I had to cheer along. Then Matt whistled when Claire made a hard drive down the field that advanced a first goal for Argyll, and we all yelled and applauded at one of Gage's heroic saves, and soon my palms stung from clapping and my throat was sore from yelling encouragement to basically everyone—because why not?

During halftime, Matt pulled me up with him to walk with the other guys over to the sidelines. You weren't supposed to talk with players at the half, but I'd seen the Lincoln guys do this, and now here I was, right up here with them.

"Nice receive," Jonesy called out to Kreo.

As she and Wendy ambled over, Wendy's eyes narrowed like a snake's. She was looking at me hard, and I knew whatever she said in Kreo's ear, that it was firstly about me and secondly something mean. Sparkling fears burst through me as my fingernails bit my palms. Was I shaking?

"Hey, are you cold?" Matt asked.

*You're not spazzing out.*

"Maybe a little."

He wrapped a protective arm around my shoulders. But no, nothing was happening to me—not outwardly. Wendy's final up-and-down, followed by a dismissive twirl of her hockey stick, would be the worst of it.

The second half of the game turned out to be a heart-stopper, and when it ended with an Argyll victory, mostly thanks to Gage's goalie work, I felt guilty thinking how I could have come and watched Gage anytime during home games. Gage was a star, I'd noticed that even parents on the opposite team knew her name—some of the Lincoln guys did, too. Why hadn't I ever broken our "stay away" rule to come support her? Not even once, not even as a surprise, to celebrate that one of my closest friends was also the best athlete in our class. And today I was here only because of Matt.

Gage might have been thinking the same thing. "Such a *claimer*, Lizzy, that you came to see *me*." She kept her voice jokey as she brushed past, slinging her stick over her shoulder like a musket. But I'd known Gage way too many years not to recognize when she was hurt.

I'd have chased her down, except what would I say once I'd caught up? Some hurried, flustered apology? I'd have to do better than that.

Claire had played great, too, but in the time I'd gone over to Gage, she'd vanished.

"Ready?" Matt's hand in mine shifted my attention.

I turned. "Yep, let's go. The others are right behind us."

His car was a deep blue-green Saab, somewhere between new and not bad. It had a secondhand vibe with a clean-car smell. Kreo and Jonesy climbed into the back seat, while I took shotgun next to Matt. My mind kept spinning back to sophomore year, and the time Kreo threw a semiformal sweet sixteen at her family's golf club. Kreo'd sent out the invite to forty guests, rejecting exactly thirteen of us. Before that party, nobody had ever put such an exact bracket around who was in the social basement.

"Great game, Kreo," I told her quietly.

"Aw, thanks, Lizzy," she chirped.

That same Saturday, Gage and Mimi and I had gone to Six Flags, where the only rule was never to mention Kreo's party, although the shame of the day hung thick over every ride and game and bite of cheeseburger.

But that was two years ago. Now I was a different person, a cooler person. A girl who hung out with Matt Ashley person.

No matter what Wendy had whispered in Kreo's ear.

At Tommy's house, everyone except me knew Furley, the family's labradoodle. We loaded up with snacks before climbing the stairs to Walt Powers's room of plaid twin bedspreads and sailing prints. An eggshell-blue sheet had been taped to the wall as a backdrop above one of the beds. Walt shared Tommy's tousled dishwater-blond hair and tortoiseshell eyes, but he looked more like a college philosophy major than a high school jock. He had the respect of the room as he made adjustments to a camera on a tripod.

"You first. Just kick off your shoes and climb up," Walt instructed me. "The tilted-upward angle is key on a Pennsylvania driver's license."

Kreo smiled warmly. "This better work, huh, Lizzy? I'm so finished with being denied into, like, *everywhere*, right?" As if we'd shared a dozen memories of being banned from bars and clubs.

I agreed with a smile and got up onto the bed, where Walt adjusted me in the camera's focus. Pop! The flash exploded before I was ready. Spots blitzed hot and red before my eyes. "Oh!" I sank to my knees. Like a dog collared to an electric fence, that zap had thrown me.

"Hey, you okay?" I focused on Walt, closely inspecting me.

"Uh-huh."

"Sorry. I should have warned you about the light." His face relaxed into a grin. "While you might experience some short-term ocular discomfort, the long-term benefits of excellent clubbing will be worth it."

"Ha, okay." Gingerly, I scooted off the bed as Kreo took my place. Still blinking, I leaned back against a far wall.

"IDs will be cut, laminated, and ready tomorrow. But you can pay my forty smacks now," said Walt. He finished setting up Kreo and—*Pop!*—took the shot.

"Yay!" Done, Kreo bounced a couple of times before she jumped off the bed and withdrew her Dooney & Bourke wallet from her matching purse—the same purse my mother had coveted last Christmas, and then decided was too expensive.

She delivered Walt a pair of twenties from a thumb-thick stack.

I could feel my money folded right at my ankle. Casually I bent down as if to adjust my sock and extracted it.

Jonesy was next. No matter how much I blinked, the fiery pattern of spots wouldn't fade from my vision. I felt like I was on a boat, tilting and swaying.

Someone had spoken to me.

"What?"

"Lizzy. You okay?" I had no idea how long Matt had been watching me.

"I . . . no. I think I'd better go home."

He nodded as if he'd expected this answer. Normal or seizure? Was anyone else looking over? Had Jonesy seen Wendy's spaz imitation of me? Did everyone at Lincoln know? Did Matt?

Quickly, before I had to think too hard about any of it, including the new hit to my savings, I handed over my forty bucks, and two minutes later, we'd spun out the door.

"I'm so sorry," I said, once we were pulling out.

"Don't be sorry, just tell me what's up."

"I've got a headache." I rubbed my temple. "And homework. Like a ton of it. Probably that's why I started getting the headache." It sounded like a lie.

He leaned over and checked an empty bottle of Tylenol in his glove compartment, shaking it to be sure. "Sorry."

"N-no, *I'm* so sorry," I stammered.

"Oh, hey, don't—you seem really upset. What's to be sorry about?"

I couldn't bring myself to confess it, but I wanted to give Matt something authentic, something better than "headache," and so I blurted out the whole story of Kreo not inviting thirteen girls to her birthday party, and how Mimi, Gage, and I felt like such losers, how we'd gone to Six Flags and how happy I'd been for my friendship with them—which made me feel bad to have upset Gage this afternoon.

"It's all about your real friends, your true group," Matt said. "And those girls put me to sleep. I made out with Wendy Palmer at five or six different mixers and sleepovers through the years. It's like everyone wanted us to be together. Everyone but me, that is." He grinned over at me. "Hey, I saw your smooth move, by the way."

"Me? Saw what?"

"I saw you take your money out of your sock!" He laughed and jerked out of range as I reached over to pinch his side. "What? I'd never bust you! All your secrets are safe with me—including that you need a wallet update, and that you had to wear your brother Owen's underpants to school the other day."

"Okay, first off, I obviously tell you too much, and also those underpants were an emergency situation! That's not *a thing I do*— it's just that I had no underwear! Remember you promised you'd never say a word to anyone."

He was laughing. "Promise, promise. I'm the vault."

Now I felt even more self-conscious. Matt was basically rephrasing Claire's description—that I was an authentic nerd. "Okay, well, thanks. I'm holding you to it."

"It makes me feel good, that you trust me," he added seriously. "I remember when I first met you, how you made me feel like I could tell you anything." A furrow appeared between his brows. "I should have called you that very first night I got your number."

I wondered what Matt would say if I confessed my condition? Not that I ever would. It was a piece of me that was as sunk and locked as a Houdini box inside me.

"You can definitely tell me anything," I said instead. "Dorky confessions work both ways."

He nodded, but then we were quiet until he pulled up to my house, when he leaned over and kissed me light on the lips. "I'll call you."

This time, I was pretty sure he would.

# eighteen

THE NEXT DAY, I asked Claire about Halloween.

"No way I'm dealing with Halloween," she said, slamming her locker shut, and giving me one of her half-mast stares. "I feel like we talked about this?"

"Oh." I stepped back. "I've got a good ID now, is the thing, if we wanted to—"

"Trampy nurse, trampy teacher, trampy bunny. I'm not into those costumes."

"You'd said something about going to clubs in the city but—"

"Halloween is amateur night at the clubs, every high school freshman will be trying to get in. And this weekend is a bust, anyway, since Aunt Jane's got me doing chores, because of what happened with Tosca. See you Monday." She was gone without a look back.

"Bummer," said Matt when I told him on the phone that night, though he didn't sound perturbed. "The only Halloween party I know about is a random invite from my friend Dave."

"Who's your friend Dave?"

"Just this guy I know from soccer camp, and he's all the way out in Paoli. Isn't Wendy having people over? She's closer to home."

I hadn't been invited to Wendy's party. "I'm sure Wendy's house is just about watching scary movies and sitting around." I cleared my throat. "Should I tell her we're coming over? Or . . . you could."

"Yeah, sure. If everyone else is going."

"Although . . . thinking about it . . . it'll be a lot of the same people at Wendy's. The Paoli party might be more new and different?"

There was a pause on the line. "Okay, why not."

When I hung up the phone, it felt like I'd landed a plane.

I USED MOST OF Saturday to try out different outfits, wishing endlessly that Claire were around to do my eyes and approve my choices. Standing on the toilet trying to see myself in sections of the bathroom mirror, I could hear Claire's voice in my head—*Don't wear your baggy tweed coat. Borrow your brother's barn jacket and your dad's black scarf. The more black the better.*

It was a "casual costume" party, according to Matt, so I'd bought a witch's hat at the drugstore, and when Matt picked me up, he'd outdone me in white pants, a blue T-shirt, and blue-tinted hair.

"I'm a Smurf," he explained to my brothers. Peter was immediately silenced by the presence of a Lincoln Academy senior, but Owen was a little more curious.

"Which one?" asked Owen. "There's lots. Grouchy Smurf and Vanity Smurf and Jokey Smurf . . ."

"I'm Awesome Smurf," said Matt.

Owen looked perplexed. "There's no such thing as Awesome Smurf."

"There is now." He flipped a stick of Trident from his overcoat for Owen's catch.

"Remember, home by eleven," Mom said, a curfew I hadn't even known was in effect until that moment. But I could tell that both my parents were impressed that after all these years, my very first date would be such a good catch. Even with his blue hair.

"I think you won over the family," I told Matt when we were safe in his car.

"Good. Your folks are cool," he said.

"They keep it well hidden. Just exactly where are you seeing coolness?"

Matt shrugged. "Just, they're easy. Compared with mine."

"Like how?"

"Like I had to change into my Halloween costume in the car. My parents don't ever want me looking stupid or whatever." He turned up the music. "Public Enemy," he said. "I can tell you don't like it."

"It's not my thing, but it's your thing, so I do like it."

"What's your music?"

All of Claire's bands—Joy Division, New Order, Psychedelic Furs—were on the tip of my tongue. "I don't know," I answered honestly.

Dave Jimenez lived deep in cow country. Long stretches of fences and fields eventually gave way to a dirt road at least another mile past the turn at the Jimenezes' mailbox. "This feels pretty Halloween-y," I joked as we bumped along until we finally got to a long ranch-style house surrounded by blackness, thundering with Van Halen, and packed with kids spilling over the front porch, where the beer keg was set up.

"Happy Halloween, Smurf and Witch." On the porch, a tall guy in a Lone Ranger mask sprang from the dark, as if he'd been waiting for us. He carried a plastic cup in each hand. "You should never drink anything purple," he said as he delivered one to me. "Purple is the color of poison, right? But it's the grain alcohol you gotta watch out for."

"Um, I guess so." I took a cup and looked down into its purple liquid surface, as Matt signaled to keep moving, a maneuver that the Lone Ranger blocked.

"Ashley." He pushed up the mask, and now I was staring at a guy who was so movie-star hot that I couldn't look away. "Is this how you come into my party? Sneaking in like a thief? You suck, man." I could tell he was a little drunk. "I'm your fricking host, asshole."

"Dude, sorry." Matt gave a half laugh. "Didn't recognize you."

I didn't see how that could be true. Even masked, Dave's face was chiseled like the guy on my paperback cover of *The Great Gatsby*, all bedroom eyes and curved lips and cleft chin.

Matt knocked a fist against Dave's shoulder. "And this is Lizzy."

"Lizzy, hey. A friend of Matt's is you know the rest."

"Thanks." I didn't know what to say. The guys' connection seemed itchy, like a memory of a prank gone wrong between them. I sipped on my drink.

"Go slow, have fun. I'll catch up with you kids later." Dave gave Matt a return jab on the arm, a little harder and meaner, and left us.

"Seems nice," I said. The music from the speakers was painfully loud as we edged our way into a sunken living room where costumed kids were dancing or huddled on the couches. Matt yoked me with both hands from behind, like a human seat belt, his arms doubling around my waist.

I leaned back to talk in his ear. Matt's ear! Like a sweet little shell you'd keep. "What's the deal with Dave's parents? How does he get away with throwing a party this intense?"

"His dad travels a lot, he must be away now. His mom died a long time ago. Dave's known for these ragers since cops would never come out this far. I think it's mostly Pruitt High kids— where Dave goes." Matt paused. "He's got lots of friends."

"Yeah, he seems like a fun guy."

"We never hang out during the school year, so it's kinda strange to see him out of context."

"He's good-looking."

"All the girls say that." Matt spoke abruptly, sounding almost insulted, and I wished *I* hadn't said it.

"Want to dance?"

"Yeah, this living room reminds me of Friday nights at Skate City."

"Ha." I smiled like I knew, but Mimi and Gage and I had never got up the nerve to hit Skate City, a middle school hotspot where the only thing worse than the popular crowd was the popular crowd speeding past us breakneck on skates.

We danced close but careful, the surfaces of our bodies light as the touch of a leaf to a current of water. When Dave reappeared with a fresh drink for me, he managed to insinuate himself between us, dancing first with me, then with Matt and me both, then just me again, pulling me in. Dave might have been the best-looking person I'd ever seen in real life. His silky dark hair was brushed off his hairline to the back of his head, and his smooth skin glowed against his paper-thin peach sweater, its wool so delicate that one tiny pull would ruin it. I tried not to stare at him too hard while memorizing his features so I could sketch them later.

When the song ended, I wriggled out of Dave's grip as Matt reeled me in.

"Enough already," said Matt. "Stop poaching."

"Who, me?" But Dave got the hint. He reached for a tall, pretty girl on the edge of the crowd, who knew him well enough to spin laughing into his arms.

"It's hot in here," I mentioned. Sweat from Matt's forehead was seeping into his hair, turning it a bright oxidized green. His arm was damp around my waist, and as we kept dancing, I couldn't help but think that he was trying to steer us away from Dave, who simultaneously was trying to put himself in my sight line. At one point, he stood dead center in the room, in conversation with the tall girl, a boarding school type—leggy in her tiny dress, with thin gold bangles up her arms. When he looked up to catch my eye, we both had to smile—I was busted. Whatever game he was playing, I should stop being part of it.

It was impossible to imagine Mimi and Gage here, though I wished they were. It would have been nice to have some friends. Would they be dancing? Drinking these purple drinks? At some point, I'd scored my third cup of punch, which didn't seem like a big deal—it wasn't too potent.

And then it hit me.

"I might need to get out of here."

"Yeah, sure." Matt kept a grip on me as I lurched from the living room. Fear of losing it, fear of a blackout—I could practically hear my ticking clock. Dr. Neumann had warned me endlessly about not mixing alcohol with medication.

At least Matt seemed to get it. His hand kept a grip as he steered us outside to cool down under the stars.

"Sorry," I said as we settled on the porch steps. I closed my eyes and breathed.

"It's fine. Dave was hounding us anyway."

My eardrums felt bruised by the music. "He's got a big personality."

Matt laughed. "That's one way of putting it. He's what my parents would call a bad influence. But yeah, Dave's an original. He's totally outside the lines."

"How's that?"

"Well, for one thing, I guess, is how he's always looking for the bigger picture. He's all about getting out there, getting lost. He's been mountain climbing in Peru, white-water rafting in Costa Rica. Last summer he went to Berlin to protest the wall, and every year he does a youth wilderness trip where they throw you in the middle of the woods and you've got to figure out how to stay alive."

"I've heard about those youth wilderness trips—Gage was thinking of going on one, if she can get over the nature-is-your-bathroom thing."

"Yeah, Dave does all the things other people talk about doing. Whenever I talk to him, he makes me want to get away from the same tired shit."

My head was spinning. I wished I could lie down for a couple of minutes. "What's your same tired shit?"

"I guess another summer lifeguarding at Little Egg Harbor."

I nodded, although Little Egg Harbor sounded pretty wonderful to me. All the rich families had houses at the shore, but my family didn't and we never went anywhere. Over a summer, we'd escape the heat for weekends at my grandmother's place out in Chester County, because she had a swimming pond nearby, and for one week in August we rented a cabin in Cook's Forest State Park. I'd really liked Cook's Forest as a little kid, but for the past three years, I'd wanted to die from the boredom and bean dinners.

The car ride home made me feel even wobblier. Why did I drink three drinks in an hour? I closed my eyes so traffic lights wouldn't shine so harsh into them.

"Are you always the designated driver?" I could hear my voice slurring the question as we arrived at my house. "For your friends, I mean?"

"It's better for me to stay sharp, or I say stupid things." Matt cut the engine and lights. "Even cough medicine screws me up." He leaned over and kissed me. "You taste like grape Kool-Aid."

Dizzy as I felt, I turned into his kiss, and soon Matt had pushed himself across the driver's seat and crossways over my body. I could feel the sharp edge of his nose, the deeper land of his lips on mine. The warmth of his breath sent a waterfall of chills down my spine.

His next kiss was full on, and I let my mouth open as I kissed him back—or tried to—I'd kissed only one other guy before, working as a bus girl at Friendly's in Berwyn last summer. Dennis Purdy had worked the take-out window, and he hadn't been too experienced himself, with his bullying tongue and no technique. It was mortifying to think that Matt would judge me as badly as I'd judged Dennis Purdy. It was also depressing to think that after all these years of imagining Matt Ashley kissing me, I now wouldn't hold up my end of the fantasy because I was too drunk.

His hand tugged the fabric of my T-shirt, pulling it free from my jeans. Nerve endings spiked at the touch of air on my skin. I wriggled down as he eased my seat back. Everything about Matt was lightweight yet strong, as if he were made from a supple wood—from the bones of his shoulders to the press of his thighs and his hard-on. I was completely unstrung with the sensation of his hand pushing under the elastic of my leggings, past my lacy underwear.

"Not Owen's," he whispered, his finger under the lace.

"Not tonight."

As his fingers spidered along my hip bone, I heard my breath dig in, my skin holding the print of his mouth everywhere he left a kiss, though my mind was racing, wondering what he expected back, if I should be more active, maybe now was the time to pull on his zipper? I didn't think I was ready to do that.

But my head was so swampy, and the car's tipped-back angle had put a lurch in my stomach. Mom had put a bottle of Colors of Benetton in my stocking last Christmas, and I'd always liked it, but right now it seemed to cling too hard, an overripe sweaty cinnamon-orange smell. So much was happening all at once, and when Matt pulled back to stare at me and ask if everything was okay, I shook my head. "I'm so sorry. I never drank hard alcohol."

"Wait—ever?" He laughed into my silence. "You'll need to sleep it off. Take some aspirin now so it can start to work." He lifted himself off me.

My stupid brain, marinating in this deep, unexpected tub of booze I'd sunk it in, couldn't figure out the right thing to say.

"Good night," I whispered. "I feel bad. Like, beyond just being drunk bad."

"Don't feel bad." He put a finger to his lips as he opened his car door and then came around to my side. I got out of the car and leaned on him as he navigated me to the front door, where we shared a quick, fumbling good-bye kiss. At the next moment of lightning horror that I might vomit right this second, I yanked open the door, sprinting to the powder room just in time to kick off the far worse part of this night.

# nineteen

AFTER AN HOUR OF heaves that left my ribs aching, I managed to take a couple of aspirin before I crawled upstairs to bed and fell into a spinning sleep. I woke into deep night blackness with my head stuck in a rhythmic *bang bang bang* like a rock in the dryer.

My skin felt like cling wrap that was barely holding all the parts of me together.

After a third trip to the bathroom, I curled up on the tile floor and wanted to die.

So this was *bombed. Plastered. Smashed.* All the words made sense now.

By morning, I was back in bed. My headache had eased into a bruised thudding. I drifted in and out of sleep until Dad tapped on my door and said he'd give me a lift to my Sunday shift at Ludington, if I could be ready in ten minutes.

The shower was like a stream of BB pellets on my tender skin, and in the car I kept my temple pressed against the glass of the passenger-seat window.

Dad pulled into the McDonald's drive-through and ordered our breakfasts.

"When did I graduate from orange juice to a large coffee?"

"Since you got your first hangover," he answered. "Drink a lot of water today."

I allowed a nod. Waiting for the lecture.

"Look, Banana," Dad started, "young people are always testing their personal limits, and I realize there's a young man involved—"

"Dad."

"—and may I just say, a very nice-seeming young man, but let me note here, don't forget you can always bring Mimi and Gage. They're good girls and a good influence, they know you best and—"

"Dad!"

"—and you're only sixteen years old, and Mom and I don't want you to be in situations where your friends aren't around to help you make the right choices."

"Dad, if you could hear yourself! Mimi and Gage don't want me to drag them around on my dates!" I pressed my fingers to my temple. This conversation was not helping my head.

"It's just a suggestion." Dad looked hurt as he brushed corn-meal flecks of his McMuffin from his brown nylon accountant's pants. "The other thing I want to say, and then I'll release you to the wilds of Ludington—is that you need to watch your health more than other kids."

"I was not even close to a—"

"Because there isn't a doctor alive, including your own, who'll tell you that alcohol doesn't have an extra implication for you."

"Fine. I'll be more careful."

"That's all I'm asking." He leaned over and pulled me in to kiss the top of my head. "Don't forget who you are, Lizzy."

The library's blinding track lighting made me want to hide in a closet. Mrs. Binswanger's beady eyes watched me drag around, limply reshelving books, and I was relieved when she clocked out and left.

I'd forgotten my book bag, so I couldn't do any homework, even if I'd been in any shape to solve physics problems or translate Ovid. Mostly I kept stumbling through last night. I was getting together with Matt Ashley. Even if I'd slightly ruined it by being too drunk, had I done all the other stuff right? Did he think I was slutty for the way I'd let him touch me wherever he wanted? Had I breathed too hard, made too much noise, or not enough? Was he thinking about it the way I was thinking about it?

I found a bottle of Anacin in the circulation-desk drawer, and spent the rest of my shift working on an ink graphic of my palm for art. I wondered what a fortune-teller might know about my hand that I didn't. I'd have given anything for a palm reading on that final score for last night. At least tonight, with the time change, I would get an extra hour of sleep, which was all I wanted once I came home from work.

The next morning, I woke up ahead of my alarm clock and felt like myself again.

New day, new week—

Holy crap, no.

*No no no no.*

Leapfrogging to my desk, I flipped through the forms. Why had I thought I was almost finished? How could I be so stupid? This was a three-essay application, and I'd typed out only the basics, along with some essay notes in longhand.

Nothing was ready. *Nothing.*

I'd needed all of Sunday, and instead I'd let it dribble away from me. I'd staggered around like a deadbeat, using up precious hours to nurse my hangover, popping painkillers and drinking Cokes to settle my stomach.

With frantic fingers, I shoved the form into my notebook, then pressed my hands against my burning cheeks. This wasn't like me. This wasn't how I did things, quick and messy. Now I'd have to take the application to school to cram work whenever I had a free moment.

I couldn't even confess it to Mimi and Gage, considering I'd held tight to my "too much work" lie all weekend, and I had to say no to their multiple invites to the mall, the movies, and Rock-N-Bowl for Sunday pizza and bowling.

"Hey, Lizzy, why the long face?" asked Gage in homeroom.

I rolled my shoulders. "I'm tired."

"I could pick you up after Ludington today. We can microwave chimichangas and pass out candy," she offered. "I rented *The Shining.*"

"And I'm coming, too," added Mimi. "Say yes. I feel like it's been forever since we did a Three Musketeers night."

"Sorry. I've just got too much work," I said, truly regretful. I really wanted to make it right with Gage, especially after last Thursday. But I wasn't lying. The application would take me hours.

"Oookay. Just let us know when you're ready to hang out with us again," said Mimi. "We miss you."

"But we won't hold our breath."

Gage's comment was a joke, of course, but I sensed hurt feelings beneath.

After my library shift, dinner, and the last trick-or-treater, I was at my desk drafting my final essays for Princeton onto legal paper. It was almost three in the morning when I sealed the envelope, and I was too wired to sleep. Eyes broiling, I made an ink sketch of Matt from a memory I had of him throwing a stick to Furley, arm arced, neck angled. As I drew, I let myself go through all the reasons why he might not have called me, then, sketch complete, I dropped like a stone into bed.

The next morning on the way to school, when I asked Mom if she would mind detouring to the post office, she was plainly shocked.

"Isn't Princeton due *today*?"

"All I needed was to type the essays. It's no big deal."

"Your *first-choice* college—where is this cavalier attitude coming from?"

"I did it. It's done. I think you're overreacting."

Mom's eyes were obscured behind her mirrored sunglasses but her mouth was a hook of disappointment. "I think all I'm doing is *reacting*. November first postage on a November first deadline is shaving it razor thin, don't you agree?"

"Mom, cut me some slack. It's not like it's overdue."

But she was right. Not that I'd admit it to Mom, who seemed to know anyway.

I stared out the car window until we'd arrived at the post office, but my anxiety stayed with me long after I made a wish, poked the envelope through the mail slot, and listened for its hushed slip to the bottom.

# twenty

THAT AFTERNOON IN ART, I set up my spot with Mimi and Gage before Claire glided in. She immediately changed the music from the Grateful Dead to Echo and the Bunnymen and sat alone at an empty table.

But when she saw me, she waved me over, a first.

She'd never confronted me about Jay's letters, so I was hopeful I was in the clear on that. As I approached, I saw that she was deep into yet another self-portrait, this one in linoleum block. Something about the short stabs of her cross-hatching looked more authentic to Claire's face—severe, guarded—than her past efforts.

"How'd the weekend end up?" she asked when I reached her.

Dave Jimenez's Halloween party felt like eons ago. I glanced at Gage and Mimi across the room, to make sure they couldn't hear. "Matt and I went to his friend's house. He had this awesome costume party." Then I added, "But I forgot to finish Princeton. I had to cram, and I mailed it in this morning. My mom was wigging out."

"No shit." Claire put down her stylus to give me all her focus. "Guess you don't want to go there as much as you thought you did."

"Are you kidding? It's like *the* goal of my life. I just forgot."

"Remind me why it's the goal again?"

"Do I have to have a reason besides that it's one of the best schools in the country?"

"What's your connection? Is there some Princeton grad who inspired you?"

"My uncle." Uncle Grant was technically my mother's uncle, and he was a source of enormous pride in Mom's family. I'd met him only a few times.

"And what's he all about?"

"He's retired, but he was a trial lawyer and he swam in the Olympics."

"So you want to follow in his footsteps?"

"Not law and swimming. But you know what I mean. Success-wise, yes."

"Sounds like Princeton is the perfect place for you, then," said Claire, with a dismissive ripple of her fingers. "Listen, I've got an idea. Let's go clubbing this weekend. There's one that just opened last month, it's called the Bank—it's an actual bank in Center City, over on Spring Garden."

Glee lifted me up. "Matt's been wanting to go into Philly—oh, unless you don't want—I mean, I know you barely know Matt but—"

"Totally, Matt, too."

"Sounds cool, I'll let him know."

I returned to my table feeling pretty pumped. Mimi and Gage hadn't heard a word, but it was obvious from their decision not to speak about it that I wasn't "claiming" my private conversation with Claire.

My Claire-glow stayed with me until dinner. I'd barely taken my first bite of lasagna when Mom started in. "Lizzy. I told your father about our pit stop at the post office this morning. We think you're losing focus on what's top priority this year. Especially with all this new, social zipping around."

"I'm not zipping that much. There's lots of girls at Argyll who are way zippier than me." I tucked on a friendly smile.

But Mom's face told me that breezy wasn't the right strategy. "Let's be clear, Lizzy. Right now, this year, you are making one of the most important choices of your life."

None of us said anything to that, and after a few seconds, Dad seemed obligated to chime in. "Mom and I work too hard to—"

The ring of the kitchen phone interrupted, loud enough to silence table talk. Since I got the majority of phone calls, it served only to emphasize Mom's point.

I stared at my lasagna, chewing at my bottom lip. I couldn't dash to the kitchen, but what if it was Matt? What if I missed this call and he never called me ever again?

Nobody moved. I counted off six rings before the call routed to the answering machine upstairs in my parents' room. The second beep meant that whoever had called had left a message.

*Please, please let it be Matt.*

"Colleges look for slumps in a transcript," continued Dad.

"Exactly." Mom nodded. "Just because you've applied early doesn't mean you can take a vacation from—oh, for heaven's sake." The phone had started ringing again, a nagging follow-up, as if the caller had flat-out refused to accept that nobody had picked up on the first go-round.

"Shouldn't I just get it? Tell whoever it is that we're eating?" I asked in a tiny voice.

Tight-faced, Mom nodded.

I dashed to the kitchen.

"Hello?"

"Lizzy? Is that you? I've been trying to get ahold of you—I left a message."

He sounded so far away that for a moment I wasn't sure if it was really him.

"Matt? What happened? Is everything okay?"

"No, it's not. Not at all. It's Tommy's brother, Walt." And now I heard Matt's voice shake openly as he forced the next words. "Last night, he killed himself."

# part two

## winter

# twenty-one

THE SUNDAY MORNING OF Walter Ryan Powers's funeral was soft and gray. A mist had settled in that weekend, and it surrounded us with a kind of static despair. Nobody could stop whispering about it, not even in the church. In hushed asides, we were all still struggling to make sense of an act that had completely shocked everyone in Walt's radius.

The service was held at the Church of the Redeemer, which I'd passed a thousand times but never been inside till now. Matt and I stood in the front pew along with the rest of Tommy's closest friends, and it was so crowded that mourners spilled from the vestibule out the front doors.

The only other funeral I'd attended was Granny Swift's, two years ago, a quietly boring hour suitable to the death of my eighty-nine-year-old great-grandmother. I hardly remembered it beyond some croaky voices eulogizing Granny's pear streusel and her volunteer work for UNICEF and the Mercer County conservancy.

Walt's funeral felt different. Everyone seemed to be staring around in a state of dazed disorder. Walt's college friends and Tommy's high school friends had turned out in huge numbers, wearing borrowed suits with wrinkled collared shirts and badly knotted ties, while the girls—myself included—stood straight in our best dark dresses, our sweetheart necklines made more demure by blazers and overcoats. But the readings, hymns, and poems kept striking that same blunt blade of shock that Walt Powers's life was over.

Matt had to get up and speak, too, because Tommy was falling apart and didn't think he could manage it. Matt had practiced his words with me over the phone. Now I watched him walk to the front, and he didn't seem nervous at all, more like a campfire storyteller as he spoke.

"Walt was like my big brother," he said, his voice deep and controlled. "But a big brother with superpowers. He taught Tommy and me how to swim and how to ride dirt bikes. When he won a free Atari from collecting box tops, he let us play with it that first day it arrived. In high school, when he started working summers for Ralph Nader, Walt always had time to explain about how to treat the environment. Whatever he was telling us, we wanted to listen, and whatever he was teaching us, we wanted to learn. Whether it was racing bikes or playing games or going out to clubs, Walt wanted everyone to be included. Last summer, he got into writing screenplays—with plans to one day direct and produce his own films. For him, making movies would be another way of sharing a dream and an experience." In Matt's pause, I knew he was doubling his effort to keep his words steady; he almost succeeded. "I can't believe those dreams and experiences won't come true for him."

"You did great," I whispered when Matt returned to my side in the pew. "I hope your parents got here in time to listen."

"They aren't here," he whispered back. Then, playing off my surprise, he added, "Suicide is a crime in the Catholic Church."

"Oh." Was that true? How could anyone feel anything but the worst kind of pity for a kid who was so unhappy with his life that he got his dad's handgun from the house safe, took it to college, and then while his roommates were at Halloween parties, locked the door to his dorm room, put the gun to his temple, and blew his brains out?

But by now I knew better than to press Matt on his parents.

Outside in the parking lot, I waited by Matt's car, arms crossed, pulling my sweater tight around me against the chill, while he looped through a last round of condolences with Tommy's extended family.

"Hey, you."

"Theo!" He appeared out of nowhere, looking like a full-on adult in a dark suit that was cut more crisply and stylish than the standard Lincoln baggy pants and boxy blazer. He seemed like he'd touched down from way farther away than just college. "Did you drive all the way from school?"

Theo nodded. "I'd have driven three times longer for Walt."

Of course, Theo and Walt were in the same class at Lincoln. "It's a shock, I guess."

Theo reached into his pocket for his car keys. "Maybe for some. You never really know what a person's going through."

I felt confused. All week, all anyone was saying was that it was a shock. But Theo didn't elaborate.

"You need a lift?" We were right by Theo's secondhand metallic blue Mustang—a car that was firmly in the Not Bad category, with points for unique.

"No, thanks." Though for a crazy moment all I wanted was for Theo to rescue me from this church, this sad, stifling morning.

"You sure? I was thinking of driving out to Longwood Gardens, just do some thinking." Theo and I both had a thing for Longwood Gardens from years ago, when the Kims had taken everyone on a "cultural" trip that bored Mimi so much she'd gone back to wait in the car. Theo and I had been mesmerized by the fountains and water lilies.

Suddenly I saw myself next to Theo, walking together along the garden paths, where I could talk openly about how I was still reeling from how Matt's parents boycotted Walt's funeral.

"I wish I could," I said instead, "but I feel like I'd be ditching my friends. My other friends, I mean. Obviously, we're friends, too, you and I." I was stammering and flustered and I wished I didn't want so badly to jump in Theo's car and escape Matt's jock pack, along with the promise of a bleak afternoon at Tommy's house.

"No problem, Blizzard. See ya later. Stay strong." He chucked me under the chin, and my tiny crush-fantasy afternoon with Theo dissolved as I watched him go.

It was funny how I'd known Theo pretty much my whole life, and yet in the six months he'd lived apart from his family, he'd become someone so newly intimidating. He'd also lost some of that Lincoln Academy touch, too, that extra aggression and competitive style that was part of the deal when you went there. Theo seemed to be past the teams and herds and status scrabbling of high school. I wondered how different I'd be, or Matt, or any of us by this time next year.

That night, I took my fake ID from where I'd stashed it in my sock drawer, trying to remember every tiny thing I'd noticed about Walt. Stretching out on my bed, with the ID next to me, I tried to pull up the feel of that afternoon as I sketched Walt in my notebook. I wanted to capture his deft fingers as he'd angled his tripod, how his shaggy hair gave him a look of a guy who spent afternoons on beaches or boats. There'd been such an easy way he'd dealt with us all, too, tolerant and laid-back.

"Why do you really think he did it?" I asked Matt later, as he dropped me home that night.

"He had some problems," Matt answered. "We were pretty close. He talked about things to me, sort of." He paused. "Not that any of it matters anymore."

"How's Tommy?"

"Bad. He's gonna need us around more. He wants to go to hang out, get some chow at Al E. Gators on Tuesday afternoon. Are you up for that?"

"Yeah, sure."

"Cool, I'll pick you up after school?"

"Great." I smiled. Though of course the circumstances with Tommy were awful, I loved whenever Matt arrived on campus. It was the easiest way in the world to announce to everyone that I was dating Matt Ashley without having to say a thing.

"MATT ASHLEY'S ALL ABOUT you these days, huh?" Gage remarked Tuesday afternoon as she walked with me down the hall. I'd seen Matt's car parked, and I knew he was in the senior lounge.

"I guess."

"He's definitely cute, and he seems nice enough. In kind of an upstanding, heroic citizen way."

"He is! We should all hang out sometime."

"Like, as a double date but with Meems and me? Might be awkward." Gage laughed self-consciously. "Are you still on for our three-way call tonight?"

"Yeah, for sure. Even though Bush is leading in every poll in the country."

"Polls don't know everything." Gage, Mimi, and I had to be kind of undercover Democrats at Argyll, where most girls—like their parents—believed that Dukakis was a joke. And that night, after witnessing George H. W. Bush's totally unsurprising victory, we all stayed on the phone in a three-way blue bummer until the diversion of my call waiting. I knew it was Claire.

"I'm gonna take that," I said.

Mimi made a kissing noise. "Tell Loverboy I say hi."

I didn't want to say that Matt's strict parents would never let him call super late.

"Hey," said Claire when I clicked over. "Looks like men still rule the world. Want to watch MTV and draw?"

"Sure."

"Hang on." I knew Claire was covering the phone as Aunt Jane barged into the library for a testy conversation about whether Claire had seen one of the cats.

"You think you can get away this Saturday?" Claire asked when she got back on.

"That'd be so great. I'm not sure I could handle another Saturday night of Rodney Dangerfield jokes at the Powers house." The past weekend, a group of Tommy's closest friends— Matt and me, along with Tommy, Jonesy, and Kreo—had hung out there, hunkered down in the paisley-cushioned family room. We'd watched *Caddyshack* followed by *Airplane*, as Mrs. Powers occasionally wandered in to tell us she'd bring in some snacks, but then never did.

"It'd be fun to walk around the city, before it gets too cold."

"I'm sure Matt would be psyched." Here was my chance. "Can I get Matt to invite his friend—"

"I don't want a setup."

"It wouldn't be like that. Couldn't you just meet him? I think he might be kind of perfect for you." Dave Jimenez plus Claire Reynolds seemed like an exact fit, two charismatic puzzle pieces notching seamlessly together.

"Uhhh." Claire's sigh gusted through the receiver.

"That sound you just made was a yes, right?"

"Ehhh . . ."

"He's really hot."

"I'm not on the market. Just tell him it's only for the boy-girl symmetry, okay?"

"He's perfect for you. You won't regret it."

"I already slightly regret it."

But I knew better. Dave, Matt, Claire—two months ago, I never could have imagined these people would all be connected through me. And yet here they were, all in reach, and I was the linchpin, the center of it all.

# twenty-two

OF COURSE CLAIRE KNEW about a tavern that sold a brand of hard cider carried by only a few select places in Philadelphia.

"It's brewed by Amish people," she explained.

"Pepper McDonald forgot to mention secret cider in her Amish people assembly," I said.

The two of us were sitting together on the Paoli local, *clackity-clack*ing into 30th Street Station. Claire hadn't wanted the hassle of Saturday-night parking, so we'd met up on the train. Her plan also meant we'd catch the 11:50 p.m. later tonight, the last local out of Philadelphia, and then walk from the Merion train station back to Lilac House. It was a little unnerving, but I'd kept quiet on concerns about serial killers lurking on the road or in deserted parking lots.

Inside 30th Street Station, we split a small McDonald's fries—the waft of hot grease in the station's drafty cold air was too tantalizing to resist—and then we plunged into the city, treading the blocks until we were tired, and then hailing a cab the rest of the way to the tavern that was tucked at the end of a cobbled one-way street. Inside was a silk scarves and black overcoats crowd, too stylish for me, but we managed to get a back table, where we ordered chicken tenders and beef nachos and hard ciders—and immediately got carded.

I removed Walt's fake ID from my wallet and passed it over. The waitress took her time. I kept my eyes on my menu, my lips pursed in phony concentration as the waitress flipped the card and scrutinized the back.

This was going on way too long. Would I get thrown out? Detained until the police arrived? Fined? Cuffed?

But the waitress handed back my card, and then Claire's, without a word.

"How do you know about this place anyway?"

"Jay."

"Jay," I repeated. "Shoulda known."

Claire put the edge of her thumb in her mouth, working a cuticle. "We spent time in Philadelphia," she added. "I thought I told you."

"Nope. I remember everything you tell me about Jay."

"I don't know why I still talk about him, I hardly ever think about him." But Claire wasn't a good actress—any mention of Jay's name left her rattled.

"Did you come here together?"

She nodded. "Last year, for the cider. We went Halloween-costume shopping and then, yeah, we had dinner here."

"I thought you didn't like Halloween."

She gave me a look. "It was fun last year, and I don't want to get all sentimental about it, but at the same time I didn't want to be at some dumb high school keg party trying not to think about it is all." She shrugged. "Anyway, we found this great costume store, and Jay bought a yeti mask, but the yeti body was huge—and Jay's only five eleven. So when we came back to school, he gave it to a kid who pinned it to his dorm wall, like a bearskin." She was smiling, and I saw so clearly the echo of last year's Claire in her face that it bothered me how absent that girl was from today.

When the ciders came, I raised my mug. "To Walt Powers," I said.

"I never met Walt," said Claire as we clinked. "I never met anyone who killed themselves. There's this pond at Strickland, it's called Lovell Pond, and they say a girl drowned herself there, back in the fifties. She'd gotten pregnant, and she didn't know what to do, who to tell, how to handle it."

"That's so sad," I said. "Terrible." My mind was racing. Unwanted pregnancy. Was *that* the scandal of Claire and Jay? Was she sending me a hint that she connected her own story to that tragic girl of Lovell Pond?

"Tommy Powers breaks down in front of us," I offered. "None of Matt's friends really know what to do for him, except to constantly hang out together and eat. Like everything can be solved with more burgers and milk shakes."

"So that means you have to hang out in a big pack, too."

"For now. Matt's still really upset about Walt. Being in the group makes him feel safe, I guess."

Claire made a face. "*Safe*? Doesn't sound too hot."

"It's not. The guys are always with us."

She wriggled her eyebrows.

I was turning warm. "I mean, we make out a little bit when he drops me off. I keep thinking it's because of Walt, nobody's really settled down yet, but—do you think it's weird?"

"Safe is . . . important," she answered slowly. "Sometimes a safe person is the thing you need most. Maybe it's because you're too young, that you're such a kid Matt doesn't feel the pressure, like he doesn't have to come on too macho, all hot and heavy."

I nodded, then scooped up a nacho once the platters of food arrived, like I was totally diverted by the meal and not at all upset with the conversation, even though it had pushed right into my bruise, my secret tender worry that Matt thought I was too young, too immature, not sexy enough. Luckily we spent the rest of dinner talking music and art and which teachers got on our nerves.

When the check came, Claire's Visa was declined.

"Crapsticks, I'm sorry. Aunt Jane gave me this card, but unless it's for supermarket errands, every time I put a charge on it, the bank calls her, and then she has them suspend my account until we discuss it. It's this power game she plays. Can you cover me again?"

I tried not to feel annoyed. I'd already bought Claire's train ticket, plus the cab here. Dinner should have been on her. I'd never have picked this trendy tavern if I thought I'd have to pay for it.

Underneath my prickly sense of being played, I also worried how Claire would deal with the rest of her costs tonight.

We stepped out into the street and hailed a taxi to Spring Garden, another six dollars from me.

"I hope there's no cover," I said helplessly as we walked the block toward the club, where a crowd of kids had gathered, rubbing their hands together and jumping up and down to keep warm.

"Of course there's a cover—it's ten dollars and all you can drink. Hey, does Matt have a twin?"

"What do you mean?"

She pointed into the herd right by the entrance, singling out Matt and Dave, who looked nearly identical in their baggy jeans, dark wool peacoats thrown back on their shoulders, thermal shirts beneath. Claire was their triplet. Earlier when we'd been getting ready in her icy library bedroom, I joked that her shirt looked like a lumberjack's underwear. But it was obviously perfect club clothes, and I was all wrong in this gray roll-neck sweater.

At least I had the Doc Martens I'd splurged on last week, even if they were overshiny with newness.

Matt's gaze on me was a private gift. "Stripes." He took my hand as he then introduced Claire to Dave, who rewarded her with one of his leading-man smiles. I could tell he liked what he saw. Claire seemed relaxed enough.

The Bank had been open for less than a month, and Claire figured our best chance was to sidle in on the early side, before the college students showed up. One look at the line told me that plenty of other high school kids had the same idea, and the three-hundred-pound bouncer didn't look to be in a hurry to open the doors.

"Dave's got an apartment near Liberty Place," Matt said after a few freezing minutes of our inching along.

I startled. "Oh, yeah?"

"It belongs to one of my dad's clients," said Dave. "He lets him use it anytime. Nobody's in it now, and I've got the key."

"It's on the twenty-fourth floor," said Matt. "We were up there earlier."

"We did each other's hair," said Dave in a lispy, fluted voice. A few kids, hearing him, laughed.

"I'm staying over tonight," Matt told me.

"Cool." Claire didn't seem to care about any of this information. But my heart was thudding at the thought of going back to some random apartment with Matt.

*Take a chill pill, Lizzy.* We hadn't even gotten into the Bank. Nobody was making any decisions yet.

At the club's entrance, Dave's and Claire's IDs passed, and they disappeared. Through dungeon-thick doors, we stepped into a vaulted marble space and a heavy bass beat. It really did look like a bank that had been hijacked by a club. Purple and red strobes flashed from the upper balcony DJ booth.

Strobes weren't good for me, since they could trigger a seizure. I looked down at my boots and counted back from ten, then let myself reconnect.

The whole place was dark, with one far wall banked by dozens of TV screens, all flickering with the same old black-and-white movie. Everyone was pulsing to the beat. It was hot, too—I pulled off my sweater and added it to the lumpy hill of scarves and coats in a deep corner of the room. As my eyes adjusted, I could see that my bra was visibly pink under my T-shirt, but people were wearing so many getups—from bubble skirts to biker shorts—that a peekaboo bra didn't seem like a big deal.

When Dave pointed to the bar in the back, I shook my head. "I'm good, thanks." I didn't need a repeat of Halloween.

"I'll see what they've got." Dave looked to Claire, hoping she'd join him, but she shrugged him off. Matt and I stayed on the floor as Dave left us, soon to reappear from the smoky bar zone with two beers and two full plastic cups balanced in his hands. After a couple of minutes, I ducked off with my drink and set it over on a far window ledge.

The music shifted to the more chilled-out sounds of Art of Noise. Dave and Claire had migrated to a corner. I'd had some last-minute doubts about them—that he'd be too bold, that she'd get aloof. But they'd clicked even better than I hoped. Free to dance, I loved how each mix strung into the next, a nonstop reason to stay out on the floor.

Matt seemed as happy as he'd ever been since Walt's death, busting out on the dance floor with anyone who wanted to join us. When we took a break, hot and sweaty and sharing a cup of water by the cooler, he wound an arm around me, and the soft surprise of his mouth pressed against mine burst me awake like a flower blooming in time-lapse mode.

"It's nice to be with you and not have all the guys around," I confessed.

Matt nodded as he looked around, taking in the dance floor, the DJ. "You can be yourself here," he said. "So many styles of people. Nobody's telling you what you're supposed to be." But he looked more wistful than gleeful about that.

When I slipped into the ladies' room a little later, it was like a whole other all-female party was happening. Girls in ribbed tank dresses and claw-moussed perms stood hip to hip, their eyes judging their reflections as they resmeared lip glosses. Matt was right, there were more intriguing types of kids in a downtown club than in our schools.

I scooped some pink glop from the communal vat of hair gel and gave a scrunch to my bangs. I hadn't gotten a trim since Claire told me to grow my hair, and now the front drooped over my eye.

In a far corner, a girl was dealing with a gross popped blister on her heel.

"You need to cover it," said her friend. "You don't want to be, like, exposed."

The blister girl looked worried. "We should go, maybe."

"I've got a Band-Aid," said another girl, who'd been doing her eyeliner, Claire-style, in the mirror. She dug in her purse and handed one over. "My bag's, like, nothing but condoms and Band-Aids. You can't be too careful, right?" Others murmured agreement.

The music had morphed into acid house, a man bloodlessly intoning "Give it to me" over a robotic loop. I looked over to where Claire and Dave were standing by a back wall, talking intensely. Matt and I traded a smile as we moved to join them.

When I caught Claire's eye, I tapped my watch. "Hey, it's half past eleven. If we grab a cab now . . ."

But Claire was already shaking her head. "Let's go back with the guys."

"Yeah, it's the least you can do, to keep the party going," said Dave.

"We're not your consolation prize," said Claire. "It's just a better plan than taking the train home late tonight."

Dave grinned. "Don't sugarcoat it for my sake."

Outside, we grabbed a cab that took us to a needle-thin high-rise on Liberty Place, and it was a relief when Matt picked up the fare. I'd hardly ever been up so high over the city, and I felt strangely trapped, like a princess in a tower, though the apartment itself wasn't much. The furniture was covered in clear plastic, a crackly dead fern rested on the radiator, and its one bookshelf was stacked with textbooks about accounting law.

"Remind me why your dad needs this place?" I asked.

"He brings his dates here," Dave answered. "He doesn't want me finding out about his swinging bachelor life."

Matt and Claire kicked off their boots at the door and were already in the bedroom, hauling out pillows and blankets to make a living-room lounge pit. I sat on the edge of it, with my back against the plastic-sheathed couch. I pulled off my Docs and wriggled my cramped toes. The others had been drinking more than I had—they were goofier, and I felt overly sober. Then Dave emerged from the kitchen with a bottle of white wine. "Who's thirsty?" He didn't listen for answers as he uncorked it and poured four juice glasses, then handed them all out.

"I'm not in for any stupid drinking games," said Claire as she settled in against the opposite wall, propped on pillows, glass in hand.

Dave laughed. "Okay, then how about this—anyone want to hear my badass ghost story?"

We all chorused yes. I sipped my wine and immediately felt calmer.

"Hang on, first I gotta take a leak."

In the pause, Matt jumped up to switch off the lights "We need some ghostly atmosphere. Dave's badass ghost story needs all the help it can get." On returning, he sat right next to me and dropped a light kiss on my lips.

Now it was pitch-black. I could hardly see my hand in front of me. When he kissed me again, I kissed him back, and our kiss tasted exciting, like wine.

"Some kids with bad IDs were getting turned away at the door as we left," Matt said quietly as I shifted into the weight of his arm around me. "I keep thinking how Walt would have been psyched to know that one of the last things he did was give us a night like this. He loved big open spaces, where you could meet all kinds of different people and be chill."

"That's awesome," I said. "We're carrying the torch, like a secret club."

"If that's a club, I want in," said Claire. "Even though Walt didn't make me a fake ID."

"Hey, who *is* Stephanie Moser, age twenty-six, of Morristown, New Jersey?" I asked. I'd seen the ID when Claire and I had been carded at the restaurant, earlier tonight.

There was a pause that made me wish I could see her face through the darkness. "A gift," she answered. "Stephanie gets me in everywhere. Even though she's four inches shorter and eight years older than me. Bartenders and bouncers only see whatever. Pale skin and dark hair."

"Mine belongs to my cousin," said Dave as he joined us. "Okay, I know nobody can see me but I've got the bottle. Who wants a top-up?" We all laughed and held our glasses out into the dark as he refilled us, and then went to be near Claire on the other side of the room.

"I never met Walt Powers, sorry to say," Dave added, "but I won't turn down a membership."

"To belonging," Claire said softly, and Matt and I clinked.

Dave began his ghost story, and I could hear in his voice someone who knows he's got a good one, and then after he'd managed to terrify us all, Claire was telling the story about the ghost of Lovell Pond—and then their voices dropped to a whisper. Matt and I were kissing, not too noisily, I hoped, as our hands dipped under each other's clothes, exploring.

"I'm getting a second bottle," said Claire from far away. I heard shuffling and then a kitchenette light snapped on, and Matt and I pulled apart, smiling shyly.

"Hey," he said.

"Hey."

Claire opening the fridge seemed like a good moment to excuse myself to head for the one bathroom, at the end of the hall. When I snapped on the light, it woke me up a little, a whole different space from the dark togetherness I'd just left. My face looked strange in this midnight mirror, my makeup smudged off, my hair rumpled. When I closed my eyes, I could feel the strobes in the walls of my eyelids, and I could still hear acid house, *Give it to me give it to me give it to me.*

I had to relax. It was okay to relax. Even though Matt was down to boxers and a T-shirt, my jeans were still on, and he wouldn't do anything I didn't want to do. He wasn't going to push me to have sex or anything. Yet I was still anxious, because all of them seemed so cool and sophisticated, and I felt like an impostor.

But I shouldn't have worried, because when I came back, Matt was almost asleep. While I could hear Claire and Dave giggling and whispering animatedly, Matt reached one sleepy arm and pulled me in next to him, and I cozied into the hollow, and closed my eyes, and let myself drift off.

# twenty-three

*Oof.* I woke up in the morning next to the couch—exactly where I'd fallen into a deep, uninterrupted sleep—with the aching print of last night in my body.

It wasn't until I sat up that I saw the others still asleep and sprawled on the other side of the room, so far away from me that I felt like some ghoulish observer. When had Matt moved over there? They all looked innocent as puppies in their nest of blankets and pillows. Claire was curled up and facing Matt, who was on his back, one hand resting on his stomach and the other thrown across Claire's middle, while Dave faced her from behind, his arm flung up and curved over her head like an umbrella.

I took them all in—Matt's angelic pixie face, Claire with her jutting nose and racehorse cheekbones, and Dave's marble-chiseled Hollywood profile. Slowly I stretched out my arm, my hand, my

fingers star-fished as if I could gather them all up. In their still-
ness, they all seemed intimately mine, and at the same time so
unknowable.

Finally I reached down, picked up a free pillow and hurled it
at Matt, startling him awake.

"Ahhhh!" He rubbed his eyes.

"When did you guys decide to have a ménage à trois?"

"I woke up about an hour after we crashed, and those two were
still drinking and gabbing, so I decided to join the party." Matt
grinned, and then decided his best plan to change the topic was to
crawl over and throw himself on top of me, tickling me.

"Stop, stop!" I laughed as I squirmed out from under him.

Now Dave and Claire were awake, stretching and yawning.

"I'm starved," she said.

"My breath rots," he added.

There was mouthwash in the bathroom, but nothing to eat in
the apartment. Dave mentioned a neighborhood diner, and after
some rushed tidying up, we walked blinking into the bright and
icy November morning and followed Dave's lead to Lonnie's, his
favorite greasy spoon a few blocks away.

When Claire broke off to walk a few paces ahead, Dave leaped
to keep pace with her. "Slowpokes! Keep up!" he called over his
shoulder.

Matt's hand folded over mine.

"So how late were you all up?" I asked, a little bit forlornly.

"Oh, man." He smiled. "The sun was coming up by the time
we crashed. We kept shooting the shit. Claire's so cool. I see why
you like her."

I tried to feel comfort in his steady grip. Matt was still mine. But I'd lost something, too. For a moment, I'd been the connective piece uniting the four of us, but this morning the balance of power had readjusted, and at its center was Claire. Of course Matt and Dave were both transfixed by her. Just to follow behind her—right now my view was of her wool coat and matchstick legs, her glossy hair, black as paint beneath her beret—was like falling halfway into a dream. She was never better than when she was a cosmopolitan girl, breezy and knowing, hard to resist. Next to her, I must have seemed so young and plain, a wren hanging out with a Lilac House peacock. It was hard to stay totally confident, even with Matt's pace perfectly matched with my own, his hand clasped in mine, and the memory of his mouth burning up my skin last night.

As we settled into a booth at Lonnie's, I felt even more kiddish as Claire, Dave, and Matt talked about a bunch of things I couldn't comment on—like getting stoned on pot brownies, where they'd partied last New Year's Eve (I'd been at my grandparents' house), and a bunch of people I didn't know who all played hockey for Fieldstone. I listened quietly and sketched Dave's profile on a napkin.

"Hey." He looked startled when he saw what I'd done. "Can I have this? Actually I'm just gonna rob you." He snatched up the napkin and folded it into his coat pocket. "It's too good not to keep."

"She's the best artist in the school," said Claire.

"Easily," agreed Matt.

It was strange to be admired by people I considered to be more exceptional than I was. I felt both embarrassed and happy.

We ordered, and a few minutes later, platters of pancakes and omelets landed in front of us. A man, thin as a coat hanger under his old-fashioned gray fedora and overcoat, waited at a complete standstill for the waitress to finish unloading the tray. He gave her wide space as he moved past.

I couldn't stop staring, my gaze traveling with him as he passed. I'd never seen anyone in real life with his sickness; the nothing weight, the waxen skin, the liverish welts on the edge of his nose.

"Did you see that guy?"

"Yes, shh." Claire nodded. "We get it. We saw."

Under the table, Matt's hand found mine. "You can't catch it from air," he assured me. Which I knew, but then I became conscious that I was holding my breath. I thought of the girl with the bloody blister at the club, how tense the other girls had been about her exposed, ragged heel.

"You get it from fluids," I said.

"Beware the evil HIV dogs," muttered Dave.

"Don't say it that way." Claire twisted her mouth. "It's grim enough without your idiotic misinformation. You don't need to beware that guy, and he's got more than HIV, he's probably got full-blown AIDS."

Dave squirmed. "I wasn't saying it any way."

"You said it like a homophobic bastard," Claire answered matter-of-factly.

The guys started laughing, but I was *still* holding my breath. I made myself exhale, and breakfast continued.

When the bill got dropped, Dave quick-drew his American Express, and I was grateful I didn't have to stick out my own card for the slap of another charge.

From Lonnie's, we launched ourselves in the direction of the train station. Claire would get off at Merion, I'd detrain in Bryn Mawr and walk to Ludington, Matt's stop was Saint David's, and Dave's was Paoli. But splitting off from Claire freaked me out. I'd left my overnight bag in her bedroom, and at the bottom of it, stuck in the back pages of my paperback copy of *Song of Solomon*, was Jay's envelope of letters.

My plan had been to replace them in that carved wooden box where I'd found them. The problem was that yesterday there hadn't been a right time, since we'd never gone to her house.

"It's not a problem. I'll bring it in on Monday," Claire told me.

"Thanks." I smiled. Nothing to hide here!

Dave paid Claire's ticket, and Matt paid mine. We sat together, my leg over his, his finger absently tracing circles on my palm as we looked out the window, its sparkling view of the Schuylkill skimming past in a final blaze of fall, college rowing shells gliding soft as moccasins across the water.

"Look." I nudged him. "The water is the same color as your eyes."

Matt leaned up to stare. "If you say so."

But I knew so. I wished I had my notebook and some paints, to chip off this moment of seeing the navy-blue water and feeling this rush of recognition for everything I loved about Matt's face. I didn't even know what image I might have captured. I just wanted to preserve the emotion, so that I'd never forget it.

Claire's stop was first. "See ya," she said as she hopped up. "That was fun." She'd never before seemed so free-spirited—because of me, and because I'd connected her to Dave and Matt, who'd been just right for her, I reminded myself, as we all blew her mock kisses. The light in her eyes, this weekend, was partly my doing.

I watched her as she sprang onto the platform and into the bright morning sun, her cheeks going insta-rosy from the cold.

Claire would never go through my stuff.

"Can I just say Claire Reynolds is radical," said Dave, moving to sit across from Matt and me, and speaking out loud the very thoughts in my own head. "Nice work, little Lizzy. Great night. She's a keeper."

"Yeah, I know. Totally." Chasing down Claire's friendship had been one of my most ambitious social leaps. But as for Claire being a keeper, I wasn't totally confident that was up to me.

# twenty-four

"CAN I BORROW YOUR car?"

"Where are you going?" Mom and Dad both looked up from the TV. They'd just settled into their favorite hour of the weekend and the ticking clock start of *60 Minutes*.

It was Sunday night after dinner, and I had a plan.

"I've left some of my homework at Claire's. She's twenty minutes away. I need to pop over. I won't stay."

"I'll come with you," said Mom. "You can still be the driver if you want. I'd love to introduce myself to Jane Sleighmaker. Now that her niece is at Argyll, we're all hoping she'll re-up her commitment to Annual Giving. The business office is doing more research, but we think she's got deep pockets."

"I'd rather go by myself."

But Mom was already out of the living room, pulling on her coat. She tossed me the keys with a smile.

I should have called ahead, except there was a good chance that if I did, Claire might invent a reason for me not to come over. So the trick was making it look spontaneous.

On the drive over, I plotted my moves.

*Sorry!* I'd exclaim when she opened the door. *Mom and I were in the area, so I thought I'd come pick up my bag—since my toothbrush and English book are in it.*

It was an easy lie, except that when we rolled up to park in front of the massive unlit house and I sprang from the car to ring the bell, it was Claire's mom who cracked open the door.

"Hi, Mrs. Reynolds." Claire had introduced her to me as Suze, but faced with her twitchy, surprised face, I was tense. "Is Claire around? I left something here."

"Claire!" Mrs. Reynolds's voice broke like a boy's as she shrilled, "Clay-ayre! Clayyyyyre! Come here right this minute! Were you expecting your friend?"

Feet pounded down the hall. Next Claire appeared, nudging her mother to the side as half of her face peeked through the sliver of door.

"Lizzy? What are you doing here?"

A cat escaped, brushing past my calf as it flung itself into the night. It was followed by another, and another.

"No, no, no!" Mrs. Reynolds was screeching. "No, no, no! Claire, shut this door!"

Claire's angry eye was staring me down. "Are you with Matt?" she hissed. "Who are you with?" I could hear cats at her feet mewling in frustration, clawing to get out.

"My mom, that's all. She wanted to meet—"

"Hi, Claire!" My blood chilled. Mom was standing right behind me.

"Mrs. *Swift*?" Claire's eye widened, and I knew, too late, that this visit was a mess of wrong, and I needed to get out of here before I made it any worse.

"Sweetie, is your aunt Jane here? I wanted to say hello—"

"Mom, no! Get back in the car!"

Mom was talking over me, attempting to budge me out of the way. "Hi, Claire! I wondered if your aunt Jane was available. I'd like to introduce myself?"

"You want to meet my aunt?" Now Claire sounded shrill.

"I'm so sorry!" My eyes begged Claire's forgiveness. "We were doing errands, and I came for my bag. Let me get it and we'll go, Claire. Promise."

"Who's that?" Aunt Jane's distinctly sharp and reedy voice cawed from above. "What's going on?"

"Mrs. Sleighmaker? Hello!" Mom was still trying to make it work. As she gave a final push into my space while tugging on the doorknob, a cat flexed and jumped, snagging at Mom's pant leg.

"Ouch! Pssst! Scat, pussycat!" Mom shook her leg as the cat dug in, while Claire seized the distraction to yank at the door, nearly squashing another cat in the process.

"I'm sorry." This was awful. Cats were yowling in chorus.

"Don't let your mom—"

"Mom, go." I hurled a glare at my mother, who had detangled from the cat and was now pulling up her pant leg to examine the wound. "Go back to the car! Claire's aunt doesn't want to see you."

Claire pushed the cat outside and slammed the door. Mom swore softly. "Would you look at this?" Her exposed winter leg glowed pale as paper, showing up the dark jagged scratch. "What is going on in that house?"

"Please go back to the car and wait for me, Mom!"

"Fine, but don't be long, I need Neosporin for this!" She stormed off.

A moment later, the door reopened just wide enough for Claire to push my bag at me. "I really wish you'd called."

"I'm so sor—"

*Slam.*

In silence and darkness, I returned to the car, a sting of tears in my eyes. I chucked my stupid bag into the back seat.

Mom was in the driver's seat, as I knew she would be. The fact that this errand had gone so wrong had nothing to do with my driving, but even a tiny chaos meant that she could take over. My parents didn't like me on the road because of my condition, and they'd use any excuse—even though my driver's license was as legal as anyone's, since my last unconscious seizure was over two years ago.

"Those monster cats came out of nowhere," Mom complained after a few minutes. "They should get those beasts declawed, and put out Beware Of signs."

"Beware of Nosy Mothers. Claire *knew* you were gawking at the house."

"I was not!" Mom grimaced. "Good grief." She paused. "But that's a real Edgar Allan Poe story, isn't it? All those disgusting animals! And it smelled absolutely vile—Lizzy, I'm not sure I want you spending nights in that house."

"On what grounds? Fear of house cats?"

"Wild cats."

"Look, Mom, don't tell anyone at Argyll about this, okay? Claire's aunt is a nut, but it's a private thing, like Uncle Ron being in AA."

"Lizzy, of course I won't spread stories. It's not my business."

I wasn't comforted—Mom could be a gossip. I'd hate anything to get back to Claire, who trusted me—even though I had broken that trust with these stupid, stolen letters that had become way more hassle than I could have possibly anticipated.

At home, up in my room, I dug into my bag for the paperback. The envelope wasn't there.

My body went cold. Impossible. I checked again. Rechecked for a better answer, the right answer. I dumped out the bag. I shook *Song of Solomon* so that its pages flapped. Nothing. Gone.

After a minute, I unfroze to get up and look in my Holly Hobbie purse. Maybe I hadn't moved the letters, after all? Except that I knew I had.

I took a long bath to calm down, stoppering and unstoppering the tub to refill it with hot water as needed. Clipped my nails. Out of the bath, I sketched my water-wrinkled hand. Wished I had the nerve to dial up Claire. Wished she would phone me.

All that night until I fell asleep, I flipped restlessly through different scenarios—had Claire figured out my theft beforehand, or was she on red alert when I showed up at her house? Had she found the letters right before she returned my bag? Would she confront me tomorrow? How would I defend myself?

My breath hurt. No thought gave me peace. No plan seemed obvious. When I finally fell asleep, my dreams were a tornado of worry.

# twenty-five

AT LUNCH MONDAY, WENDY Palmer was in front of me at the cash register. My body tensed just to be near her, and although it had been years since she'd targeted me outright, her contempt was always in her pebble-gray eyes. When she turned to look my way, it took everything in me to meet her gaze.

"Hey, Lizzy. Come sit with us," she coaxed. "Claire's already over there, see?"

I looked. Claire often bypassed lunch, but there she was between Kreo and Liz DeBatista at the Nectarine table. I'd headed to the cafeteria early, and Gage and Mimi weren't here yet, but I didn't want to snub them. And zero part of me wanted to sit with awful, sniggering Wendy, but of course I needed to deal with Claire.

"Okay." My hands were clammy as I followed Wendy. I was nervous to look Claire in the eye. I'd stolen from her! Stolen love letters and read them and shown up uninvited at her house to get them back, and she knew it.

Did she hate me for it?

"Hey, Lizzy," she said, as if everything was normal between us, as if last night hadn't happened.

"Hi." I dropped next to Maggie Farthington, who shoved over obligingly. A double whammy, dealing with Nectarines and Claire. The backs of my knees were already sweating against the plastic chair seat. As I unloaded my tray, I breathed in through my nose and exhaled through my mouth, the way Dr. Neumann had taught me.

At least Claire didn't *seem* angry anyway. Was I wrong? Was it possible she didn't know, that something else had happened to that envelope?

"So, girls! Heard you two double-dated with Dave Jimenez this weekend." As Wendy spoke, she emptied a pouch of Crystal Light lemonade into her glass of water. Lunch for Wendy was never more than this drink, plus rice crackers. "I swear, that guy could star in a Calvin Klein campaign." She shifted conspiratorially toward Claire. "Are you really into him?"

"He's sweet," Claire conceded.

"Maybe you'll be the one to put him in his place. He's got way too many girls in love with him," said Wendy.

Now I understood why Claire and I had been summoned.

"We all went to the Bank," I said, to rub it in. "That new club."

"Mmmmm!" Kreo purred at me. "So Walt's ID worked out, huh?"

"Yep." We exchanged a smile. Now this was a new weirdness, a chummy-chummy lunch with the Nectarines. Out of the corner of my eye, I saw Gage and Mimi carrying trays to our usual table by the back window. I made myself look away.

"Lucky you were in the city Saturday. It was such a shit show at Thatcher Bell's house," said Wendy. "Did you hear about Leslie and Stephen?"

"She's absent today," I observed. Leslie Spivio sat next to me in my morning Ancient Civ class. "What happened? Did they elope?"

"Not even," Wendy snorted. "But they had their wedding night, sort of."

"Palmer, please." Kreo rolled her eyes. "That's a sick way of putting it."

"What do you mean?" asked Claire. "What happened to Leslie?"

Leslie was the friendliest Nectarine, the peppy do-gooder who we always voted to be class president or vice president, who looked the part in her penny loafers with actual pennies stuck in them and her hair in a fishtail braid down her back. Everyone knew plenty about Leslie and Stephen's romance because on the first day of school, he'd sent her two dozen roses. The FTD flowers delivery guy had arrived in the cafeteria while all the girls applauded and Leslie's face turned pink as a peony—but anyone could tell she loved it.

Wendy pledged, a hand to her heart. "I was downstairs the whole time, watching *Beverly Hills Cop* with everyone else. So you didn't hear it from me."

Kreo took over. "Stephen told Thatcher that he and Leslie were fooling around in Mr. and Mrs. Bell's bedroom, and Stephen said it just ended up in a bad direction. A really bad direction."

"I'm not following," I admitted. "What do you mean, *bad direction*?"

"You're such a kid, Lizzy—do you really need it spelled out? He went too far," said Wendy impatiently. "He got ahead of himself. He pressured her."

"He pressured her . . . all the way?" I asked.

"As in rape?" asked Claire flatly.

The whole table winced from the scorch of that word.

Liz looked annoyed. "No need to get into all the details."

"Yeah, it's so disrespectful," added Wendy.

"But Leslie should report it," said Claire. "Especially if she's not eighteen yet."

"She is eighteen," said Wendy. "She's totally legal."

"Report what? Report to who?" Kreo scoffed.

"People! This is a personal situation." Wendy always spoke with the loud confidence of a beautiful girl, even though she wasn't quite—despite the year-round tan and her perfect caramel-blond highlights, she was too pinched and flinty eyed. "One, Leslie's been dating Stephen for a year. Two, she knows he's sloppy when there's alcohol involved. Three, it's basically the *job* of the girlfriend to keep a boyfriend from getting out of hand. I'm not saying Stephen had the right to do what he did, but she's putting it out there, and he's a red-blooded American guy, so whatever."

"It sounds like you *are* saying he had the right," said Claire.

"Okay, Claire, now you're just being a priss." Kreo smiled to show she wouldn't hold a grudge against prissiness. "They wear promise rings."

"A promise ring doesn't mean 'Yay, I can do whatever I want,'" said Claire.

I'd been quiet, picking at my salad. Why was Claire pushing so hard for Leslie?

"It's going to turn into she said, he said," said Liz. "Like the Preppy Killer guy."

"What are you talking about, Liz? *She* didn't get to say anything. *She*'s dead." Claire looked scornful.

"Well, to be honest, I feel sorry for Stephen catching all this heat," said Wendy.

I looked up. "Stephen's doing just fine," I said. "Stephen got exactly what he wanted, whether it was offered or not."

I hadn't thought what I'd said was so funny, but some of the girls laughed. "Yeah, save your pity for someone who needs it, Palmer," said Kreo as Claire caught my eye in quiet affirmation. And while Wendy smiled along, I could tell my comment, and the laughter, had bugged her.

"The sad part is since it happened out of school, Stephen gets off free and clear, but no protection for Leslie," said Claire, quickly sobering the table. "And nobody will do anything except waste hours gossiping about what qualifies as rape." If Claire blinked right now, a tear might spill.

She blinked, and turned away.

"Okay, enough with that *word*," said Maggie softly.

"And if we could all check in for a minute with *reality*," Kreo added, "Leslie is Stephen's girlfriend—they aren't strangers. There's no need for extra protection. It didn't happen behind a Dumpster with a total random. And the way I understand it? From the way Stephen told it to Thatcher? He said Leslie was being a tease. She wanted it just as much as he did, until the second she didn't. But by then it was out of hand. That's how Thatcher put it."

"'Out of hand.' Jesus." Claire pushed back her chair, stood up, and left. We all watched as she walked out of the lunchroom without a look back.

"What?" asked Kreo. "I was only repeating. I'm just the messenger."

"She seemed way upset," said Maggie.

"Is she gonna bus her tray?" Wendy looked annoyed. "I don't want a demerit for that."

"I'll take care of it," I said.

"Claire's a wild card, huh?" Kreo asked the question, but the Nectarines were looking at me for an answer. "She wears what she wants, goes to class when she wants, she's in French with me and if she hasn't done the homework, she doesn't even apologize, she's just like '*Je n'ai pas fini.*'"

"But she's not a free spirit, you know? Her spirit feels, like, not free at all," added Liz, as philosophical as I'd ever heard her. "She's a *heavy* spirit."

"Anyone who can hook Dave Jimenez has got magic powers." Wendy tapped a finger on the table. "What's Claire's deal anyway, Lizzy? For real?"

"Oh, I, I um . . ." I hated all this attention on me. The Nectarines, as a group, had never sought out my company before except to tease me, and my new barely accepted status was only because of Matt.

Wendy's gaze on me was both direct and amused. "Now don't spaz out, Lizzy. It's a simple question here."

My cheeks were so instantly red, I knew everyone could see, but to act bothered by Wendy's jab would be even more shameful.

"I don't know a ton about Claire, but I'm guessing she had a friend at Strickland who got hurt the way Leslie did? Or maybe . . ." I swallowed and shrugged, letting the silence speak for itself, that maybe it was Claire herself who'd been hurt.

"Everyone has skeletons." Wendy winked and grinned at me.

I checked my watch—"Uh-oh, gotta run. I'm late for year-book meeting"—and then quickly stood up and reached for Claire's tray, stacking it on mine. Head down, I made a break for it, dumping the dishware at the cleanup station, then slipping out of the lunchroom as if I were running to catch up with my fake emergency meeting. But I couldn't stand another moment of let-ting Wendy bat me around like a cat toy.

All through afternoon classes, I fiddled with my facts. Did Claire think the school was letting Leslie down by not protect-ing her? Or was this more about what had happened at Claire's old school? Claire's whole Aunt-Jane-made-me-come-here story about why she left Strickland had never washed for me—I'd seen with my own eyes how Aunt Jane bristled at Claire, how much she resented her niece's presence at Lilac House. Aunt Jane would have paid any amount of tuition to keep Claire away.

I'd told the Nectarines the truth. We had no history with Claire. Her past life was like an iceberg, mostly submerged.

But I still couldn't figure out what to do about the letters. What if I got up the nerve to come right out and apologize to Claire? What if I told her it had been what it was—the worst impulse ever—and I felt horrible about it?

After lunch, I couldn't find her, and I had a hunch she'd cut her afternoon classes. Sure enough, when I ducked out to the lower school parking lot, the orange Beetle was gone.

At Ludington, I waited until Mrs. Binswanger left and I'd taken over the desk. There weren't many kids here at five o'clock, but I gave my best impression of official business as I picked up the olive-green receiver. My fingers felt sweaty as I punched in for information to Strickland's dashboard, and was connected to the alumni office.

"Hello! I'm a former Strickland student," I began in my apple-polisher's voice. "I wanted to order a copy of your last year's yearbook."

"You'll have to send us a check or money order," said the woman on the other end, and next thing I knew, I was scribbling down the address.

"How long will it take for it to arrive?"

"Let's say between four to six weeks after your check clears."

Simple as that. The woman hadn't been suspicious or even put me on hold to look up my name.

I made out the check to Strickland for thirty-six dollars. Too much money! I wasn't in my right mind. But I had to know more. I needed to know who Claire Reynolds had been before she came here to baffle us all.

# twenty-six

"ARE YOU SURE I'm allowed over?"

"Well, you're not *not* allowed over."

"Knew it!" Matt just laughed since it was too late to worry now.

"Thanksgiving week—it's different rules."

"If you say so."

"I say so." I tried to sound confident. We were at my house, upstairs in the den. Mom and my brothers wouldn't be home for a couple of hours. I'd been impulsive, not wanting to say good-bye to Matt when he'd dropped me off from school, even though I hadn't cleared his invite with my parents.

So in he'd come, and I'd opened a bag of chips and popped open two cans of ginger ale, and now we were both cozied into the armchair recliner with *Dance Party USA* on low in case anyone came home early. "I like your house. It feels like people actually live in it."

"When you get back from your sister's after Thanksgiving, could I come over and meet your family?"

He kissed me.

"That's not an answer."

"It's just my parents are super stiff. Not fun to be around."

"Let me be the one to decide that." I tweaked his chin. "It makes me feel like you're hiding me. And your mom's so sweet on the phone." *Sweet* wasn't the word, but the couple of times I'd phoned Matt and gotten his mother, she was very polite.

Matt gathered my fingers in one hand and kissed their tips. "Next week then, but you were warned." With another softer, longer kiss on the lips, he then paused, distracted by a thought. "Hey, about this whole Leslie and Stephen thing. What's she saying happened?"

"I haven't talked to her." Not that I would have, Leslie wasn't a close friend of mine. "But she was absent yesterday and today. Sometimes girls cut Thanksgiving week, but Leslie's usually serious about school."

"I heard Stephen was in really bad form last weekend. Leslie's brother Dan's a Lincoln grad. I heard he's gonna kick Stephen's ass over Thanksgiving. But then some of the guys were saying, since Leslie's eighteen and they've been pretty serious, it's not such a big deal." Matt shook his head. "My gut says if Dan knows the story, and Leslie's staying home, then it's bad, you know?"

"Yeah, that's what most of us think. Even Claire was upset, and she doesn't get involved in school gossip."

I decided to just go ahead and blurt it out. "Do you ever think I'm young for you, Matt? Since I won't be eighteen till this summer? Does that, I don't know, affect how you see us?"

Matt looked at me like I'd made a strange joke that he wasn't sure he should laugh at. "Does it feel like I'm not into you?"

"I didn't mean to say it like that."

But really I'd meant that I didn't mean for him to react like that, like I'd unnerved him. All at once, he scooped his hands under my sweater, squeezing my waist, and pulled himself over me, his breath warming my neck. "Does this feel like I think you're young for me? Hmm? Or this?"

And then conversation was pretty much over until a quarter to five, when I started to get paranoid that my family might come home. Luckily, Matt didn't make me have to hint too broadly before he left, assuring me he'd call every night of break.

Thanksgiving week had been crammed with school quizzes and makeup tests, but everyone was in vacation mode by half-day dismissal the next day. Claire went to see her dad in Florida, the Ashleys had gone to Matt's sister's home in Boston, and Gage's family took off to visit friends in Delaware—but she'd be back for the Kims' annual Leftovers Friday night, of course. None of us had ever missed that one.

IT WAS A SWIFT family Thanksgiving tradition to go to Gran's house in Lancaster, where we celebrated the day with Aunt Carlene and Uncle Ron, plus my cousins Billy, who'd just started at Cabrini College and who everyone had referred to as "the Big College Man" at least a dozen times since we'd arrived, and Pamela, a high school senior, same as me.

"Help yourself, there's plenty of everything!" Gran announced after grace as we all filed to the sideboard buffet.

"And as usual, you don't even need teeth," muttered Billy as we stared down celery soup, creamed turnips, mashed sweet potatoes, turkey drowned in gravy, custard-soft asparagus, and pumpkin pie.

"Got any tapes?" asked Pamela afterward as we were drying dishes. Pamela and I never followed the family custom of NFL in the den after the meal.

"Yep."

We sat in Gran's breakfast nook and unloaded our cassettes for the trade-off.

Pamela was always meticulously dressed for Thanksgiving. This year, she wore royal-blue pegged pants with a matching velvet mock turtleneck, and her perfect French manicure was as high gloss as her silver LA Gear dress sneakers.

"I'm thinking of going to cosmetology school after I graduate," she said as we set out our tapes in a line. "Mom and Dad aren't totally for it. But it's kind of my thing, right, makeup and fashion?" She stared at me in her usual wide-eyed way that needed me to agree with everything she said.

"Yeah, I think you'd be good at it."

"It's like every time I see someone I think about their makeovers. Like you would look great as a blonde, I'm thinking?"

"I'm not sure."

"Like Madonna in *Who's That Girl*?"

"Madonna's a brunette now. And everyone hated *Who's That Girl*."

"Not true." Pamela never liked when I critiqued her idol. "If you wanted to start small, you could do something like this." She clawed into her tapestry satchel-bag for a magazine and then flipped it open to a model whose hair was cropped like mine, but with chunky, buttery-blond streaks.

"I'd been wondering if I should get highlights," I confessed.

"You'd look perfect."

"Maybe. I'm still thinking about it. Okay, trade." I pushed forward Serge Gainsbourg.

Pamela didn't bite. She picked up *Faith*.

"How about *Faith* for *Upstairs at Eric's*," I offered.

"Deal. I can't believe you'd trade anything George Michael." Pamela sighed. "He's the hottest."

"If you say so. I think he looks like a scruffy Ken doll."

"Insanity." Pamela shook her head. "Maybe nobody's hot because all you love is your boyfriend now."

"Matt's cuter than George Michael."

"Is he a rebel in black like you?"

Her word choice startled me, but in a good way. Did I look like a rebel, just because of my black tube skirt, black long-sleeved T-shirt, and my Docs? "I don't think either of us is so *rebel*," I said, sampling the word in my mouth, "but we like to go to clubs in Philly."

Pamela wasn't as impressed with that information as I'd hoped. "Nightclubs are dangerous," she said. "They're full of random gay guys and AIDS junkies shooting up in the bathrooms. Aren't you scared to be in there with them?"

"AIDS is horrible enough without all your bad information." I clicked in *Upstairs at Eric's* and rewound my Walkman exactly to "Only You." "You might want to grab hold of some real facts, before you talk like that." I could hear Claire's voice in my own, and I liked the way Pamela looked embarrassed.

"Hey, did you know Gran self-bleaches her hair?" she asked.

"Really?"

"She has industrial hair bleach, developer, *and* toner bottles all under her bathroom sink. Josefina sneaks it in from Nicaragua. It's more powerful than any over-the-counters. Totally strips the pigment." Her voice dropped. "I have three jam jars with me, and I'm going to loot some of her stash so I can do salon experiments on my friends."

"Try something on me," I said, half joking. Or maybe not even joking at all.

Desire brightened Pamela's face. "For real? I've got my stuff!"

"Are you sure you know how?"

"I'm practically a professional."

"As long as you don't make it look frost-and-tip, like mom hair."

"I know what to do."

Our eyes locked. Deal. We left our Walkmans on the table and clattered up the musty back stairs to the L-shaped corner of the house that was Gran's small bedroom suite, where we locked ourselves into her bathroom.

Stealthy as a burglar, Pamela went to work. Her satchel was a portable salon for the tricks of her trade. After pulling on a pair of rubber gloves, she heaved the haul of Gran's contraband from under the sink. I looked on as she shook bleach from a large white container into one of her jars, siphoned developer from a jug into another, and poured violet liquid from a narrow bottle into the third.

Then she placed the three sealed jars in a giant Ziploc.

"Wow, that was some forensics."

Pamela giggled. "Just don't rat me out! Are you ready?" She indicated for me to sit on the toilet. I sat.

"Do only the front," I told her. "And try to make it decent enough so my parents don't get completely feeble about it."

Solemnly Pamela next extracted a thin bottle of olive oil, a fine-tooth comb, and a couple of mini banana clips from the satchel. She used the pointy end of the comb to section off my hair. "We won't layer it in too crazy," she assured me as she worked the oil through the front pieces and used a washcloth to rub it in. "This protects the follicles."

Pamela used Gran's soap dish to mix the bleach and developer. With a toothbrush she'd brought, she stirred the powder and liquid, and then deployed the toothbrush to coat yarn-thick sections of my bangs.

Hydrogen peroxide fumes smarted my eyes.

"How long does it take to lift the color?"

"You're a medium-tone brown, so you need—well, this stuff is strong, so let's check on it in ten minutes." Out of the bag came an egg timer. "I wish we had a glaze, in case it gets brassy—but this developer has more kick than you'd get in a box of Clairol. Results will be dramatic and spectacular!"

Her extreme confidence made the results all the more horrifying, ten minutes later.

"Orange alert! Pamela, it looks like a crop of baby carrots sprouted along my hairline!"

"Don't panic!" Except Pamela's screeching voice and fluttering sorceress nails fit this word exactly. "Orange just means it's breaking through."

"Does. Not. Look. Good."

"Ten more minutes! Trust me! It's the halfway point!"

I was too deep in to quit. I closed my eyes, and when Pamela's timer buzzed again, and she gave the okay, I bent down and leaned my head in the sink, listening to the *scritch-scritch* of her acrylics scrubbing out the bleach, then applying two minutes' worth of toner, followed by a vigorous shampoo.

"Don't look till I dry it," she instructed, seating me on the toilet so that I was facing the shower and couldn't peek in the mirror. I tried not to think about the worst outcomes, the ratted-out bleach-job of a Bon Jovi groupie.

Pamela was short of breath when she finished, and her face was as ruddy as if she'd been handling a barbell instead of a blow dryer.

"Okay, look."

I stared at myself.

"Do you like it? Be honest. What do you think?"

Moon-pale hair lay in ribbons against my darker hair, a dramatic, not exactly natural contrast. *Rebel.* I thought of Claire, and the first time I'd run into her in the bathroom, when she told me to face the strange.

"I like it," I said honestly. "I really do. But I'm putting on a hat. I don't want to hear it from my parents and Gran tonight. So don't tell."

"I won't," promised Pamela solemnly, "as long as you don't tell anybody that one of my press-ons dropped into the gravy boat."

# twenty-seven

I KEPT MY HAT packed snugly on my head all the way home and safely upstairs, where I peeked in at my new hair only once I was in my pajamas.

It looked so cool and edgy. It even smelled different—like Gran's Herbal Essence shampoo cut with disinfectant. But the more I looked, the more I loved it.

The next morning, I came down in my hat, pretending I was cold, and when Mimi picked me up that evening for Leftovers Friday at the Kims', I didn't take it off until we were safely out of Wayne.

"No way." Mimi's stare was pure alarm, like a car horn. "No *way*."

"Don't say it like that."

"Your parents couldn't possibly know."

"They don't, but that's a temporary condition."

"Do you have a place to sleep, when they kick you out?"

"It's that bad?"

"No! It's kind of awesome. It's just so different from your old . . ." I didn't know if she wanted to say *hair* or *self.* Maybe she didn't know, either.

"The thing is, I want to keep it for a while."

"Yeah, I think you should. Be prepared for Gage, she'll make too much fun. She's mostly crabby at you for always blowing us off."

"Are you mad about that?" I asked after a bit. "Blowing you off?"

Mimi shook her head. "You haven't been around, which obviously sucks. But who am I to judge? I hung out with Noah a ton last year, right? We broke up, by the way." She put on her turn signal and burst into tears.

"Oh, no, Mimi. I'm so sorry! When? What happened?"

For a moment, the silence was alive with what she was deciding to tell me about Noah and her pain and their breakup. "I'll be fine. He did it on the phone last weekend." She sniffled shakily. "It was a total surprise. He's at his new college girlfriend's house for Thanksgiving." She dipped her head against her sleeve to give her eyes a vigorous rub. "And that's that."

"That sucks. I'm sorry."

"Thanks." She turned up the music, exhaled a baleful breath, and looked intent on the road ahead, her sign that she was backing off further talk for now. As sorry as I felt for her pain, it also hit me sharply how close I felt to her—I'd been with Mimi the first afternoon she met Noah at Wayne Sporting Goods, where he used to work. I'd witnessed their first shy and curious conversation. But next year, Mimi and I would be at different colleges, where I wouldn't be part of any of her big moments. We might never be as close again as we'd once been.

Mimi's parents had made Leftovers Friday into a tradition that I'd been showing up for since I was in lower school, when the Kims' house became my second home. Their main dish was always turkey hash with rice, along with homemade shrimp dumplings and ribs and kimchi.

Gage's jeep was already in the driveway when we pulled up, and inside, the Kims' kitchen was spiced with a peppery current of barbecue. Theo was playing Nerfoop basketball with one of the many rotating young neighbor kids who always hung around at the Kims', worshipping Theo. It might have been annoying if Theo himself had been invested in any of the worship, but it was actually sweet how he just let kids hang out and play Nerf as if they were his real buddies.

"'Sup, Blizzard." As I walked in, he popped the basketball off my head.

"Ouch!" I said, even though it hadn't hurt at all.

"Sorry." He smirked. "I hope you have good medical coverage for that injury."

"Joke all you want." I rubbed at the not-hurt spot.

"Hey, Lizzy, are you aware that your hair recently turned punk white?" asked Gage, looking up from where she was rolling out dough for the next batch of dumplings.

"I like it," said Mr. Kim, which was so out of character—Mr. Kim was the kind of professor who might not notice if the sun turned green—that Gage was silenced into shock, along with all the rest of us.

And then it was just Leftovers Friday as usual. Mr. and Mrs. Kim floated around us, checking on the oven or the pots, setting out more tableware for what always ended up being a long, casual dinner where nothing was timed, and the whole fun was waiting for this or that dish to be ready.

And this year, I had a trick up my sleeve. Theo noticed it immediately.

"Look at Bliz work those chopsticks," he teased.

I smiled. I'd been practicing—at Ludington, I'd pulled a copy of *Mind Your Manners: A Guide to International Travel*, and I kept a pair of take-out chopsticks on the circulation desk. I'd spent hours trying out their tips, picking up pennies and paper clips, honing my skills.

Mimi watched me. "Okay, something fishy's going on. Does the great Matt Ashley like to take you out for Chinese or something?"

"You're dating Matt Ashley?" Theo made a face.

"Why do you say it that way?" I asked.

As Theo leaned back in a standing stretch and then scratched long under his T-shirt, Mimi made monkey noises to show how his scratching bugged her. But I liked the way Theo moved in slow, deliberate motion, sleepy and defiant. "I dunno, Blizzard. He's like a blond Clark Kent."

"He's not—he's just good at everything."

"But you can see he's had it so easy his whole life," said Gage.

"He hasn't!" I protested.

"But maybe he's a little bit fake?" Mimi added helpfully.

"He's not at all fake! You'd never say that if you knew him!"

"That's not our fault," said Mimi. "You don't let us get to know him. He's your secret."

"I'm not hiding him, and he's not fake!"

"Speaking of fake, Theo's new girlfriend's name is *Violetta*," said Mimi. "How fake is that, right?"

"She probably made it up when she got to college," said Gage. "Actually, Lizzy, I'm surprised you haven't changed your name to something edgier, in preparation for college. Like Ingot or Manchester."

Mimi laughed, but Theo, checking in on my mortified face, reached across the island to tousle my hair. He'd ruffled my hair a thousand times—Mimi's and Gage's, too, it was just a Theo thing—so it was silly to feel such sparks from his touch. "Blizzard is cute, no matter what you call her," he said.

"Phone call for Theo," called Mrs. Kim from the other room.

Mimi made a noise of relief to watch him go. "It's so cheesy how my brother talks to you. He takes total advantage. And you just giggle and let him."

"I don't think he said anything cheesy," I said. "Also, I don't giggle."

"Kind of though, you do," said Gage.

"It's not as much what he says, it's how he says it." Mimi looked too prickly for me to disagree. "Anyway, I don't know why he bothers flirting with you. Violetta is so beautiful and she's a double major, English lit and biology, and she can speak four languages."

"That's so sickening, her so gorgeous and him a model," said Gage.

"Theo's not a *real* model!" Mimi laughed. "And Violetta isn't a model, either. I'm just saying she's beautiful based on pictures I saw, and the fact that Theo is shallow."

"Still, they must be the most disgustingly model-y couple on campus," said Gage with a sniff.

I deftly pronged a dumpling from the bamboo steamer. In the other room, I could hear the rumble of Theo's voice. I wondered what he and Violetta were talking about, if their conversations were anything like Matt's and mine. I imagined Violetta sitting on her bed and staring at her phone, getting up her nerve to punch the Kims' phone number—the first number I had ever memorized, after my own family's. Crossing her fingers that it'd be Theo picking up, so she wouldn't have to ask Mimi or one of his parents to put him on the line.

Later Theo went out with friends and the rest of us crashed out in the TV room. Mrs. Kim brought in dessert served on her blooming-cabbage-roses tea set, with a plate of lemon pound cake and Fudge Stripes cookies. The brown sofa that took up a full quarter of the room nestled us all in close. I hadn't been to Mimi's in a long time, and I loved the homey feeling of being tucked in with the familiar furniture and photographs. I could feel this year and memories of years before all rolled up like a soft hug.

The only thing on TV was *Perfect Strangers*, which was awful but I always suspected Gage was sort of in love with Balki, since I watched this show only when she was around. Mimi dozed off in the armchair, another tradition—she swore turkey put her to sleep. Sitting together, legs up on the coffee table, Gage and I hooked our feet, something she hadn't done since we were kids.

"I was thinking you'd blow off Leftovers Friday," she said.

"Me? No way."

"You've gotten so cool."

"Shut *up*."

Larry and Balki were flailing around in a muddy riverbed—a high-budget episode for holiday viewers. Gage was trying to act like she thought the comedy was stupid, but I could tell by her attention that she found it hilarious, and it made me feel sort of protective of her. Back in fourth grade, she'd been the same way about a visiting puppet show—quietly enthralled while pretending to scoff at it with the rest of us.

She waited until the commercial to ask me, "So by the way, my parents are renting again at Mad River during that week between Christmas and New Year's. Any interest?"

"Ha," I snorted. "I don't even know how to ski. I'd have two left feet."

"If you don't want to, just say. I only mentioned it because last year, you'd said you might want to go. I didn't realize you weren't serious." Her voice sharpened.

I stared at Gage. A blush was spreading across her cheeks. She thought I was rejecting her. "I don't have ski stuff, Gagey. I couldn't pay for anything. I'd be leaning on you way too hard." The truth was awkward, but I didn't want her to think anything worse.

"I know," said Gage quietly. "But meals and everything are paid for. I can give you lessons myself, and I've got tons of ski stuff to lend you. As for my parents, I've already cleared it with them. They're psyched."

"I mean, do you really want me?" I asked. "Do you really want to take a nonskiing person skiing for a week? I'd be on the bunny slopes the whole time."

"There's a scene up there." Gage's voice softened. "And I'm hopeless when it comes to meeting new people. But last New

Year's Eve, I was sort of unprepared for it, and I ended up playing Parcheesi and drinking sparkling cider with Helena after my parents went to bed, while everyone else was partying together. If I had a friend up with me, it'd be different. I'm getting too old to hide . . . and you're better at being social."

"If you don't mind me borrowing your stuff and being on the kiddie slope, I think we'd have a good time."

"Yeah, I think so, too." Balki was back on, hamming it up. We watched for a while. Gage never said more than she meant, and she'd said a lot. So I was surprised at the next ad break when she turned to me again. "I *do* perm my hair," she confessed softly, her eyes darting to Mimi to make sure she was sound asleep.

"Oh, yeah?"

"It never works out the exact way I want. I think I'm doing it wrong, maybe. And I was thinking, if you didn't mind, you could give me some help, next time? Since your hair is a home job. I'm not saying like a full makeover."

"Sure. Count on me. It'll be fun."

"Yeah, no big deal if you can't."

"I totally can help."

"Only if you want to. It's not even anything I care about, it's nothing, only if you want to."

I kept my eyes on the screen; Gage's vulnerability was like a force field to keep me from looking at her. "Yeah, but I totally want to. No big deal at all."

# twenty-eight

"You need to know something."

I looked up from where I was rummaging around at the bottom of my locker, scavenging for stray lunch tickets. I'd been trying to catch up with this morning ever since I slept through my alarm, dressing in a rush to dash outside, unbreakfasted, on Mom's third honk. Mom liked an early start on any back-from-break Monday, but now all I wanted was a bagel and a burnt-roast cup of cafeteria coffee.

But without any cash or lunch tickets, I had no way to pay for either.

Lordy, I was so broke all the time.

And now Claire's voice sank my heart to the floor of my stomach. Here it was. She was finally coming after me about Jay's letters.

"What is it?" I stood. My feet felt stuck as I let the spasm of panic pass through my body. I wanted to run.

"Last night, right when I got back from Florida, I called Dave. That band I'd been wanting to hear, the Painted Bandits, was playing over at Wallbanger's, down on Second Street. I drove into the city and we met up. He'd brought along Matt."

"Oh." When I hadn't heard from Matt last night, I'd gone to bed with an ear tuned for a call that never came. At the time, I hadn't thought much of it.

"We all hung out together. It was spontaneous. But then I felt bad, because it was like we went out without you included. But it wasn't behind your back."

"Right," I said. "But why didn't Matt call me?" I spoke my insecurity out loud and instantly wished I hadn't.

Claire looked defensive. "Don't ask me. He didn't say anything about that to me. We were out late. After Wallbanger's, we found this dive club on Quince Street."

"So I guess you really hit it off with Dave."

She paused. "I guess so."

Her story sounded flimsy, but what was there to say? "Thanks for telling me."

"Sure. It was really no big deal." She smiled. "Your hair's freaking awesome."

Claire never gave fake compliments. "Thanks. My parents are not in agreement."

"Then they wouldn't be parents, right?"

I smiled in answer, but I felt confused as I watched Claire glide on down the hall. What exactly had just happened here?

That afternoon at Ludington, Matt dropped by with a bunch of red flowers in his hand.

"Carnations," he said. "My mom said they're the apology flower. Stripes, you made your hair stripy! Bleached it? I like."

"Thanks." I took the flowers and ran my fingers through my hair. "Apology for what? For going out last night?"

"Yeah, I was hanging out with Dave when Claire called, and it was one of those plans that seems good at the time—and then after Wallbanger's, we went—"

"To a bar on Quince Street, I heard."

"Right." He cleared his throat. "It was too late to phone you."

"It's fine." Everyone had so much explaining for me.

"You're usually deep into homework on Sundays. Not like the rest of us slackers."

"You're not a slacker. You already admitted once that your name has been known to show up on the honor roll." But my mind couldn't leave it alone, this image of Dave and Claire and Matt at the concert, then the bar, triplets cut from the same long, lean cloth, looking like college kids, sharing those private, edgy stories that had kept them all up that night in Philadelphia. Did the guys jostle for Claire's attention? Was there some kind of deeper connection among the three of them that could happen only when I was out of the picture?

"Hey, can you promise me something?" I had to ask it, forcing the gear switch that raised Matt's eyebrows. "If you're in love with Claire Reynolds, will you please just come clean and tell me?"

Matt drew back from me sharply, unsettled. "Is that what you think?"

"I don't know what to think. All this talking about last night, and me not there. You and Claire both have made a thing about it. As if something happened. Which makes me think—was it so innocent?" My casual shrug couldn't compensate for the catch in my voice.

He leaned in, his fingertips anchoring him to the desk as his eyes made the promise to mine. "I'm not in love with Claire Reynolds. Not now, or ever."

There was a heartbeat in that next moment when I could feel my hope lifting for a next, possible confession—*I'm not in love with Claire because I'm falling in love with you, Stripes.* But Matt didn't speak those words.

# twenty-nine

THE MASTERCARD ENVELOPE WAS waiting for me later that evening, when I got home from my shift. Mom had left it on the kitchen table. My heart was pounding as I ripped it open.

$374.03.

I'd barely been able to pay my credit card bill last month, and this month was worse by double. My two library checks, totaling just over one hundred and fifty dollars, wouldn't even begin to cover my latest run-up of charges.

I sat. The new pair of Doc Martens made up a full one-third of the statement costs. My black Benetton jeans, Claire's and my way-too-expensive Philadelphia tavern dinner, that time I'd picked up Matt's and my Lupini's milk shakes—nothing was forgotten, but the bill was even higher than my mental tab, because I'd also spent on so many little, forgettable items: a pair of dance-uniform tights and a pot of pink glitter gloss at the drug-store, the twelve-dollar charge for an Argyll '89ers senior class mug, a Philadelphia Flyers sweatshirt for Peter's birthday.

I'd taken out more ATM money than usual this month, too, and I also had to tally for the cleared thirty-six-dollar check to Strickland for the yearbook. Lately I'd wanted so many things, and I'd spent so recklessly to get them. How would I possibly pay this down?

There was one quick, partial solution. Skating past my parents, who were watching Dan Rather in the living room, I went upstairs and called Mrs. Binswanger.

"More hours?" she sniffed, interested. "I *have* been wanting to stop my Wednesdays. But I thought fifteen hours a week was as much as your mother said you could work."

"She'll see it my way, I promise."

If I took Mrs. Binswanger's Wednesdays, I'd clock in four more hours a week. And if I went cold turkey on my spending, I could use the next three months to pay off the card in installments.

When I came downstairs to help with dinner and tell Mom my plan, she was predictably displeased. "Lizzy, we let you keep Ludington because you can do some studying there, and because more than one hundred and fifty dollars a month equals a pretty good allowance, wouldn't you say? Why do you need more spending money than that?"

"Okay, first of all, it's a paycheck. I wish you'd stop saying *allowance*, like this is something you and Dad are providing. Second, I can handle the extra hours. Third, I need to pay down some new charges on my credit card."

Mom snapped to a different kind of attention.

"What kinds of charges?"

"It's been expensive—as you know—to be a senior at a school like Argyll."

She winced. Day to day, Mom and I both saw how typical Argyll-family lifestyles differed from our own budget-pinching ways. Her voice softened as she reached out a hand. "Do you mind if I take a look at the statement?"

I pulled it from where I'd tucked it into a notebook. Mom stared at the page for a long time, her face furrowed in her looking-at-bills expression I knew all too well.

"Well, those boots, really Lizzy, you could have waited for Christmas, Dad and I would have been happy to get them. The designer jeans also seem like a splurge? But what I really don't understand is your spending fifty-six dollars for dinner in Philadelphia."

"It was me plus Claire. Her card was declined."

"Jane Sleighmaker's niece, Claire, from the cat mansion?" Mom looked up.

I nodded.

"You're kidding me. She could easily pay this. Is thirty dollars, her half of dinner, all she owes you?"

I flinched at the idea of "owe," but if I added last month's sushi and the cover for Liz's party, and all those train and taxi costs around and from Philadelphia, Claire's tab with me was over sixty dollars. "A little more."

"How much more?"

"Maybe double."

"Okay, so how about you end this nonsense right now, of picking up costs for a Sleighmaker." Mom looked exasperatedly relieved, as if she'd solved the whole dilemma. "Jane Sleighmaker has *millions*. The business office just did some research on that family, and I am not exaggerating. We're going to approach her for our capital funds campaign."

"You don't get it, Claire's aunt is a total tightwad. There's no way I can—"

"*You* don't get it, Lizzy. Your carelessness has put you in the red for almost four hundred dollars. You'll be charged twelve percent interest on whatever it is you can't pay this month. This is how people sink into perpetual debt, and the timing couldn't be worse. Do you think that the student loans you'll need to take out for Princeton are chump change?"

"Listen, I can handle this, okay?" I was shaking my head back and forth, wishing Mom would stop, but suddenly she grabbed both of my forearms in a lock.

"No," she said. "*You* listen. I'll let you take the extra shift at Ludington, but you've got to ask Claire Reynolds for your sixty dollars back."

"Mom, you're not listening to me. There is no way."

"Find a way."

"Ludington isn't so bad. With four more hours each week, I can earn about fifty extra a month, and if I'm careful, I'll have it all paid back by the end of January."

"There's a difference between what you could do and what you *should* do. It's not a lot of money on Claire's end. Not compared with all the work you'll need to do. Explain to her that you lost control of your spending. It happens. It's not the end of the world." Mom cupped my face in her hands, imploringly. "Claire seems like a good girl. Would you have asked Mimi or Gage to pay a debt?"

I nodded. Of course I could have gotten Mimi and Gage to pay me back.

But they also knew my situation, so they never would have borrowed.

"If Claire's a real friend, she'll want to get you out of your predicament. Right?"

"I don't know." It probably wasn't crazy, what Mom was asking me. But just imagining that talk with Claire, I was already coming undone.

# thirty

"You're blowing this out of whack." Matt switched lanes to get off at his exit. "Claire's not hurting for cash. She'll repay you, easy." Even though we'd talked about it on the phone late last night, I couldn't stop thinking about it.

"It feels awkward to ask."

"It's worse if you don't. Last year, my friend Jake went to his girlfriend's prom and he wanted to wear my formal stuff, including my tie and cummerbund. I was cool to lend it all to him—but he kept forgetting to bring it back for months, till I called him out in front of all the guys."

"I could never do that."

"Yeah you could if it's the only way to get your stuff back."

"Right, but . . ." Matt didn't understand that it was different with girls. Or maybe it was different with new friendships. Or maybe it was just different with Claire.

The Ashleys lived in an important-looking brick house that Gage and I had driven past last year, on my dare, right when she'd just gotten her license and we had nowhere to go. It was quietly thrilling to walk through its red-painted front door now, though I halfway wished that Gage were with me, just for the laugh.

Inside, I felt the hush of prim decisions, from the tick of the grandfather clock to the sheen of the silvery silk wallpaper. On my side, Matt had gone quiet.

"So pretty," I whispered.

"You've been here before, right? Downstairs."

"Nope, never."

"My party, remember?" He gave me a quick look. "You told me . . ."

My cheeks got hot. "It looks different in the daylight." But now it seemed stupid to lie to him. "Okay, I'm busted. I was too intimidated to go to Matt Ashley's homecoming party. I lied to impress you."

He burst out laughing. "You *goofball*."

"Matt, is that you?" Mrs. Ashley's voice floated to us like that of a ghostly hostess. "And did you bring Lizzy?"

"Yes!" I called.

"This way." Matt took my hand, and together we walked through a living room so formal I could feel a nervous prickle on the back of my neck. A grand piano made a display of silver-framed wedding pictures. I pointed to a pretty bride in a recent-looking photo.

"Your sister, Erin, right?"

"Yep. This is our multigenerational Ashley-family wedding gallery. I'm next. My spot's already reserved." Matt tapped the corner of an empty frame.

"Seriously?"

"Mom is a planner."

It seemed ridiculous to me that anyone would put an empty frame on a piano. "You might not get married for ten more years!" I objected. "Fifteen, even!"

But Matt was already leading me through the living room, and then down two steps into a smaller room where his mother stood on a stepladder before a regal cone of Christmas tree. Stacks of opened boxes on a side table held tissue-wrapped ornaments. Matt's mother looked a bit like an ornament herself, glassy and breakable.

"So this is Lizzy." She dropped her hand on my shoulder and patted it twice, which made me feel like a noble service dog. "Can you believe we're already into December?" Her smile wasn't unkind. "So much to do, with these holidays."

"Yes, at school, too. Your tree is beautiful."

"Thank you. Every year, we get a Canadian blue spruce. The decorators come to trim it and do the lights. But I hang the ornaments. I'm the family touch. Will you hand me that?" She pointed to an ornament.

"Sure." I wondered what Mrs. Ashley didn't like about a good old Pennsylvania Douglas fir. The Swift-family tree was always plump and strong, even if it was decorated with a mess of junk my brothers and I had made in art classes over the years. My mom tried to keep the ornaments in shape, though it wasn't like they'd ever known greatness, birthed from Styrofoam or macaroni and yarn.

But still. Our tree looked like Christmas. This tree looked like a hotel lobby.

I passed Mrs. Ashley a spindly wooden reindeer by his pretty gold clothespin, which I'd been holding open for her to clamp to the tree.

"Ouch!"

"Oh, no! I'm so sorry!" So awful—I'd accidentally snapped the tip of her finger. "I didn't mean to do that!"

"It's fine, it's fine." But her eyes went as wide as those of a child who's been smacked, and when she hopped down from the step-ladder, sucking on her finger, I felt like I'd committed a secretly intentional, sadistic act. "Matt says you're very bright, Lizzy." Her voice accused me as she cast an eye over my bleach-striped hair, the print of pink glitter gloss on my mouth.

"Lizzy applied early to Princeton," said Matt.

"That's wonderful."

But no, I wasn't wonderful to Mrs. Ashley, I could feel it. I wasn't Nectarine-y enough, I didn't have the tennis bracelet or the hairband or the Joan & David flats. I didn't accessorize nicely with the Ashleys' manicured, Merchant Ivory sitting room and imported Christmas tree and their Golden Boy son.

We heard the front door slam.

"Dad's home. Two for one." Matt's smile was grim. "We'll need to keep out of their way," he added quietly, though I didn't see how we were creating a disturbance.

"Heigh-ho!" Matt's dad said to nobody specifically as he headed to the bar cart. He was small and bald and apparently not very interested in who was in his house.

"Hey, Dad, this is my friend Lizzy."

"Pleased to meet you," I added.

"And you." But Mr. Ashley seemed more pleased to get busy with his scotch and ice tongs, and to start telling a happened-at-the-office story that was for Matt's mom alone. The Ashleys weren't kid-friendly parents, not that this surprised me. I wasn't sure why I needed them to like me so badly, why I wanted to linger even as Matt took my hand. "C'mon, we've got our own den," he said quietly. "You can meet the young'uns, my little brother and sister."

When we left, the Ashleys didn't even seem to notice.

The "den" turned out to be a barely made-over basement. It was messy and smelled like mildew, with a carpet that felt spongy under my boots. I could see how Matt could throw a party here—there just wasn't much to look after or destroy. Right now, the creaky tank of an old console television was blaring an ancient rerun of *Gilligan's Island*. A gum-snapping college-aged baby-sitter who didn't introduce herself was sunk in the couch, wedged between Matt's little sister and brother, who I knew were in fourth and fifth grade. The kids were cute in that Irish-pixie Ashley way, and the den seemed like a sad place to keep them. If there was a housekeeper—a house like this surely had one—it felt like she hadn't been down here in weeks.

With his palm at my back, Matt kept us moving past the den and through a door, into a boxed-in laundry room, and then a supply closet, which he slammed into darkness.

He was at me in an instant, his lips slightly parted in a kiss that felt strange and hungry as his hand went straight up my shirt.

"This is like Seven Minutes in Heaven," I murmured when I could collect a breath. I'd never been invited to any of those boy-girl parties back in middle school, but Gage and Mimi always had an ear out for those daring stories of pilfered beer and kissing games, like Truth or Dare or Spin the Bottle or Seven Minutes in Heaven, when a girl and boy would slam themselves into a closet, and a timer would be set.

Matt snorted. "I played that game with half your class."

It was such a zingy thought, so exactly how I loved to imagine Matt, hot and in demand. "And now you play it with me," I whispered.

"Mmm." His mouth was demanding a deeper kiss, his hand cupped over my bra, and then under it, his fingers circling my nipple. "My parents really wouldn't want us doing this," he murmured. "It's basically a sin, in their book."

"Why not?"

"Just, with my brother and sister so close, and them upstairs."

"A little bit of sin feels okay."

In answer, Matt tightened his arms around me, kissing me intensely as shivers played catch through my body. I sensed maybe that Matt was excited by this weird idea of disobeying his parents. It excited me, too.

I unbuttoned the top button of Matt's school-uniform khaki pants and unzipped his fly to his flannel boxer shorts. I couldn't tell what he wanted, but when I closed my hand over the flannel around the outward spring of his dick, he pressed in closer, his breath urging me. Okay, but—what next? What was his dick about, exactly? Wasn't it sort of an up and down thing, a rhythm like brushing your hair if you're in a hurry? I'd seen something like that in a movie but it was in a car, and they didn't show it, and Matt wasn't showing me now.

I relaxed my hand. Maybe it was more of a gentle slide or massage.

"You don't—" His voice was hoarse as he broke off. "Have you ever given a hand job before?"

I'd thought about trying it at my house, but the room had been too bright, not the right atmosphere. This felt different, more secretive. "Show me how." My voice notched above a whisper. "I want to know."

"Not over clothes."

"Oh, right. Right." I pushed my hand through the opening in his boxers and was immediately relieved that this secret skin seemed so friendly to the touch, like a new-made sculpture of warm firm clay, and then the slightly softer head. "Whoa."

I still wasn't sure about the specifics of how to do it, though, and it seemed like my slow back-and-forth wasn't even close to correct, since Matt's dick was changing in my hand, actually shrinking from me and retreating like a disappointed animal.

And now Matt was laughing softly, zipping himself up, and I'd never been so glad for the darkness that hid the shame on my face. "It doesn't matter, Stripes. You don't have to do this. Some other time, maybe not in the laundry room."

"No, let's . . ." I wanted to do more. I just didn't know how to ask for it.

Matt kissed me one more time, a sweet kiss that didn't care about my inexperience, though Claire's words were at me like bees—*you're such a kid he doesn't feel the pressure*—as we looped back into the den.

The babysitter raised her eyes oh-so-slightly to smirk at me, and I wondered if she'd seen Matt lead other girls into the infamous supply closet. Girls who knew what they were doing, girls who'd been expertly practicing hand jobs since middle school, while my nerdy friends and I'd spent weekends playing board games, snarfing Chipwiches, and fantasizing about a day we'd be everything we couldn't be in real life.

# thirty-one

"HEY, DO YOU WANT to see *Dead Ringers* with me this weekend at the Ritz Cinq?" Claire had virtually ignored me in Tuesday art class, and for the millionth time I'd figured she was done with me, so her Wednesday-evening call took me by surprise.

"I want to," I said, "but my parents are keeping me locked up on the grounds of debt."

"You sound stressed."

"Maybe stressed about my Latin test. I don't know why I didn't take French like any normal person."

"Because all the nerds take Latin." She added, more thoughtfully, "You know, my shrink is helpful for stress, when I need a place to dump my problems. Don't you see someone, too?"

"No, I don't. Actually you asked me that before."

"Did I?"

My voice was as tight as it had ever been with her. "It's like you think I *should* see someone." When what I wanted to say but couldn't was, *Yeah, I see someone for my epilepsy. You know I have that, right?*

Her answering laugh shrugged me off.

I couldn't figure out how to ask Claire for the sixty dollars on the phone. But after I hung up, I felt the pang of regret. After all, she owed me. Claire had more spending money than I did. Maybe not a ton, but I could tell by her lipstick brands and cassette tapes, and the fact that her gas tank was always full, she was doing okay.

Friday at lunch, I risked my mom's annoyance to bill my student account with a fresh pack of lunch tickets. I used up a twenty-five-cent ticket for a cup of black coffee. I needed that bounce.

Claire was in the art room. In one hand, she held a bagel while she worked on a washy green watercolor painting. When she saw me, she smiled. "Is your mom relenting? Can you come out to the movies? Do you want to invite the guys?"

"No, she's not, and I can't—I wish I could, it sounds like so much fun. But listen, me being grounded actually relates to this other thing." I pushed myself a step closer. "You know how sometimes I've covered some expenses for you? When I've charged meals and cabs to my credit card? Anyway, I feel embarrassed to ask, but"—I took a breath—"I need a refund."

Claire rattled the tip of her brush in her jam jar of green water. She daubed at the paint cake. "You know my sitch, Lizzy. I'm so broke all the time. Maybe if you need to borrow, you could try Gage?"

"Well, this is more about you paying me back. Because I'm kind of in a state of emergency, money-wise." My blood was in a coffee-heated boil. "Obviously I hate to ask, because you've been so cool to me."

"I guess I don't get it," said Claire after a moment, and there was no mistaking the ice on her words. "I didn't realize I was *borrowing* money from you. But I can ask my mom. How much?"

"It adds up to about sixty dollars."

Now Claire looked plain stunned. "What are you talking about? It couldn't be more than twenty-five bucks for some over-priced bar food and a hard cider."

"But there was also the Hinata bill last month, and the train into Philly. A couple of taxi rides. Liz's party cover charge." I felt so incredibly petty, tallying it.

Claire's answering silence was painful, as if she were holding us both underwater and counting the seconds before she finally spoke again. "Lizzy, that black cardigan sweater I gave you, the one you always wear? I gave it to you because Jay gave it to me. I didn't want it anymore, for certain reasons—but it's probably worth about two hundred dollars. It's cashmere."

Of course I knew the sweater was cashmere. It was the only cashmere thing I owned. "I've got to dig out of this debt, Claire. It's not personal."

"It feels pretty personal. It also feels kind of like an ambush. Are you sure this isn't about when Matt and Dave and I went into the city?"

"No!" My voice squeaked in outrage. "That has got nothing to do with this. Why would it?"

"I was annoyed when you took Jay's letters, and I should have dealt with it. I should have said something, but instead I clammed up about it. I know when I don't talk to you it upsets you, so that's what I did. Now you're annoyed that I'm hanging out with Matt and Dave, and you're trying to upset me, too—making me pay you money I *borrowed*." Her fingers clipped angry quote marks for the word as her eyes bore into me. A fresh sweatiness itched my neck and under my arms. "Maybe it's time we deal with this, and give each other a break."

"I'm s-so sorry for taking that envelope," I stammered. "It was stupid. I was too curious, and it was a bad impulse. I've been trying to figure out for weeks how to make that right. I'd planned to slip it back in its place when I stayed over at your house last time, except we ended up spending the night in the city. But I'm not trying to get you back for hanging out with the guys. Money is a whole other problem for me, Claire."

Her head tilted. "What did you think of them?"

"Think of what?"

"Jay's letters. What was your opinion?"

Was this a trick? "I don't know. Um. Bad handwriting, I guess. To be honest, I felt so awful that I took them, I feel like my main opinion about them is just my guilt."

Was I imagining Claire's disappointment with my answer? Her face was already stony again. "Look, are you seriously asking me for sixty dollars?"

"Do you think this makes me feel good? It's totally the opposite. I feel like a jerk."

"Money doesn't grow on trees in my life, either. Give me the weekend."

"It doesn't need to be the weekend. It can be whenever works best for you."

"You don't mean that."

"I do."

"You might wish it, but you don't mean it."

"You're making this so different from what it is. It doesn't have to be like a business deal between us. I really think of you as my friend."

"Maybe I don't know what I think of you." She was looking at me with something I was too scared to believe was open dislike. "Three days. Count on it."

Then she plucked her paintbrush from the jar, dismissing me.

# thirty-two

"YOU'RE GROUNDED FOR MONEY you have to pay back?" In the silence, I could sense Matt trying to puzzle it out. "Actually it reminds me of how my dad says this superwitty thing, that he should ground my mom for the damage she does to her Neiman Marcus card."

"Oh, yes. That is hilarious."

"Since the thing about my dad is he's not sexist."

"Also, I bet that joke gets funnier and funnier, the more he tells it."

"Totally." Whenever Matt brought up this topic of his hyperconservative family—his chauvinist dad and his passive mom—he needed it to be a joke. But I could always hear that it bothered him. Perfect on the outside was the Ashley-family way.

"The other night I told them I was thinking about heading to Hawaii after graduation, to surf, pick up jobs along the way. My dad acted like he hadn't even heard me. Next day, I see the summer intern application to his law firm, Drinker and Lewis, on my desk. Mom's put a Post-it with a smiley face that says if I fill it out, she'll drive it in and drop it off."

"You're looking at it now, right? I dare you to fill it out in crayon."

Matt laughed. "I should."

"Seriously, though. Fold it up and put it away."

"Yeah, I hate looking at it. This assumption I should be a lawyer because Dad's a lawyer and Uncle Ed's a lawyer and my granddad was a lawyer—so who cares what I want, why should anyone listen to me?"

"If they're not listening to you, then you don't have to listen to them. At least put it out of sight."

I heard Matt's desk drawer open as he shoved it in. "Hey, if you're grounded, I'm gonna hang out with Tommy and the guys."

"If you get bored, come by Ludington on Sunday."

"You know I will, Stripes. The least I can do is make a conjugal visit."

As bummed as I was not to do anything with Matt, at least being grounded would give me time to write Claire an apology. I practiced a few drafts, made a final copy at Ludington, and had it enveloped and ready by Monday morning, when I slid it through her locker.

Monday night, there was no call from her.

"You're reading too much into it," said Matt, who did call. "Give Claire the time to pay you back. She'll come around."

I hoped so. Claire wasn't at the next morning's assembly, and so she missed Maggie Farthington's talk on *Roe v. Wade*.

"First assembly that had me halfway awake," said Gage at lunch.

"All I could think was if the rumor was true," Mimi admitted. "Do *you* know, Lizzy? Her boyfriend went to Lincoln, he was in that jock scene."

In fact I did know the rumor—that Maggie herself had an abortion last summer—was true. Matt had told me in confidence, because he was close friends with Karl Adler, Maggie's boyfriend at the time. They'd broken up even before Maggie knew she was pregnant, and Karl had graduated last year and now went to school in Michigan. But over Thanksgiving, he and Maggie had gotten back together, and Karl told Matt that Maggie felt really brave and scared about giving the assembly.

"So clap really hard," Matt had said on the phone last night.

"It's the kind of assembly I want to give," I said. "One where you can tell people are actually connecting with me." Then I wished I hadn't said it, because I could feel Gage and Mimi thinking: *Then do yours on your epilepsy.*

I'd never spoken about my own condition with the others. Not my absences, or my meds, or Dr. Neumann—nothing. If Gage and Mimi ever talked about it, and I always hoped they didn't, it was all behind my back.

Gage had straightened in her seat and was looking past us. I twisted around.

Claire was approaching.

"Here." Her hand was outstretched and her face was neutral as she delivered the envelope. It was the same generic business envelope that I'd stuck in her locker, and for a scalding second I thought she was returning my own letter to me.

But no. This envelope was unmarked. I'd scripted her name onto the one for the note I'd written.

I took it—it wasn't even sealed, so I had a clear view of three twenties, newly minted.

"Thanks." I'd have felt worse if the money had been soft and crumpled, but these bills looked as if Claire had popped by an ATM and withdrawn them from the cash piles in the Sleighmaker vault.

"Okay," said Claire. "We're square."

A tiny hammer was pinging minute flashes of pain over my eye. "Thanks a lot, Claire," I said again.

She turned and left.

"What was that about?" asked Mimi.

"Nothing. She owed me some money."

"I know you're friendly with Claire, but she's so random. How does she get away with wearing a black turtleneck for a uniform? And she skipped morning classes today." Mimi shook her head. "Her grades must be in the toilet."

"Her whole day is basically a silent anarchy of flipping off the school," said Gage.

I lifted my shoulders like *dunno*, though I certainly wasn't thinking about any of what Mimi and Gage were talking about. Claire was so angry with me. I never should have told Mom that Claire owed me money. I never should have chased it down. For sixty dollars, I'd lost Claire's trust, the only thing that mattered to me.

"Do you even know where she's applied to colleges?" Mimi asked me.

"California," I answered. "She told me once, she wants to head west."

"Imagine, my letter is just sitting there," said Gage. "I'm sure my mom's holding a flashlight underneath, trying to read it."

"You're both getting in," said Mimi. "It's not even an exciting discussion."

"Don't jinx us," I told her.

Colleges had mailed out all early-decision acceptance letters last Friday, which meant they'd probably arrived today. It had been on my mind all weekend, and especially this afternoon. Still, I was glad I didn't have to pull a shift at Ludington, and that Matt had wrestling tryouts so he couldn't pick me up. I'd already planned to ride home on the school bus. Long and pokey as my route was, I'd still beat Mom home and snag it.

My parents weren't like Gage's parents, swooping into my mail with flashlights. But I still wanted to hear from Princeton in solitude.

As usual, the mail lay on the living room carpet, where it had fallen through the slot. When I went through it for the first time, I missed it completely because I'd been looking for something thicker—an envelope plumped with inserts from the bursar, dining services, and student housing. That's what acceptance letters looked like, I remembered from when Theo got his.

So I hadn't anticipated its wafer thinness beneath Mom's over-sized Spiegel catalog.

Thin meant bad.

Still, my mind was careening around my reason, hounding down a way to make thin mean normal. I ripped the envelope from the top.

It was weightless because it was a formality? Just a quick, official nod from Admissions?

I'd get the thick envelope next week. Yes, that was it.

I sat on the floor. Words jumped around, passing through me in tiny zaps, competing for priority.

*. . . have carefully considered . . .*

*at this time deferred . . . to be reconsidered . . . regular pool.*

I hadn't gotten into Princeton. Not in. I'd have to wait and see in April, with all the other applicants. Panic was confetti in my head. I'd have to tell my parents, I'd have to tell everyone, I needed to start right-this-second applying to more colleges. My stomach was acid. Silver flashes pinged my eye again; literally, I couldn't see straight. But today, a seizure wasn't my main concern.

Upstairs I kicked off my boots and fell into the sloshy snoozing comfort of my parents' waterbed. I pulled up the covers and let the rejection sink into my bones.

And then I called Gage.

All year, every year, since the beginning of middle school when homework and grades and prizes began to mean something, Gage and I were neck and neck. We were the only two students who consistently landed on the highest honor rolls. We both knew what cram sessions felt like, we knew the 3:00 a.m. thrill of solving a physics problem, the endless memorization of time lines and the try, try again. I couldn't think of anyone better to help me through my defeat.

"Hey-ey!" The lilt in her voice meant yes. Gage Renee Hornblow had been formally accepted into Harvard's Class of 1993. "Did it come?"

"Deferred till April."

"Oh, no, *Lizzy.*" Racing out of her joy to enter my gloom, her voice was so exactly what I needed that tears smarted in the corners of my eyes. "But it's not like you got rejected. Rejected is a whole other can of worms. Your real chance is April. Don't cry, Lizzy. Come on. Do you have everything lined up and ready to go out?"

"There are some other applications on my desk." I wiped my eyes with the back of my hand. "I haven't even started."

Gage sucked in a breath through her teeth. Gage was different from me—she'd been so paranoid that she wouldn't get into Harvard that she'd completed a storehouse of applications earlier this fall, to be safe.

Me, I'd let my optimism wing it, all the way to a crash landing.

"It'll be okay," she said. "It's a setback. I'll help you get cracking if you want."

"Thanks. And there goes my winter break," I added, in semi-afterthought. "As my parents freak out."

"Right." Gage hadn't thought of that, or that now my parents would never let me go skiing at Mad River. They weren't crazy about the idea of my doing anything so wild as downhill skiing with my condition. January 1 deadlines would be the perfect excuse.

"I'm really glad for you, Gage. You worked hard."

"You did, too, Lizzy—and it's not over yet."

But I'd be deep in the shame of it tomorrow. That I knew. The jolt of my getting deferred by Princeton would be more like salty gossip than a juicy rumor, but it had enough flavor to pass along. My name would be spoken in whole new *Did you hear?* whispers for the rest of the week.

But now it was just me and Gage, her good news and my bad news, and all of it cradled in a friendship as old as memory.

I stayed on with her for a while.

My parents would be upset, my classmates would be shocked, I was wrenched with what-next nerves, but losing Mad River made me saddest. I'd really wanted to spend that week with Gage, to restrengthen a friendship that had felt a little bumpy these past couple of months—it would have been exactly what I needed. Instead I was out on a tightrope, with nothing but a lonely uncertainty stretched out in front of me, and no voice in my head convincing me that everything would be okay.

# thirty-three

Princeton hadn't accepted me, Claire wasn't talking to me, and by the end of the week when my first semester marks came in, I was in trouble with Argyll, too. My grades had dropped in everything but AP Art, where I'd landed an improbable 96. Even with that boost, my 90 in Ancient Civ, 84 in Classical Studies, 86 in Latin, and 91 in English had struck me down with an average that, for the first time ever, fell below a 90.

"I'm guessing that these low marks feel like punishment enough, Lizzy, but for Mom and me, it's the last straw. You're grounded starting next week, for winter break," Dad remarked during dinner cleanup that night. "It's hard for us to understand why you're not taking your life seriously anymore. Did you even figure out a topic for your senior assembly?"

"Uh, yeah." The Mary Cassatt kitchen wall calendar was above the stove. "I'm doing it on Mary Cassatt."

Dad blinked. "Well, that's nice. Your mom's favorite artist."

"I thought that would make her happy."

And when Mom heard, she was. Maybe it was Mary Cassatt that paved the way for my parents to let me keep one final date with Matt that next week, to say good-bye before his two weeks away to Club Med in Cabo, Mexico. I knew a lot of families that did these mysterious Club Meds in a world parallel to the one where my own family lived. Matt had done a ton of them, and he wasn't even excited about this one.

He picked me up after dark and told me it would be a surprise, and to dress warmly. I hadn't realized how much I *didn't* want to see Claire and Dave until Matt's car pulled up and I saw he was alone. I'd tried to downplay how wrecked I felt about Claire's and my feud because it seemed insecure, and Matt was so sure it was just a temporary misunderstanding.

"Where are we headed?"

"You'll see."

We exited at Valley Forge, and when we turned into the park, I still couldn't figure it out. It was after five, with none of the usual RVs and tour buses in the parking lot.

"Are we going to reenact key battles of the Revolutionary War?" I asked as we parked and got out. "That could be so romantic."

"Valley Forge National Park *is* romantic, goofball," said Matt. "And the rules here are loose. Like, if you get here before dark, you can have a picnic."

"All I've got in my bag is gum."

Matt popped the trunk and took out a picnic basket. "Luckily, I've got apples and cheese and crackers, and even a Bartles and Jaymes."

"Whoa, that *is* romantic."

"Gotta have faith. I'm not always a dumb jock."

"Well, except that this picnic isn't historically accurate—George Washington's soldiers mostly drank gruel flavored with pepper and old socks."

He shut the trunk and slung an arm around me. "This wine cooler might not taste much better. I rooked it from the Powerses' wine fridge—they go through it so fast, they'll never notice."

Matt had even brought a blanket, and he knew where to spread it out, on a hill clearing with a view of the fields that he said was off the beaten trail of the park rangers, who didn't start patrolling until after nine.

"Are you too cold?" he asked.

"No, it's nice." I bit into a crisp apple and suppressed a shiver.

Matt pulled me in from behind, so that his legs were on either side of mine. His hands kneaded my shoulders. "I feel bad you aren't doing anything cool for break," he mentioned.

"Oh, is this a guilt shoulder rub?" I laughed.

"Everything's a guilt thing when you're Catholic."

"I'll take it. It feels too good." I gave over a couple of minutes to the pure enjoyment of Matt's muscle power. "Do you think you'll quit going to Mass, when you're in college?"

His fingers paused a moment. "I might," he admitted. "If God is really the way my parents think, I think I should probably stop hanging out with him on Sunday."

The backrub felt so good, and so did the closeness of Matt's body, and the darkness, and the fact that we were completely alone—nobody for miles—and after a few minutes, I pushed back against Matt's chest so that he knew to lie down, and then I flipped over to face him. We kissed, and finally the cold started to feel good, mingled with our heated breath.

"We might get caught," I whispered. "Imagine if some of those park rangers were out here, watching." That idea of getting caught had cranked Matt up before, and sure enough, I could feel him get hard, and this time—thanks to my discussion with Mimi, who as it turned out had all kinds of pointers in the art of this job, I understood exactly what to do. Gentle, no friction, keep the rhythm steady but mix up the pressure . . . When he came, fishing a paper napkin from the picnic basket to clean himself up while I discreetly looked away, he seemed so surprised that I didn't know what to say, and we didn't speak about it at all on the drive back.

"See you soon," he said, giving me a small kiss and still looking a little shocked by the whole thing when he dropped me off at home.

"Don't do anything I wouldn't do," I answered, and for the first time, I realized I could say that without being totally ironic. I'd done some things. I'd done something tonight. It made me feel half triumphant and half ashamed, and I wondered if that's how Matt felt, too.

A LITTLE LATER, ALONE in the kitchen with a cup of tea and nothing around to read but my brothers' discarded skateboarding magazines, I could feel the chains of this dreaded vacation settle in around my ankles. Matt was gone. The Hornblows were heading to Mad River, in Vermont. Mimi was around, but every other year the Kims hosted their extended family from Korea, and this was that year, and Mimi was expected to pitch in.

Matt had warned me it would be too hard for him to call long-distance from Mexico, so I didn't really expect him to. But over the next days, whenever I heard the phone, I hoped.

Meantime, I was stuck with a whole lot of Peter and Owen, who seemed to be extra underfoot, turning every room into a burrow of crusting cereal bowls and discarded sneakers and sweatshirts. On one of my rare outings, I tagged along with the family for some Christmas shopping, which didn't put me in a holly-jolly mood, either. It wasn't like I could splurge for anything, with the debt I was in. I bought some festive tins at Pottery Barn, and one day when the family was out, I baked cookies, with oatmeal or raisins or chocolate chips or nuts, depending on preference. It was a cop-out, gift-wise, but I was so broke, what else could I do?

Our parents used major holidays to give the necessities, like winter boots and jackets, but on this Christmas morning, my fireplace stocking held a card with a check for $150 along with a stern message from Santa informing me that this money should be used to pay off my Mastercard.

I appreciated the check, but the note felt like a lump of coal.

To help time pass, I set tasks for myself. One afternoon, I purged my oldest clothes for the Salvation Army. Into a white kitchen garbage bag went my ankle-length, celery-green pleated paisley skirt, my butterscotch-brown Little House on the Prairie boots, my deep-V cropped checkered blazer, my eggplant turtleneck, and a pair of pleated dress pants that Peter had outgrown and given to me that had never fit me right. My modern dance clothes were just as ugly: thick pink sweatpants, shiny blue tights and silver leotards, an unending supply of shapeless T-shirts.

When I was done, the bag bulged, and my closet and dresser looked so empty I could have been a hotel guest in my own bedroom. But it also felt good. My future didn't wear these bright patterns and flowery prints. I was graduating from that girl. Wherever I landed come fall, it was the one thing I knew for sure.

A few afternoons, I also braved phoning Claire's house. Her mom answered every call, and once I was put on hold for long, humiliating minutes. When Mrs. Reynolds came back on the line, she told me in a stilted voice that while she'd thought Claire was in the house, she'd been terribly mistaken.

"Please be sure to let her know I was trying to get ahold of her? I know she's going to visit her dad for most of the holidays."

"Yes, of course. She'll want to be in touch with you, too, Lizzy."

We hung up, both of us embarrassed by her lie.

Claire left without calling me, Matt never phoned, and vacation dragged on. My bedroom was a study zone, my desk cluttered with Bic pens and index cards, legal paper and loose notes, soda cans and coffee cups. Gran had catapulted me into the new technology by giving me a Christmas-present boom box with a CD player, along with one lone CD, George Winston's *December*. The instrumental carols reminded me of walking alone down a country path at twilight, and the music kept me focused as I edited my essays and inched through earnest, personal explanations of why I'd be perfect for each college—though I couldn't see myself at any of them.

STIR-CRAZY ON NEW YEAR'S Eve, I jumped a train into the city. It was the first time I'd ever gone into Philadelphia alone, but my trips with Claire had bucked up my confidence. I planned to see one of those weird foreign films they showed at the Ritz Five, but I told my parents the trip was for AP Art, because I needed to draw my hand in different locations. I even carted along my notebook and drawing supplies.

My lie ended up shaping the afternoon, because once I got there, I decided to skip the movie and walk over to Moore College of Art to look at a student sculpture exhibition in the lobby. I then hit some galleries in Old City, where I sketched people and copied artwork and drew my hand.

At the Philadelphia Museum of Art, I saw the painting at once, as clear as if it had shouted my name from across the room. The billboard scale, the bold lines and bright colors, the fierce drumbeat motion in the composition. Of course, it had to be him, and I had to know more. I jotted down all his information in my notebook. Finally something had sparked.

So long, Mary Cassatt.

Walking alone through the city, my colored pencils clinking lightly in the sling bag over my shoulder, I felt more like myself than I had both these past two weeks of being stuck in my room. I stopped for a cheese sandwich at a café, and it tasted like the most delicious cheese sandwich ever made. With a little bit of time to duck into a final gallery, I discovered one on the same block—a light-filled space of tall rooms and a wooden floor that creaked like a boat. The gallery was so quaint that when I first spied her, I didn't recognize her, although when I did, I wished I hadn't.

Instead I looked closer, even though I felt like a Peeping Tom. The oiled brushstrokes were so aggressive, challenging me to stare up and down the shape of her, lounging boneless on a bed. Her flesh was bright: peach, banana, and mustard flesh tones. You could almost feel the warmth of her skin in contrast to the cool, pearl-white rumpled bedsheets.

The placard beneath the painting confirmed it.

Phillip Custis-Brown
*Jeanie*, 1985
Oil on canvas
73.7 cm × 92.1 cm (29 in × 36¼ in)

Mrs. Custis-Brown's name was Jean. I shivered. It was just so weird, that explosion of teacher pubic hair, those raisin-dark teacher nipples. I imagined Mr. Custis-Brown, thumb crooked to get the jut of "Jeanie's" hipbone and the curve of her inner thigh just right. I felt kidnapped, like the Custis-Browns had secretly grabbed me by the hands and pushed me into a forbidden, velvety room of scarf-draped lamps and red wine and nakedness.

Mrs. Custis-Brown had looked embarrassed that day, when Claire played the Gainsbourg, but she'd only been pretending to be a prude at her workplace, where we girls saw her as the perfect match to a husband who was like the human version of Peter Rabbit.

But the joke was on us, because Jeanie Custis-Brown wasn't embarrassed by anything. It was like she was laughing at me, and visions of her naked body stayed smeared across my closed eyes as I rode home on the train.

I was used to girls with secrets—like Leslie or Kreo. Even I had a secret. But not every secret made you its victim. Some secrets were bold. Some secrets, like Mrs. Custis-Brown's, were your double life, where you were defiant and wild.

Maybe that's where I'd been wrong all along about Claire?

Maybe the real Claire always had been right in front of me, and I'd gotten her totally inside out and backward. What if Jay was the victim here? As in, Claire had found the one guy who'd been ridiculously easy to manipulate, and she'd gone after him hard—baked him lemon squares, knitted him a cute woolly hat, created mixtapes. She'd come on so charming that Jay had fallen madly in love with her, to the point where he didn't realize she was casting a spell until, too late, he learned it was just a power game, and Claire never cared about him after all.

Claire's reluctance to talk about Jay—what if it was because she'd hurt him, and she felt guilty about it?

It also made sense if I imagined that Claire had done to Jay what she'd done to me. I'd been so enthralled with Claire, and she'd dropped me so easy. For all I knew, poor Jay was still writing her wistful notes from Paris, or whatever place he'd buried himself after she'd totaled his life.

His letters were probably as pathetic as the one I'd put in her locker.

By the time I got off the train, trading its dry heat for the damp, dog-nose cold, my temples were pounding. If I'd had a quarter, I'd have called a parent to come pick me up at the station. Instead I trudged, shoulders hunched, every step a thud of throbbing accusations.

Claire never had been a real friend, and she'd never needed one, either. I'd been a ready ear and a willing sympathizer whenever she needed a diversion. But the minute I'd bothered her, the minute I'd asked her for something, she'd tossed me to the curb.

"Good gracious, Lizzy, don't slam the door like that!" Mom jumped up from the kitchen table as I entered. "What happened to you? You look awful."

"I've got a headache."

Within minutes, I'd been sent up to take a warm shower. I came back down long enough to eat a bowl of tomato soup with a grilled cheese sandwich plus two Tylenol.

Then I burrowed under my bedcovers. Some New Year's Eve.

When I woke up, it was black. My digital clock read 11:27. As much as I wanted to roll over and go back to sleep, it seemed wrong, especially since my headache had subsided. Might as well wave good-bye to the last minutes of 1988.

But there was nothing to do. The house was stone silent, the boys and my parents were all asleep, and every bedroom door was closed.

Parties were happening everywhere, and I wasn't at any of them. I imagined all the Nectarines champagne-toasting in front of a roaring fire at some luxury ski lodge. I imagined Matt feeling up Miss Gunne Sax somewhere in dangerous proximity to his parents, all hot and bothered by the risk of being caught. I imagined Gage at the Parcheesi board with her sister and her glass of sparkling cider—and even that seemed more joyful than ghosting around my dark house.

In the kitchen, I nearly broke my wrist scooping out a bowl of too-hard coffee ice cream. There was a slush of junk mail on the counter, including a rolled-up flyer and a small, opened package from Good Hardware, its packing twine stuffed into the empty box. I rolled the rubber band off the flyer and wound the rough string of twine in a coil around my finger.

Settled in the den, I flipped open my sketchbook.

I turned on "Dick Clark's New Year's Rockin' Eve" to see the crowds in paper-foil top hats freezing their butts off in Times Square. Richard Marx was next up to perform, so I switched to MTV's "Big Bang '89," which featured Bobby Brown and looked a little bit more promising.

Leafing through my sketchbook brought a blast of the day back to me. It was crammed with doodles and sketches, a longer study I'd done of a guy leaning over to tie his shoe in the café. I'd sketched the bold, bright museum piece, too—and it burst back into my head with all the intensity of that first second I'd seen it, the same vibrant figures, the same feeling of jam-packed togetherness that made me think of clubs and concerts and all the places I wanted to be, reminding me that hiding also meant missing out.

When I finished my ice cream, I snapped the post office rubber band over my wrist and triple-tied the twine around my hand. I picked up a pencil, and nudged deep down into that soft magic that took over whenever I began to sketch. I needed it especially tonight. Art was all I had.

# part three

## spring

# thirty-four

"Hey, Blizzard. Happy New Year."

"Hey, Theo. You, too." I yawned, wedging the phone closer to my ear. "Mimi's not here." In fact, I'd seen Mimi only once over break, when she'd picked me up for lunch at Saladalley on Christmas Eve—and she'd barely had time for that meet-up.

"Actually it's you I need. Are you free today?"

"Oh." I was now awake and on guard. "Depends what it is."

"You can't tell Meems. Because she offered to help, and I shafted her."

"Okay . . ." What was this all about? What did Theo think I could do better for him than his kid sister? "What's up?"

"I've left it to the last second, but I've got to find Violetta a birthday gift to take back to school. A good one."

Aha, a girlfriend-gift mission. I felt the pinch of disappointment. "Theo, it's New Year's Day. Everything's closed."

"King of Prussia Mall stays open till five today. I'll come get you."

"Why am I being singled out for this VIP field trip?"

"Full disclosure? I think you might be ten percent less of a dork these days, Bliz. So I'm enlisting you to help buy my excellent girlfriend something special."

"Now you're just gettin' on my noives."

I could hear Theo's smile on the other end of the line. "See ya in twenty. I'll beep."

Twenty minutes later, I was running out the door to jump in.

"Thanks for this," he said first thing.

"I only got sprung because I lied to my parents that I was helping with the blood drive at the Red Cross, and you were giving me a lift over and back."

"See, because parents trust me. I'm basically the town hero. National Merit *and* All-American? They should build a statue in the park already."

"As soon as they learn to make one out of hot air."

"Nyuck nyuck nyuck nyuck."

At the mall, we browsed for over an hour, finally choosing a book of poems by Elizabeth Bishop, and then at the Macy's counter, a tiny crystal bottle of Chanel No. 5—after we'd sprayed and sniffed a dozen different scents.

"A late Christmas gift?" The old lady at the register winked at Theo. "Smart of you to have your girlfriend come along and test our fragrances herself. Saves the embarrassment of having to return something, mm?" She winked.

"Yeah, I'm careful like that," said Theo, throwing an arm around my shoulders and giving me a bone-crushing football buddy squeeze. "Anything for my little honey."

"It feels a little cheap for our five-year anniversary," I added, which made the lady's eyelashes flutter in surprise as Theo laughed outright.

But it was weirdly fun to be mistaken for Theo's girlfriend, even if the reality was that we were out shopping for his actual girlfriend, and Violetta was someone I'd never even met. Theo looked hot in his barn jacket and unlaced work boots, his hair overgrown in a way that Mimi said their parents hated for being "girlie," but I thought softened the razor cut of his jawline. And I enjoyed the sweet nature of the errand, even when we'd moved to the even-more-awkward lingerie department. Theo's expression was so serious when he talked to the saleslady about finding something "classic but personal," and wanting to get the size and style exactly right.

"You've got your debate-team face on," I told him as we waited for his selection, a plain black silk camisole, to be gift wrapped. "Remember when you were in sixth grade, how you'd instruct Mimi and me to try and stump you—but you'd made a double set of flash-card questions, one for you and one for us, so you could never lose?"

"That's why I was lord of the middle school debate."

"Excuse me, did you just call yourself lord of the middle school debate?" We both were laughing. "And you say *I'm* a dork?"

"Blizzard, I seem to remember you being at my house many a Saturday night wearing owl footie jammies with attached wings."

"Hoot! Oh, wait, my retainer's still in!" I pretended to whip out an imaginary retainer, which Theo'd had to wear for years— then jumped out of the way as he aimed a kick at my shins.

Later we sat with our bags at a table outside the Orange Julius. "These presents put a dent in your wallet," I observed. "Does that mean Violetta is the one?"

"The one for now." Typical Theo. "Actually I'm kind of feeling like Violetta's birthday has dominated the past ninety minutes. How about you catch me up on *you*, Bliz? I know from Meems you got deferred, which sucks. Sorry to hear."

"That was bad," I said, "but it was kind of the cherry on the cake."

"How so?"

I took a breath and went for it. "Everything feels like it's slipping out of my control lately—my first-semester grades slumped, I racked up major debt on my credit card, my whole winter break has been one big college application to a bunch of schools I'm not sure I care about—and honestly at this point, I'm not sure I care about Princeton, either. But disappointing my parents after all they've sacrificed for my education just crushes me, for real. I miss Matt, too, but I'm also kinda jealous that he's off at Club Med having the time of his life, hanging out with all the bikini girls. And finally, I think I've pissed off a new friend I made this year, Claire, possibly to the point of no return." I went into detail on that, with the letters and the money.

When I finally stopped talking, I felt like I might burst into tears. I took a deep breath. "So now you're pretty caught up on me."

Theo didn't change expression, just stirred his icy Julius with a little plastic coffee stirrer. Then he gave himself a moment for a slow, overhead arm stretch.

"Well, okay. First off, the hardest voices to tune out are your parents' voices in your head. I'm always working on that, especially when I'm trying to figure out what *I* want to do, what makes *me* happy versus them. Separating out what you want from what the 'rents want is a step in the right direction. So that's a positive."

A positive? "Well, that's a different way to think about it, I guess."

"And it sounds like you're not totally trusting your man," Theo continued. "I was never tight with Matt Ashley, but one thing I always thought about him is that he's a guy you can trust. He wouldn't go out with you if he secretly thought you were too young for him. But . . ." He held up a finger.

"But what?" I leaned in.

"But if you two don't get serious in the next month, you never will."

"Oh." I blinked, startled. "Why do you say that?"

"Guys move only one direction. Forward. Not in circles."

"Matt moves forward!"

Theo lifted his palms. "Then the Club Med bikini girls are no threat."

Was I threatened? A sentence from one of Jay's letters to Claire had haunted me ever since I'd first read it: *I feel like I'm going to do this thing, go forward in this way that breaks everything apart between us and messes us up forever.*

In that one thought, Jay had sprinted out faster than any of Matt's moves. Matt was too careful to break things apart and mess us up forever. But wasn't that a good thing? It's not like Stephen Clancy had moved forward with Leslie the right way. What was the basic movement of Matt and me? I'd never pinned a single satisfying conclusion to how that last night in Valley Forge had gone, especially whenever I remembered the surprise on Matt's face, and how he didn't seem to know what to say to me after.

Okay, but maybe Theo was talking about direction, not speed or distance.

Theo must have sensed my dismay. He grinned. "Look, it might be different for me. I function best in relationships where I feel like my girl would rather jump off a cliff than be without me."

I threw my crumpled napkin so it bounced off his chin. "Theo, you egomaniac. I don't even know why I ask your advice."

"Too late, I'm giving it. And as for your pal Claire, sometimes being ice-cold—hard as it feels—is a cover-up. Could be she was just embarrassed that she had to go begging for cash from her aunt. You have to own some of this, right? You put her in a crappy position."

Under the table, my fists clenched. "I get it, but I also tried to do the right things, too. I wrote her an apology, and I called her five times. I wanted to work it out."

"Blizzard, don't sweat it. You're a great person, one of my little sister's best and oldest friends. Any girl would be psyched to be your friend, and any guy'd be psyched to date ya." He said it casually, his tone taking the steam out of it, but as always, Theo could get me swoony with one hand tied behind his back.

Later, when he peeked in on the bag of Violetta's birthday gifts, a private smile playing on his face, I couldn't help prickling with envy.

# thirty-five

"You."

"You, yourself." Before I could stop myself, I jumped into his arms for his hug, which he gave me, in a crushing squeeze.

"I missed you," he said, his voice muffled in my ear. "I missed our talks. I missed telling you everything that happened to me every day. I kept wondering what you were up to. I kept wanting to tell you incredibly stupid private things."

"Me, too," I said, my voice equally snuffed into his shoulder. I felt like I could have drowned in my own relief, hearing Matt tell me that he missed me.

When we pried apart to look at each other, and then he pulled me close again, this time for a kiss, a familiar sweetness that melted through me before he released me with a smile, then twirled and dipped me. "Don't kill me for saying this, but I always wanted to learn those dumb dances you see on TV shows. Like, how funny would it be at prom if you just busted out a tango, right?"

"Yes, yes, yes!" I let him spin me one way, then the other. "Learning tango and wearing a cape. I have days when I really feel like—it's absolutely a cape day."

Matt laughed. "Dracula or superhero?"

"Dracula, obviously."

"Obviously." We were still dancing. From upstairs, the sound of the TV changed as it went to commercial. Matt looked up. "Who's here?"

"Only my brothers, but they're watching sports, they won't bug us. Let me make you some cocoa?"

"Sure. It's freezing outside." Then he asked, as he followed me to the kitchen, "So, you ready to go back?"

"Overready," I said over my shoulder. New Year's Day was Sunday this year, so we'd had today off, but school reopened tomorrow. "It's my official last day of being grounded. Today we took down the tree and did like fifty hours of house cleaning for January back-to-school. Swift-family tradition."

"Yeah, Mom returned our decorations to the vault and started marking Christmas gifts for return and exchange. Ashley-family tradition."

As I was rummaging for the hot chocolate tin, Matt came up close. "Wait a sec, I've got something for you." He reached into his back pocket and pulled out a small box. "Merry Christmas."

"Oh my gosh!" He'd told me he'd planned to get me something over break, but I wasn't prepared for how pretty the box was. The last week I'd seen him, I'd given him an early, signed edition of *Dune*, one of our favorites. I'd found it in a second-hand bookshop in Radnor, and it had cost me forty dollars, but I couldn't pass it up.

The paper gave way to a white box, and inside the box was a velvet jewelry case. Popping it open, I found a loose red stone, threaded with blue, cut into the crooked shape of a heart. "It's a Mexican fire opal, naturally heart shaped," Matt told me as I rolled it into my palm. "They were selling them in Cabo."

"Oh."

"You can get it made into anything, like a ring or a necklace, whatever you think it should be."

I turned it over. The opal was gorgeous, but the gift itself seemed slightly vague and unfinished. "What do *you* think it should be?"

He frowned. "I don't know. Maybe it's the key to unlock what you want most." He laughed unhappily. "Or maybe it's just a really sucky gift."

This wasn't going right. "No, Matt, I love it. Thank you." And I tried to feel more thrilled about it, though of course I didn't have any extra cash to turn a loose stone into a fine piece of jewelry. Quickly I kissed Matt on the lips, my fingers touching the back of his neck, pressing against him. Matt held me a moment, before gathering my fingertips and kissing them quickly. "I really missed ya, Stripes."

"My mom and dad are close by—they might be home any minute," I whispered. "I dare you to put your hand up my shirt." In response, Matt just turned red, and seemed so genuinely embarrassed that I felt bad. "Kidding, kidding," I said quickly. "Will you grab the milk?"

I stirred in the cocoa powder as Matt sat at the table and told me about Mexico, the surfing and the beach bonfires. He wore a rope bracelet on his wrist, and his shirt was also new, baby-blue linen that I knew his mom had decided on, but made me feel shabby in comparison, in my plain T-shirt and jeans. My solitary confinement of winter break suddenly seemed unfair compared with the casual luxury of Matt's stories.

"Your face is grumpy."

"It's not."

"It is." Matt watched me. "I wish I could have taken you with me. A million times I wanted you there, or at least on the phone, to crack up laughing with you." He was successfully coaxing the smile he needed from me.

"I kept picturing you with some adorable preppy girl."

"I kept picturing you up all night with your applications."

"They're all done. Now I'm sweating about my assembly."

Matt nodded. "You know how my sister Erin's stage fright was epic when she was at Argyll. She did her assembly on Yo-Yo Ma and then she played cello. I was in fifth grade, and all I remember was how she talked about it for months."

"How'd she do?"

"She got an A."

"You don't get how scary it is. When you spoke at Walt's service, it just seemed like you were telling a story at the dinner table."

Matt looked unhappy. "I had to do right by Walt. I'd never have messed that up." He was quiet a moment, and it seemed to cost him effort to brighten up his voice when he spoke again.

"Anyway, I think playing sports is good practice. Being out there, screwing up for everyone to see. But I'm always nervous on the inside. That's natural. And you've got nothing to be scared of."

My knees were shaking right now, thinking about everything I was scared of. What harm would it do to tell Matt about my fear of having a seizure? Here it was, just the two of us at the kitchen table, everything close and intimate. "I guess I'm scared because I'm never onstage."

Matt's eyes searched mine as he sipped from his mug. Paranoia gripped me. He knew, he'd always known. No, he didn't have a clue. Because at this point, if he'd heard the music room story, he'd have brought it up himself. It was for me to tell him, if I wanted to tell it. It was my secret, not his.

"So I saw Claire last night," he said.

I hadn't expected Claire's name to barge into the conversation. I was conscious of the quiet in the room. The ticking kitchen clock. The faint upstairs noise of the television. "No carnations for me this time?"

"I was at Dave's and she was there. They already had plans, and we drove to the city. I thought you should know in case you felt left out."

*Left out* was exactly what I'd been. How could I feel anything different? "If the three of you would rather go out together, without me, why do you always have to tell me about it?"

"It's not like we'd *rather* go out without you. It just happened that way. They like this bar in the city. We'd been there before, it's got a relaxed door policy on Sundays."

"Dave likes the city, but not with me in it."

"Stripes, that is untrue. He thinks you're awesome. It's only that I was already Dave's friend, and now Claire's tight with him. Hey, you introduced them, don't forget."

"Sure." I wanted it to make sense, and it halfway did, but it also left me so doubtful. "Claire's icing me out because of the whole money thing."

"I asked her about that. She says you just surprised her. She said you'd made it seem like you were flush."

"That's not fair." But now that I'd talked it out with Theo, too, I could see where I'd gone wrong. I'd offered to pay for things too quickly, to be the hero so everything went smoothly.

"Look, I like Claire," said Matt. "She's been through some stuff, she's got interesting—"

"I like her, too," I interrupted. "But she's mad at me now—so if you want to spend time with her, just know that right now I can't."

Matt looked perplexed. "Aright, got it. And if you and Claire aren't hanging out right now, I'd rather be with you. There's a big party out in Glen Mills this Friday, and Jonesy says he'll drive us all—would you be psyched for that?"

"Yeah, I would, actually."

"Cool. Settled." He extended a finger to spin the lazy Susan in the middle of our kitchen table. The shepherd and shepherdess salt and pepper shakers, the napkin holder, and the squeezable bear-shaped honey all spun into a blur.

Dizzy, I blinked and looked away, but I could still feel the spinning in my body, the desire to ask more questions about Claire, about why they'd all become so close, without me. What was Claire telling Matt that she hadn't told me? I closed my eyes against the vertigo and buttoned my lips against sniping comments. "It'd be fun to do something with Jonesy and Kreo."

"Yeah." Matt folded his hand over mine. "Aright, I better beat it."

At the front door, he kissed me good-bye, and I was overwhelmed with the sensation of having him back again, the warmth of his tanned skin, the crumple of his linen shirt, that faintest hint of citrusy aftershave he sometimes wore that I loved. But when I opened my eyes to look up at him, I was tugged by misgivings that I barely had any intuition about Matt other than a scratchy, aching feeling that as much as he liked me, he also partly wanted to escape me.

No, I wasn't doing this right, but I didn't know how to do it any better.

# thirty-six

FIRST DAY BACK AT Argyll was extra noisy with everyone returning from exotic vacations. Seven other seniors besides Gage had
gotten into their top-choice schools. They seemed louder and
lazier and happier, and I felt out of sync. Being deferred was like a
backpack of failure that I had to lug around everywhere. Everyone
saw it and everyone knew.

"It sure puts the rest of us on pins and needles till April," said
Mimi as we got ready for sports, Mimi to basketball and me to
my dreaded modern dance class. The last thing I wanted to do
was leap around the brightly lit studio in my dance tights while
the full-length mirror reflected my sullen face and mediocre
technique.

"If you say so," I answered. "I don't think about it much." Not
like Mimi, who'd applied to a bunch of schools but was obsessed

with Berkeley, since it was geographically farthest from Noah. My pretend indifference wasn't fooling anyone, least of all me. But I had to slam college thoughts into a back closet of my brain, or I'd go crazy thinking about all the possible different rejections in store for me come spring.

When I caught Claire's eye in homeroom at the end of the day, she stared at a space just past my ear.

Nope, we still weren't right. Another defeat on my shoulders.

By the next morning, we'd settled back into school routines. Alison Greely's "The Origins of Pleasantries and Salutations" was the second-semester kickoff assembly. It went fine.

"Ali Greetings should give another assembly about the origins of apologies," said Wendy as we all filed out of the theater. "Then she could apologize to us multiple ways for her incredibly stupid assembly." She was talking in that loud voice that wanted everyone to start laughing and think she was hilarious, and of course a few girls did. But her casual cruelty sent prickles up my neck. Would my assembly remind Wendy to start up all her spaz imitations again? Would I be able to see her make fun of me from the podium? As bad as it would be to have a seizure in front of everyone, it was also horrible to think I'd be ridiculed just for standing up in front of the school.

After lunch, I had to hand off my prepared visuals for Mrs. Robles to make into slides.

"I'm intrigued, Lizzy." She lifted the top image.

"Thanks," I mumbled. I wouldn't breathe easy till this was over.

That afternoon, as I sped through the arts lobby, I nearly smacked into Claire, heading in the same direction.

We both stopped, wild-eyed, like a pair of skittish horses.

"Hey," I said.

"Hey."

She had her portfolio hoisted tight under her armpit. It struck me that she had no clue how I'd agonized about her over break, while she was lazing away her days in Florida—or for that matter hanging out with my boyfriend in the city the other night.

"I'm behind in my portfolio concentration," she said. "Are you?"

"I'm not ahead." I was amazed that Claire was getting in any of her work on time. It didn't seem very Claire-ish. "How was vacation?"

"Boring. My dad's condo is basically a retirement community. What about you?"

"Boring, too. Once I went into Philly. I hit a bunch of museums and galleries, I went down to South Street, did some sketches." I could feel my smile a little too eager.

Claire made a shrugging motion like steam through her body. "Nice."

Was Claire going to mention my two-page apology letter, or give me a reason why she never returned any of my calls, or let me know what she'd been up to last night?

"I wanted to—I wished I could have, that you could have—"

"Right. We're gonna be late." She broke away from me, pivoting to stride into the art room, leaving me breathless with everything I'd wanted to say to her.

I walked behind her, keeping my distance.

Mr. Custis-Brown, who always took over from his wife teaching Argyll's spring semester, was waiting for us in the studio. Last fall's sketches and watercolors had been plucked off the walls, the supply shelves were decluttered, and tables and easels were freshly reconfigured. I was glad that I wouldn't have to see "Jeanie" this semester, and be reminded about all that secret, sultry flesh.

Claire put on some Pet Shop Boys. Then she scraped her easel to the outer reaches of the room. I sat with Gage and Mimi and pretended to pay attention as they picked up the conversation about their mostly uneventful winter breaks, though I was hardly listening, my eyes snaking over to Claire, wondering if I could count anything that had just happened as a sign that we were thawing out, or that she was finally, once and for all, done with me.

# thirty-seven

THAT AFTERNOON, I HAD a shift at Ludington, but Matt couldn't pick me up to take me there, which he sometimes did. The sky was dark as I got off the train, and at the circulation desk, I found Mrs. Binswanger already in her hat and coat. There was hardly anybody else in the library, and later when the snow started to fall in earnest, Dad called the desk phone to say he'd come get me at the end of my shift.

At closing, I put away my homework and finished some tasks, returning the last of the plastic-covered books to the kids' section, straightening the chairs, and running a Bissell over the faded orange carpet.

When I saw Leslie Spivio hunkered all by herself at a back carrel, I stopped humming. I thought I'd been alone.

"Hey, Leslie." She popped up, scared by the sound of my voice. "Lights off in five minutes, okay?"

"Okay."

Leslie was someone I'd known since we were little kids, and I'd always considered her slightly annoying—she made too many classroom announcements, and was often shoving a clipboard under my nose, asking me to give a dollar for this drive or to sign up for that campaign. Girls had remarked on how Leslie had changed since whatever had happened with Stephen. But I'd never been close with Leslie, and it wasn't until this instant, across the dark, quiet library, that I took stock of how different she seemed from before.

She was wearing a sweater two sizes too big, and her hair hung lank on her shoulders. While she'd lost that pulled-together, laced-up Leslie-ness on the outside, what really seemed different was how her glow was gone. She didn't look like a girl who had the energy to sign up your name for Meals on Wheels or organize the student coat drive.

"You can leave with me through the back exit," I told her. "I already locked up the front. We're supposed to get five or six inches. My dad is waiting in the parking lot. Do you have a ride?"

"I've got my car."

"Okay."

Leslie had been in the music room, that day in eighth grade. Our secrets about each other were dark water between us, but neither of us knew how to hold out a hand for the other to cross over. What was I supposed to say, anyhow? What were we supposed to cross into? A place where everything was going to be okay? How did I know who got to be okay?

"I need to be last so I can hit the lights, too," I told her.

"Got it," she said as she reached for her coat.

Snow was falling hard by the time I raced out to the parking lot.

"Hey, Banana, you're sure quiet," Dad said after our silent trip home.

"I'm fine."

"Nice to be back at school and busy?"

"I guess, compared."

"It was a mellow vacation," he agreed.

"Mellow? I was grounded," I reminded him. "You and Mom made it horrible for me."

"Easy, champ. Your grades fell, you had debts to pay and a pile of applications to send out after you got deferred. I think Mom and I were indulging in some fairly normal parenting to rein you in a little, no?"

I said nothing. If I'd been allowed to go with Gage to Mad River, she'd have given me time to work on my applications, plus I'd have had her friendship and a few activities to break up the long hours of essay writing.

My parents were always so absolutely sure they were right that sometimes it felt like the wrongest thing about them.

The boys had eaten already, but Mom had kept my dinner warm for me. Next to my bowl of lentil chili and corn bread was a square brown-wrapped package.

"That came in the mail," she said. "It's from Massachusetts. What is it?"

"Just a sample yearbook we wanted to look at for yearbook committee." I was stunned to see it. Not that I'd forgotten, but

I'd never thought about what it would feel like when it finally got here. I was burning up in wonder. "We're checking out different styles. The school expensed it." I was scared to look at Mom, in case she guessed I was lying.

I inhaled my chili, then ran with the book clutched to my chest, panting slightly as I got to my room, where I locked the door behind me and ripped open the packaging.

The outside of the yearbook was bottle green, the cover board a finer grain than what our own school budget could afford, and the binding was more expensive, too. Its center was embossed with the words *The Strickland Lamp* beneath a tiny foil-stamped emblem that looked like a genie's magic lantern.

I ran my finger over the spine, beautiful, then opened and flipped right to the senior class pages. I'd never learned his last name, but that wouldn't matter, I'd find him soon enough. Jay could also be a nickname for Jason, James, Jeremy, Jacob—he could be a lot of kids. My eyes scanned the pages, four students on a page, maybe fifty pages, about two hundred seniors, half boys.

There was a senior named James Lancing, but his entire life seemed to be about basketball. Another senior named Justin MacCallum looked too blond and spindly to meet Claire's description.

He had to be here. I checked the smaller photo squares of the junior class, where I found Claire's photograph, smiling and all-American. The juniors offered a James Brunt and a John de la Salle—one too freckled, the other too brawny. The sophomores gave me a J. P. Barclay, a ruddy-faced class clown who was wearing a tuxedo T-shirt beneath his sports jacket. With some desperation, I turned to the freshmen. Maybe this was Claire's shame? Had she been in love with a lowly freshman? I found a Jay Luis who looked about twelve.

Of the dozen prefects, none of them had a name starting with J or Jay.

I tried searching like a psychic, feeling it out, imagining that Jay would suddenly sharpen like a familiar face in a crowd, in a microsmirk or an adorable forelock of hair falling over his eye. I imagined him looking like the haunted schoolboy Ian Curtis from Joy Division. I imagined him as bold and suave as Dave Jimenez.

On the other hand, Claire was everywhere.

We'd almost finished assembling a mock-up of the Argyll yearbook, and Claire hadn't bothered showing up for any of the official sports and clubs photos. She was a ghost at Argyll—but at Strickland, she burned with life. Like Gage, she played three different sports, and even as a junior, Claire was varsity in every one of them, front and center in all team pictures, and a cocaptain in lacrosse. Instantly recognizable and yet chillingly different, like some firebrand twin sister to the Claire Reynolds I knew today.

She was also in French club, but nope, no Jay in French club, either, and wouldn't a guy who was fluent in French and living in Paris be hamming it up in French club? In the community service section, I discovered Claire in a shot headlined "Basil County School," where she stood in a cluster of elementary school children, a few in wheelchairs, their smiling faces blanched by photo overexposure. *Strickland takes pride in our long relationship with Basil County School, tutoring at-risk youngsters with physical disabilities and emotional needs,* read the caption, along with a quote: "I always wanted to be a big sister. When I spend time with BCS, I feel like I get a bunch of sisters and brothers all at once!"—*Claire Reynolds, '89.*

It didn't even sound like her.

I couldn't find Claire in any of the poufy hair and spangle dress photographs from Strickland's winter and spring formals, but there was an artistic shot of her in the "Students at Large" section, curled up in an armchair reading a copy of *The Sound and the Fury*. Behind her, past-bloom tulips drooped over their vase.

No Jay no Jay no Jay.

I checked and rechecked, running through pages, and then I slid the yearbook off my bed, letting it drop with a thud to the floor. My body was hot with confusion. I lay sprawled there for a while, and knew when I clicked back that I'd been gone from myself, stuck in an absence.

I shook myself out and reset my thoughts.

Jay had to be somewhere in that yearbook. I'd read those letters myself. Beyond a doubt, he was a Strickland kid. He talked about the dorms, the kitchen, the campus. It didn't make any sense. There was something that I wasn't seeing, something that was right in front of my eyes.

After a few minutes, I leaned over the bed, hauled up the book, and began all over again, scrutinizing every page, every section, all the way to the endpaper "Campus Candids" jammed with current events and newsworthy highlights of the past year. Back filler, we called it. And that's where I found the photo.

It was of a Halloween party, and Claire wasn't in it. That was why I'd missed it at first. It was eerily out of focus, a group of kids in thrown-together costumes; a witch hat, a zombie, a cowboy, a girl in an outlaw mustache, and him.

I could still see her eyes shining as she'd told me about the costume store, the day she and Jay had spent together in Philadelphia.

*The Strickland Bash—It Was a Graveyard Smash! l-r Allison Weiss, Kimmy Patterson, Jorge San Fleban, Doug Isaacs, Emily Hotchkiss, Laura Lin, Jazpaul Singh, (and Mr. Moser).*

Mr. Moser, the one in the yeti mask—that was Jay.

I tore back to the faculty section. I found him in "Administration."

*James Harrington Moser, Assistant Head of the Upper School.*

*Moser*: I recognized that name, too.

James Harrington Moser also taught French literature.

My eyes burned. James Harrington Moser was not a sweet puppy, the way I'd pictured. Of course, that was probably because he was ten years older than I'd originally assumed. But his wavy brown hair and angular face made him impressive, more handsome than cute. He also seemed like too much of a grown-up to be called hot. He was a *man*. Why hadn't I known that, from his letters? He'd been so charming and unsure of himself. In his own words, he'd seemed so young.

At Argyll, the only cute and youthful male on faculty was Mr. Stewart, a freshman chemistry teacher. To most of us, his looks were kind of a joke. "Alert, alert! Jonathan Stewart alert," we'd whisper to each other whenever he walked past us, and then we'd laugh to watch him frown bashfully at his shoes. A few of the girls were slightly idiotic about Mr. Stewart, and blocked his initials on their tennis sneakers. I'd even seen his name inside a heart in a bathroom stall.

James Harrington Moser looked older than Jonathan Stewart, and he didn't appear to be at all shy, in his politician's dark jacket and striped tie. But then who was Stephanie Moser, of Claire's driving license fame? Was she his sister? A cousin? His *wife*?

I searched Jay Moser's face, and even after I'd closed the yearbook, five minutes later, I had to go back in and scrutinize him all over again.

J. Moser was a teacher, a grown man. James Harrington Moser had written love letters to one of his students, and that student was Claire. When I thought about those letters now, they seemed different, like a magic trick, now you're a student, thinking about parties and your finals and—*Poof!*—now you're an adult, thinking about taxes and your mortgage.

But he and Claire had been close, once, and when they stopped being close, she came here, with scars.

The weight of all I didn't know about them was infinite.

What had he done to her?

# thirty-eight

I'D PICKED A BACK corner behind the pottery kiln to pin up my collection of hands for AP portfolio midyear review. I'd started it Tuesday and now it was Thursday, and I was just about done. I was surprised to see all my work, all at once, and to look at how many pieces I'd completed.

I knew that art was unimportant, in the scheme of things. And Mr. Custis-Brown wasn't exhibiting the work—he just wanted us all to check in with everyone's progress, like a peer review. So I didn't know why I was sweating whether I wanted the ink drawing near my chalk study, or which piece should be in the center.

*"A-wimm-a-way, a-wimm-a-way,"* Gage sang lightly as she walked past, shaking a box of ballpoint pens. "When you're done, come see my wall."

Gage had chosen the prime space by the door.

"I love it," I told her honestly.

She smiled, running her hands through her hair so it stuck out like the arms of a starfish. "Really?"

"Yeah, of course." My eyes roved her paintings, the rough ocean collage, the glinting oils of a frozen puddle, an acrylic brown-green pond in its thickest, earthiest state. All of them were excellent. "It's so many cool ways to think about water."

We walked over to Mimi's work by the back window. She'd made simple colorful pieces using patterns and grids. You could have framed any of them for a kitchen wall.

"Solid effort," Mimi judged herself.

A few girls had started gathering around my wall of hands, so I crept off shyly, in search of Claire's self-portraits. It turned out she was hiding her gallery on a wall of Mr. Custis-Brown's office. Her back was to me as she finished fastening up her last few pieces.

None of the pieces looked like Claire. The washed green face could have been any girl, and the vampy movie-star sketch she'd made that first day was still cartoonish and wrong. There was a pencil sketch she'd done of an older lady who looked more like her mom than Claire herself. It was as if Claire didn't really know what she looked like, exactly. Every face was a vague approximation, and not one Claire reminded me of the boldly smiling girl in *The Strickland Lamp*.

I was startled when Mr. Custis-Brown came away from his desk to stand next to Claire. They were close together. Too close? Everyone liked Mr. Custis-Brown okay—although he looked gentle, his mind was sharp, and he always had a joke or a clipped-out *New Yorker* cartoon to pass around.

But did Claire like him *in that way?* Were teachers her type?

I wished I could unthink it, but Claire's secret wouldn't let me alone. Whatever had happened last year at Strickland, it had been wrong from the start, and it was partly why—if not the whole reason—Claire had left.

Maybe I'd solved the mystery of Claire's Jay, but I wished I hadn't, and now I couldn't banish it any farther than this dark, cramped place inside my head. No matter what she thought of me, I'd never hurt her with information I'd gone so sneakily out of my way to unbury.

Claire must have sensed my gaze on her. When she caught my eye through the partition, we both glanced away.

EVERY NIGHT, I LOOKED forward to my phone call with Matt, and as the weekend got closer, I started looking forward to that, too. The Glen Mills party would be a blast, he'd assured me the night before—even if Claire and Dave had made their own plans to hit some clubs on South Street.

"What's the deal? Are Claire and Dave together?" I asked.

"I guess," said Matt. "They're close. Doesn't matter. We'll have fun anyway."

I hung up feeling a little worried. Did Matt want to hang out with Claire and Dave, instead of me? And I wished for the thousandth time that Claire and I were friends again.

Friday afternoon after school, I went poking around my mom's dresser. Mom was a couple of sizes up from me, and her clothes on my body always looked borrowed. But this time I hit the jackpot with her lingerie drawer, where I found a peach-silk camisole.

It was loose, but all I needed was that little edge of lace to show beneath my oversized oxford shirt, plus jeans and boots.

I also gave myself a spritz from Mom's Opium bottle. Perfume had never been my thing, but when Theo bought that ounce of Chanel No. 5 for Violetta, it struck me how Colors of Benetton was not exactly a sophisticated choice. If a camisole and expensive perfume worked for Violetta, they should work for me, too.

When Jonesy and Kreo picked me up later on, I was out the door before my parents could try to reel in everyone for introductions. I leaped like a cat over the salted sidewalk, and slid into the back seat next to Matt.

"Hey. You smell different," said Matt.

"You smell nice," corrected Jonesy.

"Thanks." Score one for Opium, even if the wrong guy had complimented me.

"We're heading to Tommy's instead of that party." Matt's voice was toneless. "His parents aren't around, and he wants to hang in."

"Oh, okay." Disappointment rippled through me. "Not even a stop-off at Glen Mills?"

"Look, Tommy's like our brother," said Jonesy, "and if he's not on for a big party tonight, then we support. He needs our friendship. He said his Christmas was a bitch."

"Tommy's become such a stoner these days." Kreo's voice made it clear that she wasn't wild to sit around at Tommy's, either.

In response, Jonesy turned up the radio.

The family room at the Powerses' was already hijacked by the smell of pot. A real bong—until then, I'd seen only Jeff Spicoli's bong in *Fast Times at Ridgemont High*—was circulating. Tommy was beached on his favorite wicker saucer chair, dragging deep from a Marlboro. His red-rimmed eyes barely registered me. If Tommy Powers needed my friendship to get him through, he was keeping his gratitude deeply hidden.

The movie on the VCR was a raunchy ski comedy. I took the edge of the couch as Matt sank beside me. We cracked a couple of Rolling Rocks from the twelve-pack on the table and settled in. But after a few minutes, Matt got up—to use the bathroom, I figured, but when time had passed and he didn't return, I was glad to have an excuse to leave the room and find him. He seemed extra quiet tonight. I figured he'd be rummaging for snacks, or playing fetch with Furley, but no.

He wasn't in the kitchen or breakfast room, or anywhere downstairs, either.

I knew Tommy's parents weren't home, and after a minute, I risked a tiptoe up the main staircase. I hadn't been on the second floor of this house since that afternoon Walt had taken my picture, and now it felt like a darkly weighted space. I couldn't shake a sense of Walt's presence, thin as breath beneath the carpet runner, quiet as fog behind the walls. Faces in the framed wall photographs of the once-happy, once-complete Powers family seemed to watch me as I passed.

I had a strange sense Matt would be there before I'd even opened the door to Walt's bedroom, and sure enough, he was sitting on the edge of Walt's bed, head bowed and hands clasped as if in prayer.

When he looked up at me, I wasn't expecting the silent gust of his sadness. It landed like a punch to my heart.

"I'm so sorry," I whispered. "I'm interrupting. Are you okay?"

"Yeah. It's all right. You don't have to go."

But I wanted to leave. Something was odd with the way Matt was looking at me, like I was an object he'd lost a while back, and now didn't exactly recognize. I crept over and sat next to him, my arm just touching his. He breathed out, deep, as if trying to deflate whatever was trapped inside. In the sharp cold of the unheated room, I could smell the beer on his breath, the trace spice of Opium on my own skin, and the cling of cigarette smoke in our clothes.

"You miss him," I whispered.

Matt gave a bare nod. "Walt was scared, was all." His voice cracked just above his whisper. "He was just scared." Then he asked, "You think God forgave him?"

"Oh," I said. "I guess . . . I don't know."

"Do you think he's going to hell? Like a real hell, for people who do that?"

"Do what, kill themselves? No." Then I repeated, more strongly as Matt's words sank in, "*No*, Matt. No, of course not."

"Even if suicide is a mortal sin, Walt was way too screwed up in his head to know what he was doing."

I knew the Ashley family was deeply Catholic. They attended church every Sunday, they sometimes had their priest over for dinner, and I'd even spied a gold-framed portrait of Jesus hanging like some famous ancestor in their dining room. I'd never thought Matt was so Catholic that he genuinely worried about Walt's standing with God. Did he really believe in a hell, with a devil and a pitchfork for all eternity?

"Of course he's forgiven," I promised.

"I came up here thinking I'd feel close to him. Stupid of me . . ."

"I'm sure he's in a better place," I offered, though I didn't really believe any of that, either. *A better place* was what you said when someone died who'd been sick or old. Walt had been young and healthy, both feet planted firmly on the planet. "Matt, why do you really think it happened?"

"He said he was having these nightmares."

"Yeah, you'd told me that. But was he having nightmares for a specific reason?"

"Sometimes it's not the reason, it's how you deal."

"But *was* there a reason?"

"I dunno," Matt answered dully. He was so enclosed in himself tonight that I couldn't reach him. Through the shadows, his eyes wouldn't let me in. "I'm glad you came looking for me, actually. I've been hoping for a right time for us to talk."

"Oh." I sat up a little straighter.

"Stripes, you know how bad I wanted everything to work for us. You get that, don't you? Because in a lot of ways—the most important ways, maybe—you're one of the best people that's ever walked into my life."

*Wanted.* Past tense. I heard it and I didn't hear it, like the dart before the poison. Was Matt breaking up with me? Right here, in Walt Powers's bedroom? "Okay." I took a breath. "I mean, what do you think is . . . not working?" My heart was racing so fast I thought I might be sick.

"It's not you," he said. "And it's not your fault. I'm just not sure I'm ready to have a girlfriend."

"What? Why not?" I didn't even know how to frame the thousand questions in my head. "When did you decide this—what does this even mean?"

"That's the thing, I don't know."

"What do you think is wrong with me and you?"

"Nothing, really." Matt was looking out Walt's window like he couldn't bear to tell it to my face. "The first night I met you, at that mixer, I had a feeling about you. I did. And the reason I didn't call you then was because I knew that whenever it happened between us, it would be big. And it is."

"It feels big to me, too. Even just the way we talk on the phone, or how good it is whenever we hang out." I thought about Valley Forge, and how Matt never said anything about that, how it maybe hadn't felt like *moving forward*? "But I'm not the way you want a girlfriend to be. Is that it?"

He shifted closer. "You are exactly the way I want you to be. Do you remember that morning on the train, when you said my eyes were the same color as the river? I can't even explain how good that made me feel. Not in some lame, conceited way, but just to be noticed. And once on the phone you told me about how in soccer, I always try to make team plays and assist on the field, instead of going for the star shot—my own *teammates* don't see that. Or how we both knew all the characters in *Dune*. How we both think the tango looks idiotic but we want to learn it.

"And I see you, too, Stripes. You're a real artist. There's part of me that hopes we'll know each other forever. But maybe—maybe you are too young. Or maybe I'm not ready for a full-time girlfriend, but whatever it is, I'm tired of hurting whenever I feel this missing piece between us."

"I think we could find it!" I burst out. "This doesn't make any sense." But a part of me knew that it did, and that I'd felt defeated by it, too.

"I wish we could be something better for each other," said Matt.

These were the truest things Matt had ever said to me. It was like he'd thrown open a wide window on our relationship, and we were both taking huge, gulping breaths of fresh air. And yet at the same time, I didn't want to breathe it in at all, because there was nothing better than being Matt's girlfriend, and losing Matt Ashley, whom I'd adored for so long, felt like the worst thing that could happen to me.

Whatever I said next, however I left him, alone in Walt Powers's haunted bedroom, however I got myself downstairs to sit out the rest of the movie, was pretty much a blur. I stared wide-eyed at the TV screen as a pattern of light and sound, my beer a warm, tasteless liquid to keep my throat from closing in. By the time Matt joined me maybe five or maybe twenty minutes later, I knew I'd glitched and returned from an absence seizure; maybe more than one.

What did it matter? Nobody noticed. I barely noticed.

On the ride home, together and yet apart in the back seat, Matt already felt like a separate planet, or a boat drifting out to sea. He wouldn't call me anymore. We wouldn't hang on the phone, laughing for hours. We wouldn't make plans. No more linking fingers as we crossed the Argyll parking lot, no more make-out sessions in his car—strange and I guess imperfect as they were, they'd turned my body into something wild and alive and wonderfully unpredictable.

What would our breakup even feel like? I couldn't imagine that by this time next week, I wouldn't be as close with Matt. Or that in a month, I'd know him even less. The worst part was that he wanted to go. And what was "better" than being his girlfriend? How could I be anything better than that?

When Jonesy pulled up to my house, I jumped out with calm good-byes for everyone, though my heart was thumping with the force of my desire to keep it together. Right now, the one thing that might feel just as bad as breaking up with Matt Ashley was if they pitied me for it.

And I couldn't bear that. Almost nothing was worse than that.

# thirty-nine

IN BED, I'D LET the tears fall until my pillow was damp, and I fell asleep, exhausted—until at some point, I'd bolted awake again. I sat up. Checked the clock.

It was almost 4:00 a.m. Something had happened to me.

My pillows were off the bed and my sheets were as twisted as a breadstick down by my feet. A nightmare. But I didn't remember any of it.

I could hear a hollowed-out noise inside me like static. Eerie as a hush of rain or a rustle of dry leaves, though it wasn't either of these things.

After a minute, I got out of bed and went to my window, to shake it off.

Later that morning, when pear-pale sunshine had opened my eyes again, my depression about Matt took over, and I mostly forgot about my wee-hours wake-up. I stayed in bed all day. My parents, each coming into my room at different times to look in on me, were both semi-irritated, thinking I had a hangover. But since I hadn't broken curfew, and since they couldn't catch the sound of me vomiting in the bathroom like last time, they couldn't accuse me outright.

"What's going on with you, Banana?" Dad asked on his turn at check-in, handing off a mug of tea. "It's past lunch."

"Matt and I broke up."

"Ah, kiddo. I'm sorry."

"It's okay. I'm fine." I closed my eyes, sipped the hot, sweet, milky tea, and tried to seem like a person who was fine. One thing I knew for sure: I'd had too many seizures to blow off another week. "I think I need to see Dr. Neumann."

Dad looked instantly petrified as he kept his voice cheerful. "When is your next appointment?"

"A week from this Tuesday. But I missed our meeting last month. I think it makes sense to see her before my assembly."

"Absolutely right. Smart thinking, Lizzy."

"No biggie. I just want to check in with her, that's all."

When Mom joined him, she put a hand on my forehead, searching for that elusive fever. "Lizzy, I can get permission for you to skip this assembly. Mrs. Birmingham even suggested to me that you could give it privately to a few teachers in Mrs. Robles's office."

"Wait—what?" I propped up to stare at the two of them, like a pair of hawks guarding my bedside. "Delivering my assembly to some teachers in Mrs. Robles's office? Seriously? You really think I need that much special treatment?"

Dad frowned. "If you're worried about what your friends might think, you can get the school to 'reschedule' for May. By that time, it's so late in the year, nobody will care."

"Well, 'I' care." I made quote marks, imitating him, though smart-mouthing Dad was always a bad idea. "I just want to see my doctor. Why do you have to make me feel so weird about myself?"

"Dad and I were only thinking of options."

"You think copping out is an option? You think *hiding* me is an option?"

"Hey, easy does it. All that Mom and I do, we do from love."

"Lizzy, if you give that assembly onstage for everyone to see, obviously we'll be proud that you tried, no matter what."

"For everyone to see me have a fit—is that what you mean?" My heart was pounding in my ears.

Dad sighed. "You know that's not what we mean."

"But now if I *do* mess up, you both can say you told me so until forever."

Mom went to the door. "I'm sorry you've had to grow up under such a tyrannical parenting regime."

"Nothing's going to change your opinion that I can't handle my life. You've got to stop overcontrolling me. Like, if I drive the car, or if I want to go skiing with Gage, you two will do anything to throw in a wrench."

"You didn't go skiing with Gage because you were grounded," said Dad.

"I was only grounded for being deferred. I could have done those applications up in Vermont—or anywhere. You never like when I try to be adventurous."

"You were grounded for your debt," said Mom.

"Money that I'm paying back. Nobody had to bail me out."

"And your grades fell," added Dad.

"But I still made honor roll. *Nobody* else gets grounded for honor roll. It's just that you two would rather have me stay home and out of harm's way. Don't you see how you both do that?" My tears were surprising me, skating in tracks down my face.

My parents looked glum and baffled, as if I made no sense at all. They told me to get my rest and we'd talk about it later. When they shut the door, I threw my pillow at it.

I was left alone until late that afternoon, when Mom came up to let me know she'd moved my appointment with Dr. Neumann to this Tuesday.

The next morning, dragging out of bed, I gave myself an up-and-down in the mirror. My junior year, we'd studied the romantic poets and I'd even written an English paper: "Fragments, Failure, and Ruin in the Romantics." It was something about the failure of Shelley and Coleridge to do something or be something. All I really remembered about that paper was that I got the highest grade in the class.

In my heart, I always knew it was your basic bullshit thesis, and it seemed ironic to me that I couldn't remember anything about it that might offer me any actual, takeaway knowledge—other than the fact that Matt's and my "romance" had been a beautiful fragment, a heartbreaking failure, and now was pretty much a ruin.

# forty

SPYING ME FROM HER office window, Dr. Neumann let me in before I rang the bell.

"Nice to see you, Lizzy." We took our opposite armchairs in her office. "Tea?"

"No, thanks." She looked exactly the same as when I'd first started seeing her a few years ago. She still wore her salt-and-pepper bob tucked behind her ears and she still dressed in black separates, today perked by a chunky turquoise pendant that looked like it might possess secret magic powers.

Her smile was her hug, because Dr. Neumann never touched me. She was very careful about creating an atmosphere where I would feel safe, not squeezed. Suddenly I imagined Jay Moser in his yeti mask, groping Claire. I don't know why I always pictured him in that mask now. Maybe because I felt like he had tricked me. Maybe because he seemed unknown and monstrous.

"You've been busy," said Dr. Neumann. "Catch me up." She looked down at her trusty yellow legal pad. "Your assembly is this Friday."

"Yep."

"Let's explore that. You've rehearsed your talk? Are you comfortable with it? The lights, the view from the stage?"

"Yes, all of it. Today I did a run-through with Mrs. Robles. Everyone does. We have to practice and make sure the slides are in the right order and try out the clicker and the microphone. That kind of stuff."

Dr. Neumann gave her notes a glance. "So you feel prepared."

Even small talk about the assembly had my knees shaking, but my anxiety felt too hard to admit. If I started, I'd never stop. "Super prepared."

"You've been concerned about this assembly for so long. Any thoughts now that you're so close?" She wanted me to talk about seizures.

"At this point? I'm just looking forward to it being over."

"I understand. Good luck! Not that you'll need it." Her study of my face felt like she was scrubbing me for truths. "So, let me hear the rest of your news. How's Matt?"

My heart lurched as I nodded. "Oh, good."

"You were going to meet his parents, when we spoke last month?"

Five million years ago. "Yep. I met them, and his brother and sister. Really nice family."

"What else is going on?"

"Um, nothing much."

Dr. Neumann didn't need notes. It was a thing I'd learned about her, over the years. Now she stopped pretending to consult them. Like an animal that's just poked up its head from its burrow, she was on alert. "How's your new friend Claire? You'd set her up with a friend of Matt's. How did that work out?"

I felt a painful urge of wanting to call my own bluff and start again, to talk about how these first days post breakup had left me crushed. All weekend, I'd wondered what Dr. Neumann might say about it. Her advice was always smart. But now, face-to-face with her, I wasn't so sure how fragile I wanted to seem. "Everything worked out great, they're dating now," I said. "Matt and I are taking it a little slower."

"Oh, and why is that?"

"My parents weren't too psyched about my last report card, and they don't want me going out as much, so . . . I don't get to see Matt as much." I shrugged like whatever. The story seemed believable even to me.

"How do you feel about that?"

"I feel fine. It's fine."

"Do you miss not seeing him as much?"

"Not really. School is more of a priority right now."

Dr. Neumann kept her face still. "And you've heard from Princeton?"

Oops. I hadn't said about Princeton. "Oh, right." I nodded. "I got deferred."

"I'm sorry to hear. You worked very, very hard."

"I'm hopeful for April." Dr. Neumann loved that word *hope*.

"You've had a lot going on in your life lately."

Friday night, I might have had multiple absence seizures at Tommy's house. Plus I had that 4:00 a.m. wake-up, where I'd had to remake my whole bed in the dark. I'd been scared. Dr. Neumann always asked me about changes like this, possible seizures and changes in patterns.

But I'd been okay since then. "I've been fine. I've had one or two absences."

"Ah, would you like to talk about that?"

"Just same old, same old. I'm fine."

"I understand. I want to note that one of those old textbook terms coming to my mind about this session is *flat affect*. A nice thing about you being so educated about your epilepsy is that maybe we can explore together what that term might mean?"

"Flat affect as in empty inside?" *Flat affect* actually sounded like the perfect way to describe how I felt.

"Kind of, yes. It suggests a change in brain activity."

I made myself hold eye contact. "Flat affect is fine by me. You think my episodes are always a result of stress. But these past months *all* have been stressful—and I've handled everything, right? Empty is the calm opposite of chaotic."

Dr. Neumann let the silence grow between us, a tactic that always worked.

"What if you're wrong about me?" I asked. "What if my parents are, too? For so many years, I've listened to you tell me to be careful, be calm, respect the condition. But this year, I've done crazy stuff. I've jumped out bathroom windows, I've failed tests,

I've been drunk—but I never wound up convulsive. The meds are working. I can go have experiences. Isn't it about time to let me grow up?"

My fists were balled in my lap and my face was hot. Dr. Neumann was nodding along, but she always did that. "Lizzy, the aim of any treatment is to control the condition. I'm glad you've been testing your limits and adapting new tactics of self-regulation. I think you're doing a marvelous job. And it would be wonderful, in my opinion, if you began to talk about it more openly."

"What do you mean? We always talk openly."

"Really? You don't even say the word *epilepsy* out loud. You've admitted you don't talk about epilepsy, ever, to anyone. You don't wear your dog tag, you won't attend group therapies—"

"Why should I wear that dumb tag? By now, I'd have been wearing something for four whole years and never once needed it."

"Yes, but sometimes seizures just happen. We can't predict the how, when, and why. But let's explore this—you yourself have said you've never discussed the disorder with Mimi and Gage. I'm guessing that's also the rule with Claire and Matt. How can you be your real self if you can't be truthful about this issue?"

"I don't need everyone to know everything about me, for me to be authentic."

Dr. Neumann was all casual voice. "The impact of this condition on your life is real. Why not admit it? What's getting in the way? Could it be your assumptions about other people? Fears?"

I shrugged. "I don't want people to think of me as disabled."

"Your friends already know. You can't undo what they saw. You can't control what other people might think about it. But perhaps your closest friends deserve to be part of a conversation with you, and to draw their own conclusions. No story is supposed to stay the same forever. I think you want to live a new way, out in the open." Her eyes were hoping for my answer, an answer I couldn't give her because I didn't have it. "Don't you think that's safe to say, Lizzy?"

Did I?

# forty-one

"IN DECEMBER 1980, A young artist named Keith Haring noticed that black paper was being used to cover up old subway advertisements, and he saw opportunity. Instantly, Haring knew how he'd contribute to the underground world of graffiti art. It wasn't long before Haring and his chalk drawings became a mythic and unstoppable force."

My fingertips were ice as I clicked my first slide, an image of flying saucers and babies. "New York City was captivated by Haring's pictures of primitive animals, humans having sex, and men with holes in their stomachs. Haring has explained that he is haunted by this image, because he connects it with John Lennon's assassination."

*Click, click click.*

A gasp in the audience. These drawings of sex and violence weren't too scandalous in my eyes, but the shock in the theater made my heart beat harder. "Simple, effective renderings are still a hallmark of Haring's in-your-face style, and have led him to international fame as an artist and an activist. But first, let's step back in time to Kutztown, Pennsylvania, 1958."

At that, someone whooped—probably Barb Wassman, who'd been dating that guy from Kutztown. Barb's whoop was followed by laughter, the good kind. Keith Haring's images were an eyeful. I'd picked a surprise topic, and the girls were feeling it.

Except that my insides were waging civil war. I wanted to run off the stage so bad I didn't know how to make myself stay.

I forced a glance up for my first look out at the shadowy audience. I'd hardly ever been onstage before. Never been in a play, or in a music concert, or part of some dumb lip-sync act for the talent show. Where were Wendy and Kreo? Was Wendy doing the spaz face? Giving this assembly was worse than I'd imagined. Standing up here felt shameful, like being stark naked and covered in itchy hives. All I wanted to do was cry and scratch. I could hear my pulse pounding. My knees were banging together. But somehow my voice had caught a line and held steady.

There was no way to pick out Wendy, but I could hear a particular silence in the air. A waiting, a hold. Curious. Maybe *everyone* was remembering about the music room. Or maybe they were wondering how I was holding up since the breakup with Matt. Did everyone know we were over? Had Kreo told?

*Don't think about that.*

The gooseneck podium lamp lit up my notes, and a beam connected the light-box projector to the screen behind me, but otherwise everything was deeply, deathly black.

Dr. Neumann's voice was a warning in my head. *Sometimes seizures just happen.*

I took a breath and felt the clicker beneath my thumb. *Click.* "Keith Haring grew up as the oldest child in a family that included three sisters. Even in grade school, he had an early interest in making art and mischief, and sometimes he got in trouble for being a prankster and a partier. But by the time he'd graduated from Kutztown High, he was serious about one thing—his art."

I was on the high wire. Whatever else happened, I'd inched out this far.

*Sometimes seizures just happen.*

"After a couple of years at the Ivy School in Pittsburgh, Haring moved to New York City, where his provocative imagery electrified everyone. By the next summer, he'd created one of his most recognizable pieces, *Radiant Baby*." I clicked to it. "Haring once said that babies represent 'the possibility of the future, the understanding of perfection, and the purest, most positive experience of the human existence.'"

With everything that had happened between us, I hoped Claire was out there, and was remembering—in a happy way—that afternoon in October when she and I had seen that Keith Haring mural, and she'd told me about her Pop Shop pin.

My next slides showed Haring's early exhibitions, reviews, friendships, and influences. I tried not to think of Mrs. Robles lurking in the light booth, or my mom in the front row. I felt a sudden tip and tilt of the floor beneath my feet. Vertigo. I held my balance. Doubt was a silent circle of vultures in the air.

I'd almost made it. Almost, almost, but *sometimes seizures just happen.*

Pressing the flat of my hand to one side of the podium, I centered myself. "Haring often works at a very large scale. From Brooklyn to Berlin . . ."

My sentence petered out. *Nobody but me . . .*

Many times my imagination had thrown me out into the middle of this assembly, only to sink or burn up in failure. I couldn't find the next sentence on my cards. But I knew it by heart, and I forced myself to lift my gaze from the card.

"From Brooklyn to Berlin, his simple images speak a universal language that often tackles current issues from apartheid, to crack cocaine, to the AIDS epidemic." I could barely trust that my feet were grounding me, or that my thumb understood to click.

"Two years ago, Haring came to our own city of Philadelphia to create a mural with CityKids called *We the Youth*. You can see it today, on Twenty-Second and Ellsworth. Like many of his public installations, our mural is vibrant with the spirit of an urban community. Sometimes—"

*Sometimes seizures just happen.*

"Sometimes the risk with graffiti is that its art will be defaced, but you can visit *We the Youth* anytime and see this piece intact. Haring's mural at the Palladium, and his successful Pop Shop in SoHo, New York, are other examples that this artist is our successor to Andy Warhol as a reigning prince of pop art."

*Click click click click.*

"Recently, Haring was diagnosed HIV positive, and while this doesn't seem to have affected his output . . ." Though my slides changed now, to images of skulls and snakes, bones and devils. "Haring's work has a new, forceful energy."

I'd combed art magazine interviews for more details on this unhappy bend in Keith Haring's story. One article said he was doing just fine, had hardly slowed down while living with HIV, and was more a globetrotter than ever.

I hurried to the finish.

"If the past ten years are any indication, I think we can expect to see a lot more exciting work from this artist. Thank you."

My last click was my favorite. It was a larger study of that small piece I'd seen in Philadelphia on New Year's Eve, a crowded dance scene that would always remind me of my night at the Bank, the risk of chaos met by the pure joy of being there.

Applause broke out. I stepped away from the podium and ducked backstage, conscious of my sweating armpits and my heaving breath.

*Sometimes seizures just happen.* But not today.

Nobody was in the theater's wings. I sat on a folding chair and put my freezing hands on my knees and breathed. It was only when I could hear the student announcements start that it really sank in. I had done it.

When Mrs. Robles appeared through the theater's side door, she seemed pleased. "Good job, Lizzy. You sure stepped outside your comfort zone today, didn't you?" She handed me an index card.

I stood on rubbery legs. My thanks came inside a puff of air. I knew, even before I'd looked at the grade on the card, that it would be pretty good. It was actually three grades, the average of my subject (90), content (92), and presentation (97) averaged to a 93—an A minus.

Shy and pleased and braced for Nectarines, I exited from backstage around to the lobby as students spilled out the theater's doors. Wendy herself was deep in conversation and didn't see me, but a few girls gave me a high five or a "Nice."

Mom was waiting for me, wearing her best work dress and heels and an expression like I'd burped in a restaurant on my birthday.

As in, not my fault, no big deal—but embarrassing.

No surprise. I knew she wouldn't be too into my choice of subject matter.

When I showed her my grade, she smiled. "Very nice, Lizzy. I'm so proud." She squeezed my shoulder. "Though I wish I'd known ahead you were picking that artist."

"Why?"

"For one thing, I told everyone that it was Mary Cassatt."

"I love Keith Haring. I wanted the assembly to be important to me, personally."

"And I wasn't expecting all the drug references, or all of those, ah . . ." She whispered the last two words: "Phallic symbols."

"Sorry to disappoint. Sexual shock is part of his energy." I was quoting myself, a sentence that I'd put into my speech and held in my heart because it meant so much to me, but then I'd cut it, because it felt too private.

"Oh, for heaven's sake, Lizzy. It's not just me—you can see the score reflects some unease with the subject matter. Your presentation score is highest, and I bet you'd have gotten an A plus if you'd done Cassatt. I'm still proud, but I also feel like I just can't win with you lately."

"Were you worried that I wouldn't get through it?"

"It's a mother's job to worry." If misery could smile, that was Mom's face.

And I knew I shouldn't have, but I bit back. "Imagine if you could only say, *Congratulations, Lizzy—I believed in you all along.* Imagine that!"

"Your tone has become really harsh." Mom looked upset, then she seemed to take stock of all the people milling around us. She gave me a quick, closemouthed smile and turned away, heels clicking as she left me, shoulders squared against the pain I'd inflicted.

My impulse was to run to her, to catch up and tell her I was sorry for hurting her feelings. I *was* sorry. But I was also sorry that she didn't get why I'd chosen Haring, or why his passion was so important to me. And I couldn't apologize for that.

# forty-two

MATT AND I HADN'T exactly stopped talking on the phone. He
called the night before my assembly to wish me luck, and he called
Friday afternoon, to hear how it went.

"Before I get off, I meant to tell you there's free weekend
drawing classes over at Moore," he said. "I tore off the number
from our school community board. Mr. Dorsey's wife teaches
over there."

"Really?"

"I could pick you up some Saturday, and I'd wait for you. We
could have lunch."

"Yeah, sure."

Was he just trying to be nice? But he still didn't get off. We
ended up talking for over an hour. In the end, when I'd finally
hung up, I'd felt kind of destroyed that our breakup had done

nothing to end our closeness. Wasn't that what being a couple was all about? Didn't he think so, too? How would I ever move on from Matt if we stayed this important to each other?

That night, Mimi and Gage took me out to Chili's and then Gage drove us to her house for make-your-own ice cream sundaes.

In the privacy of Gage's room, spooning the last of my chocolate with butterscotch sauce, I told them about the breakup.

"Hello? And it happened a whole week ago?" Mimi looked crestfallen. "When were you planning to let us know? Aren't we still your best friends?"

"I just wanted to get past the assembly stress. And it wasn't a bad breakup. I mean, not that I've had a ton of experience. But we still talk on the phone."

"That's sweet," Mimi acknowledged. "Noah and I didn't speak again once after our breakup, except when I called to ask him to return some of my CDs."

"It makes me sad to hear his voice," I admitted. "Maybe not talking to him would be easier."

"You didn't seem affected by it onstage," said Gage. "Were you nervous?"

"The whole time! Especially when I imagined Nectarines laughing at me."

"Guys, I've never told you this." Gage looked like she didn't want to tell it now, either. "But in fourth grade, Wendy Palmer once said I looked like the evil toy that would blow up Santa's workshop. It obsesses me—how Wendy thought that back then, and if she still does."

Mimi and I both knew about that insult. We quietly traded looks.

"She'll never remember she said that," Mimi assured.

"She might," I said. "I think you have to accept that Wendy's out there, and she's always hoping you'll mess up, or that she can make fun of you for something. You've got to deal, and do it anyway."

"True." Gage nodded, and it was one of those rare times when I felt like I wasn't the baby of the group, but someone wiser.

"My assembly's in March," said Mimi. "Is 'Prohibition Era' a boring topic? You definitely win for the most sex in your assembly, Lizzy. Nobody was expecting that! People's eyes were falling out of their heads with some of those slides of yours."

It amazed me, too, that I'd been the one to give such a daring assembly—and I didn't even mind if my grade might have been docked for it. I'd do it again if it meant speaking up for art that I thought was important and real. If I told Mimi and Gage about my father's suggestion to do my presentation in Mrs. Robles's office, they'd laugh so hard. It was a funny story, and I imagined Dr. Neumann nodding: *Talk about your condition. Use the word* epilepsy. *Explore your real self.*

But this was one dare I couldn't take, I just couldn't.

Gage drove me home a little later. She had a fencing thing in Morristown on Saturday, and Mimi and her mom were hitting some clothing outlets, but I was beat, glad for an early night with Ursula K. Le Guin. The phone rang just as I'd switched off my bedside reading lamp. So late, I knew it could be only for me.

I leaped down to the kitchen, hoping against hope it was Claire.

"Bliz."

"Hey!"

"I'm at a pay phone, we're heading out to a party—but quick, give me the rundown on your big speech. It was today, right?"

"Uh-huh." I was so flattered Theo remembered, my smile covered my whole face. "It went great. Didn't pass out, got an A minus." Then before I could stop myself, I blurted out about my breakup with Matt.

"Aw, Bliz. Sorry to hear. That's rough. You'd been worried it was headed there."

"Yeah." Had I?

"You'll be okay." Now I could hear kids calling to Theo, hooting his name. "Look, I gotta go. I'm glad you nailed it today. Chin up, kid."

And then he was gone.

As TOTALLY SURPRISING AND cool as Theo's call had been, it also reminded me how Claire hadn't phoned my house in forever. She hadn't come up to me after the assembly, either, and all week she'd skipped out of school early, per her habit. So I wasn't prepared to see her striding into Ludington on Sunday evening right before closing, dressed in black jeans and a bomber jacket, her Wayfarers casually perched on her head and a long silk ivory scarf wrapped around her neck, Amelia Earhart–style.

She looked so glamorous that it was hard for me to know what to do with my emotions, or even my hands. As she beelined for my desk, every nerve in me was tensed to the point of breaking.

"Nice job Friday," she began, friendly enough.

"Oh. Thanks. I figured you'd skipped it."

"Nope. How cool that you did Haring. I felt like I was secretly part of it, when you got to the mural."

"You were," I said earnestly.

"We should go look at it again."

My heart was pounding. "Anytime, yeah."

"How was your weekend?"

"Quiet." My skin flushed, wondering if Claire had been hanging out with Dave and Matt this weekend—while I'd been stuck at home with no plans.

"So listen, Matt and Dave and I were thinking of going to the city tonight, to that bar on Quince that's around the corner from Moriarty's—we thought you'd want to join. We'll stop by your house first if you need to get permission." Claire spoke fast, maybe hoping I wouldn't notice the complete strangeness of her talking to me in such a friendly way, or the fact that this suggestion was totally off-the-wall.

"Claire," I started. "Why are you doing this?"

"We can tell your parents we're going to my house to study."

"No. *Claire*." I stared her down. "It's been over a month since we've made any kind of a plan about anything."

Claire's eyes seemed to admit to this. "Okay," she began again, more slowly. "Backing up. For a while, I felt like I had a right to be pissed with you. First with the letters, and then you totally misled me about that money, and it was incredibly hard for me to ask Aunt Jane, with all the strings she attaches to everything. But I get it. Sixty bucks equals, what—twenty hours here?" She opened her arms to show that *here* meant Ludington. "I didn't mean to be naïve about your situation. I'm really sorry about that—and your letter was really kind. I should have said that first thing. It meant a lot to me." Her face was frank. "Can we call it a learning curve?"

All I wanted was to crush our standoff into a bad memory and toss it over my shoulder. All I wanted was to declare a new day on our friendship. I'd never stopped wanting that. "Okay," I said after a moment.

"The four of us, at the diner, on the train, that morning after the club—that was our best. I always think about that morning. Our little foursome."

"Me, too," I admitted.

"So we're on?"

"*No*. Claire, don't you see how strange it would be for me to hang out with my ex-boyfriend the weekend right after we broke up?"

"Matt misses you."

She wasn't mocking my pain, but I felt like she didn't understand it. "I appreciate the offer," I told her, "but it's confusing. Matt and I talked on the phone Friday, and he didn't say anything about this weekend, you all going to that bar, or me coming along."

"He wanted me to be the one to ask. He doesn't know how to say it. Don't you think it'd be better between you and Matt as friends?"

"Is that what he said? *Better as friends?* Does he say things like that about us to you?"

Claire shifted. "Don't look at me like that. I didn't mean to upset you. Of course you still have feelings for him. I know he has feelings for you. But maybe this breakup is supposed to be the start of something new."

I could feel my limbs stiffening. I swallowed. "Sorry if it still feels like the end of something old. I guess I'm not ready."

"You can decide to be happy, Lizzy."

Claire sounded like a therapist. In fact, she sounded like my therapist. But two could play that game. "Really? Let's explore that," I snapped. "Could your authentic self have decided to be happy about Jay, when everything was said and done?"

"Jay?" Color crept up in her cheeks. "Jay—was different."

"If you say so."

I wondered if Claire could sense what I knew about Jay. Her face was inscrutable, but I knew my words had hit the target.

"Look. I'm going home after this. I'm tired." The confusing idea of seeing Matt tonight wrenched at me. Tears were gathering hot behind my eyelashes. I stared blurrily down at my stack of book returns. Opened an inkpad and took up the hand stamp.

"If you change your mind . . ."

"I won't."

She lingered a few seconds. Then she smacked her hand on the desk and left.

When I looked up, I realized that her slap had signaled what she'd left behind—a small circle of tin.

I picked it up. It was her Radiant Baby button.

On the ride home, I cooled my cheek on the train's window glass. Claire meant well, and in a way I was thrilled that she'd offered me this olive branch. But she didn't understand Matt and me. If only her "learning curve" were as simple as she thought.

At home, the whole family was leaving for Sunday dinner at the Midgeses'—a plan I'd forgotten until I found them all in the kitchen, buttoning into heavy coats.

"Do I have to go? I don't feel up to it."

"They have Chopper 1 on Nintendo," said Peter. "We're gonna play it all night."

Mom looked at me, perplexed. "It's their wedding anniversary dinner. I suppose I can say you've got a headache."

"Okay, say that."

"You know where we are if you need to call." Dad's eyes narrowed. "Are you all right, Lizzy? Sure you'd rather be alone?"

There was nothing I'd rather be than alone. "Don't worry about me."

"I think you *are* getting a headache," said Mom. "I'm glad you're staying in. You don't look well." Preparing herself for the lie she'd soon be telling, by making it be true.

# forty-three

In the quiet house, I swigged some Nyquil along with my chicken noodle Cup-a-Soup dinner so that I'd nod off early, but it worked for only about an hour. I woke up groggy and tingling with wanting to do something, but what?

Matt and Claire and Dave were together. They'd probably just started their night. Bought beers and burgers, figured out the tunes lineup on the jukebox, if there was a jukebox.

I paced and looked out windows onto the quiet suburbia all around me.

For years, all I'd done was hope for Matt Ashley. Hoped and hoped, and then it happened. Matt Ashley had swept into my life like Prince Charming and changed it forever. Suddenly we were together all the time, and then almost just as suddenly—and for reasons I still didn't really understand—we had failed.

Now Matt, Claire, and Dave wanted me to be part of something, and I'd rejected it, but why? I missed our foursome almost as much as the duo of Matt and me.

I was on the edge of the decision, but it also seemed dangerous—a sharp new blade of strategy gleaming in the dark.

*Take Mom's car.*

My mouth was dry. Yes. That was it. I'd take Mom's car, and I'd drive into the city, and meet them all on Quince. They'd invited me, and even if I wasn't "with" Matt, I was wanted, right? Because that's what Claire had meant, *right?*

Before I could veer too hard into a second guess, I was rocketing into my jeans and Docs. I smoked on some eyeliner, brushed my teeth. My roots were coming in, and my untrimmed-since-October bangs dropped heavy past my eyes. "Shetland pony," Dad had complained, but in my view, my hair looked more like the white and dark feathers of a bird.

*Took the car and went to the movies with Mimi, home by 11.*

My parents wouldn't like this note.

Mom's keys felt like contraband as I unhooked them from the key rack. Outside was freezing, and my boots crunched through a fresh skin of snow. I backed out slowly, hands locked on my Driver's Ed three and nine, my breath making clouds because I wasn't sure which was the heat button, and I didn't want to push something wrong, or invite any more anxiety than what was already churning around inside me. I was petrified the Nyquil had slowed my reflexes and that I was flying in the face of its label warning—driving a car was for sure operating "heavy machinery."

I could claim, sum total, about twenty hours of driving experience, mostly via hoagie runs to Wawa. I'd hardly practiced highways, right-hand turns, backing up, and parallel parking. This would be my first real test. North Wayne Avenue to Lancaster, a slow zipper all the way in. Nothing scary about it. It wasn't until I crossed the first traffic light into Lower Merion that my doubts caught up. I pushed through. The halfway mark. And then, twenty minutes later, the natural turn at the dead end.

I'd never learned the name of this bar. "Around the corner from Moriarty's" wasn't much to go on. But Moriarty's was a well-known Philly landmark, and when I'd looked up the address in the *Donnelly Directory*, it mentioned the nearby street parking.

At least it was Sunday. At least it wasn't rush hour.

At least, at least . . . and when I turned onto Walnut, at least there it was. Moriarty's. All lit up, right on the corner. Down the block, there weren't any cars to interfere with my parking attempt.

I backed the Corolla inch by inch and parallel to the curb. Cut the engine. Took that courage breath, then slammed outside. Okay. Yes. I was doing this, I was really doing this. My car keys were jangling in my pocket like I was a real adult, alone in my hometown city. So far, so good.

Quince Street was a one-way cobblestone, darker than Walnut, lined with skinny trees and carriage houses. At the corner blinked a ground-floor Coors Light sign, with a flickering hint of activity behind the smoked glass. I pushed through the thick wooden door and into the surround stereo's INXS "Don't Change." Good song, good omen. It was crowded, too. I squinted through the burnt haze of cigarette smoke. I could feel the unnerved flicker in the men's glances up and over at me. I wasn't the usual.

As dives went, it wasn't that dive-y. Bicycles were bolted onto the walls as a kind of loose theme, a male theme, and most of the guys wore heavy outdoor clothes, boots, and leather jackets. Masculine enough that I felt my difference. A couple of focused bartenders pulled beers on tap and served the busy wraparound bar. Up front were a pair of pinball machines, and in a back corner, I saw them immediately, tight-knit in conversation, a perfect triangle of closeness, as if there'd never been a time when they weren't best friends.

It was probably a trick of the eye, because how could the moon be in view through that grimy window? And yet, the way I saw it, the light bathed Claire's face with the same radiance of that very first night when I'd stayed over. I'd never forgotten how she looked in the library window seat, like a moonlit magic version of Claire. A bright-eyed girl I'd rediscovered tonight, with Matt, my Matt, except that he wasn't mine, because he was with Claire, and he was also with Dave.

It wasn't so much that I saw anything as that I understood everything. I'd always been looking so hard for the realest Matt, the most private Matt. But I'd never counted on what I'd feel when I finally did find him, so unguarded and at ease in the company he trusted, that it extinguished anything I'd ever told myself about him. All those lies I'd told myself. Now I saw him. Facing Claire. But next to Dave, their shoulders just touching.

Here he was. And what I felt—more than anything else in that red, roaring moment—was totally betrayed.

# forty-four

I WISH THAT I could remember everything, but this is what comes next.

It begins in the dark pocket of that room. I'm the black shadow flat against the wall, and I see what I see.

My feet are numb, and then so are my hands.

"Hey," I call over to them, but my voice is softened to nothing under the din of jukebox music and the bar crowd, the wall-mounted television. I try again. "Hey."

Magnetic waves of memory. Gage was chewing gum that afternoon; she always chewed gum in music class because she was paranoid about her singing breath. It's with me again, a waft of sweet spearmint.

*Lizzy, stop it why are you being so weird everyone's looking*

A warm afternoon. The first day we'd cracked open the windows to invite the green spring air. Our singing voices and Mr. Hock's plinking piano, drifting outside to the playing fields.

*"Nobody but meeee . . ."*

A tingling in my fingers and the back of my short-circuiting brain, a rush of heat.

*Oh my God, she's spazzing out.*

Four years later, no time at all.

*Sometimes seizures just happen.*

Claire catches sight of me as clouds burst apart into peppery fluttering, tiny flecks spattering across my vision, along with a deep sharp twist of panic that I can't stop any of this, not even one second of it.

And now Matt is calling to me, but my own voice isn't coming out, everything is seized up inside me and the noise expelled from my lungs isn't right and isn't mine, there's a sound in my ears that's not me, either, a screaming tuneless tune. Every muscle is contracting, overcharged, I can't hold on to my limbs, myself, I'm not here, I'm not me, I'm not . . .

# forty-five

I TRY TO MAKE time lines and sequences, but I never remember much better than an approximate mess of that night. Some of it is gone completely. Shock and sedatives will do that, Dr. Neumann told me. Memory loss is to be expected.

But I clung to what I could, resurfing those moments as they endlessly crashed to shore in my brain—even as they got rippled by distortion.

What I recalled best and most in the emergency room: the pain.

I throbbed bone deep with it, from the back of my skull, behind my eyes, between my ribs. Bruises that darkened along my leg from where I fell, heavily and onto one side. Sore and pulsing even in my mouth, along with an iron taste of blood.

At some point, I spoke. "My tongue hurts."

"You bit it!" My nurse was warm brown eyes and kindness in her South Philly accent. "We're going down for the EEG next. You need wooder?"

I imagined myself like a primitive stick figure, a Keith Haring–shaped body, my center marked by a red $X$. Everything I needed to do, think, feel, and understand was pulling at me in opposite directions, all at once.

The lights were too bright. A technician came and attached a few dozen electrodes to my scalp. A whisper of the recording machine as my brain waves were turned to patterns and stored. My eyes closed. I could hear hurrying feet in soft-soled shoes, jangling phones and garbled intercoms, pinging bells, and buzzers.

At some point, Claire was a strange angel hovering over me.

My eyes closed.

The nurse again. "Memba comin' in? Talk to me. I took your blood?"

I shook my head.

"Okay, so you got a small concussion. Is all you need to know, so rest."

Resting. Claire again. "Lizzy? I sent Dave and Matt back to the apartment. I said I'd be your guardian and I'd sign the release because I figured you didn't—"

"You should have gone with them." Was that my voice? "I have other people to help me. I don't need you." I began coughing, which made me feel stupid and weak, as Claire waited for me to get my breath back. "You lied."

"No, I just didn't tell. That's different. We didn't think you were coming."

"What's it all about? That bar. Is that the type of bar you all hang out at, now that I'm not around? Is Matt in love with Dave? How long did you know about it?"

"No, he's not. It's not like that. It's not that simple."

"It looked pretty simple."

"Nobody's gone behind your back, Lizzy."

"That's what you three always say when you go behind my back."

"Lizzy, nothing's going on behind your back except for honest conversation."

The thing I couldn't give them. "You hid it from me." A rebel tear spilled, my sore throat constricted. "All these secrets."

"I knew about your seizures already, it was one of the first things Wendy—"

"Stop it. I don't want to hear—"

"—and I figured if I had a secret, and you had one, too, maybe they canceled each other out and you'd respect—"

"Shut up, Claire!" Rising up on my elbows, my headache splitting me in half. "Just go already."

My eyes closed. My body had turned to liquid melting pain.

The nurse. A cup of water. My question, *How did I get here?* Her answer, *In an ambulance with all your friends.*

Maybe that happened first?

At some point, a paunchy doctor who looked like Uncle Ron, but sterner. He took my vitals and told me I was free to leave in the company of an adult. "You aren't wearing tags. It's lucky your friends knew about your epilepsy."

Epilepsy, the *X* that marked me.

I was given a brown bag, stapled. Prescriptions. The nurse. "Arncha gonna leave? You gotta friend out there, she's been waiting and waiting."

"No, I want to leave with my family."

"What's the name?"

I said it. My eyes closed.

At some point, I stood. Testing my legs, I walked carefully out to the main desk, where that same gray-fedora man from Lonnie's diner all those weeks ago was slumped, exhausted, in one of the orange molded chairs. No fedora this time, and he was weaker than I remembered. His skin stretched too thin over the gaunt bones of his face. And then I saw him again, in a hospital gown and wheeling a drip—and when I saw him a third time, now with his mother, I realized none of these men were the gray-fedora man, they were all different men. It was just that they were all dying the same way.

"I need to make a phone call."

At some point, a phone call. This must have happened first.

The Kims kept one phone in the living room, another in Mr. Kim's upstairs office. Mr. and Mrs. Kim both slept soundly. Mimi was my best bet at calm in a crisis.

"Hello?"

"Theo?" I could hear the TV in the background.

"Hello? Who is this?" Mimi sounded sleep blunted.

"I got it." Using his most unbothered, older brother voice. "Jump off, Meems."

"Can you tell Violetta please not to call after eleven? Jeez!" The phone slammed.

Theo waited a moment anyway, to ensure Mimi wouldn't pick up again to deliver a few more lecturing words. "What's wrong, Blizzard?"

My voice, croaking out facts. "I'm at the emergency room at Drexel. I don't want to go home with the people I came here with."

"You're injured or just shitfaced?"

"I had a seizure. Because of, you know, my epilepsy." There it was, the word. Out. And I was saying it to Theo, of all people. "Why are you home?"

"Martin Luther King Day's on Monday, I'm here for the long weekend. Okay, listen, I'm hanging up now. I'm coming in. Sit tight."

My eyes closed.

Later Claire told me that she'd stayed in the waiting room until Theo came through and gave my name at the desk. Of course I hated thinking about that, too. Claire introducing herself and explaining what had happened. The two of them discussing me. All that jarring knowledge of me between them.

By the time Theo arrived, I'd moved to a chair. Brown paper bag on my lap.

Theo was wearing what I knew were basically his pj's—his faded lounge-around Lincoln Academy sweatpants and a Union Jack T-shirt he'd had since he was a skinny ninth grader that now hugged his chest and biceps. He hadn't even wasted a moment to change. But he was his same Theo self, and I felt lucky he'd picked up the phone. Before we left, we agreed on the story before he called my worried parents from the hospital. He explained that we'd met up at the movies, that I'd gone with him to an alcohol-free party all the way in Overbrook, and that when I had the seizure, we were close enough to Philly that he'd driven me in for an X-ray and EEG. And that now he was bringing me home.

I could hear Dad thanking him, over and over.

Theo also found out where I'd parked, and he drove back into the city with a friend early the next morning and returned the Corolla to my trusting parents. To this day, they don't know the whole story. Not every single secret will ruin your life.

# forty-six

2/14

Dear Lizzy,

Since you've spent the past couple of weeks not calling me back, I hope you might go for a note. Even if I'm not as good with words as you. But when you wrote me that apology back in December, I read it plenty of times. It was honest and from your heart, but I didn't trust it. I've been burned by words before. Once upon a time, Jay wrote me thousands of them and I ate them up like popcorn, and as it turned out, he was the worst possible kind of person, and his words were worth less than nothing. So I didn't know what to think about yours, because I'd made such a stupid bet on him. Want to know something? After you took his letters, I kept hoping you'd come back to me with an opinion about them, and then I'd know he'd tricked you, too, and you thought he was amazing, and you'd been just as fooled as I'd been, because there was no way to see that he was a horrible lying bastard kind of a person.

The second thing I wanted to tell you, what I tried to tell you in the ER that night, and I still think you should know it, was that Wendy Palmer told me everything that first week. How Angela Ertel's parents are swingers and Lindsey's dad is in the mob, and that Jill de la Reyes's brother has spina bifida, and that Becky Schultz's dad ran off with the babysitter and Deenie Herring's brother's a fag and Maggie Farthington was at some special camp for kids with eating disorders, and that you'd had a major epileptic seizure a few years ago and almost choked on your own tongue.

Palmer didn't exactly win me over with any of that, but I guess I felt this connection to you, as a person who didn't like sharing things that made you feel worse instead of better. Or you didn't mind being partly hidden. I get that. I know how much I needed to hide when I left Strickland. I still think of myself as a girl who disappeared. But here's the other thing, I'd figured it out early with Dave. Not Matt, at first, but Dave. That night after the Bank, he told me about this older guy who came into his life and pretty much destroyed his trust. So we had that in common. It was a story Matt knew. Matt has his own stories. It'd be wrong of me to print them here, but the three of us bonded that night, and I realized that as much as I respect kept secrets, it's also a relief to share them.

I never talk about Jay at school, and if you're not doing anything Friday night, you could maybe come over? Lizzy, I don't know what else. I'm not good at this stuff, and the card's running out of room.

Just this: we know you're our fourth.

You know you are, too.

Be our Valentine.

Claire

# forty-seven

THAT AFTERNOON, WITH CLAIRE'S card in my book bag and a toasted bagel in my hand, I headed for the art room. All I wanted was to free my mind to make art. My heart was throbbing with everything Claire had written. Most of it wasn't any shock. Some secrets are obvious, like every scandal that Wendy had offered up. All of those stories had been passed around our classroom for years, like grubby show-and-tell objects. Of course my story was part of it.

As for Matt and Dave, what I mostly wanted on that was time. Maybe this was why I hadn't taken Claire's phone calls—or Matt's. Every new feeling kept catching me by the throat.

In the art room, the sound of laughter stopped me, and when Mrs. Custis-Brown peeked around the corner, she looked so flushed and out of breath I glanced away, even though she was fully clothed.

"Lizzy!" she called. "You're just who we wanted to see! Phil is in here, too. Can you come into the office for a chat?"

"Okay." I set my bagel on the table and dragged in.

This couldn't be good.

The art room office was more like an ambitious cubby, and so cluttered I felt like I knew what the Custis-Browns' apartment must look like. Mr. Custis-Brown, behind the desk, pointed me to the only empty seat as Mrs. C-B moved some papers to perch up on the desk corner. I sat heavily. Dr. Neumann was still making adjustments to my medications, and I'd been foggy these past days, a sluggish beat behind everything. I knew the meds were necessary, but I disliked the way time moved in slow motion, and how my impulses and reactions felt coated in wax.

"Is everything okay?" I asked into their expectant smiles.

"Yes, yes. Better than okay. In fact, Phil and I have been looking together at the AP portfolios. Yours is very promising, Lizzy, and we wanted to ask you if you'd applied to any art schools?"

"Not really. I guess I'm hoping for Princeton? Where I'm a legacy."

"We think your AP portfolio is pretty unusual." Mr. Custis-Brown clasped his hands behind his large woolly head, tipping it back to regard me through turtled eyes. "You have a lot going on in this concentration, don't you think?"

"What do you mean?"

"There's a real vision here, wouldn't you say? Take *Kidnapped*. Where the hand is tied up in elastic and twine. And then there's

*Drowned*, where these fingers appear waterlogged and you've twisted a bath stopper's chain to your middle finger. And the—"

"The clothespins one," Mrs. Custis-Brown broke in. "What's it called?"

"*Out to Dry*." I'd done that piece after meeting Mrs. Ashley. I'd clipped each of my fingers with a clothespin, resulting in a drawing that looked strange and dangerous. "I hope you don't think they're, like, really dark or anything." I didn't like the intensity of this conversation. "That I have some mental problems."

"We aren't labeling your work. We're mostly intrigued by it. And we did show it to a friend of ours, an art critic that Jeanie and I both respect. He wrote this"—he picked a piece of paper off his desk—"*In each piece of art, the hand is its own entity. It exists violent, helpless, and apart from the rest of the body, as if seized by a private undercurrent of deep conflict.*" Mr. Custis-Brown looked up and raised his eyebrows.

"You don't have to make it sound so smart." I looked down, skidded a finger along the hem of my uniform kilt. "Since I don't think it is," I mumbled to my lap.

"Phil and I believe you'll place out of the introductory art courses easy, and go right into advanced technique. Lizzy?" I looked up. Mrs. Custis-Brown was staring at me so intensely, her hands buckled tight over her knee. "I've only once, in all my twenty years of teaching at Argyll, given a student a ninety-six. And that was your grade last semester. I hoped it would be a signal to you."

"Oh." It hadn't been.

"There's no doubt that your concentration is exceptional," Mr. Custis-Brown added. "It's forceful and passionate and shows a seriousness of intent. We realize that you haven't spoken much about studying art after Argyll." He sat back in his chair. "Not with us anyway."

"Right." There was nobody to roll my eyes at, or I would have. Art after Argyll?

"We want to make sure that you have a full understanding of your potential, Lizzy. And how truly exciting this path might be for you," said Mrs. Custis-Brown.

"I appreciate that. I really like art class." What ridiculous idea was this? As if I could just reverse course, forget my whole academic life of the past dozen years, and everything I'd worked for, to become—what? A *studio art* major? Insane. Pursuing art—that was what you did when you weren't good at anything else.

My knees were shaking, I capped them with my hands.

"There are so many schools." Mr. Custis-Brown began to list them on his fingers. "Rhode Island School of Design. Carnegie Mellon. Moore College. The School of Visual Arts in Manhattan."

"Philadelphia College of Art," added Mrs. Custis-Brown. "Bard. Hunter. Temple."

I was nodding into their enthusiasm, but I could hear my parents, a pair of cobras in the back of my brain, hissing their rejection of these schools. I stood up. "Thank you so much. I will totally think about it. Good to see you again, Mrs. Custis-Brown."

"We hope you'll give this some deep consideration. We can write letters of recommendation, we'll find out which schools have rolling admissions policies—we know lots of people who work in the arts community, and we're here for you as a resource anytime.

"And call me Jean."

Permission for me to call Mrs. Custis-Brown *Jean*, one tiny step away from *Jeanie*, felt like permission for me to look at her naked again, which I also didn't want to do. But I tried to stay neutral as I nodded and made my getaway.

I didn't want to see anyone. Not Claire, who'd skipped AP Art anyway, not the Custis-Browns, and at the end of the day, I didn't want to deal with Matt, either—which made the news that he was on campus all the more of a jolt.

"Just saw your boyfriend," sang one of the juniors as she passed me in the hall. "He's in the lounge."

"Oh. Thanks." I reversed direction.

He was sitting on the couch, sipping a Coke, casually chatting with Maggie and Kreo, as if a million things weren't between us now. But my heart tugged a little, knowing how Matt must crave to be exactly the way he was presenting himself—as the perfect Lincoln ex-boyfriend, so unquestioned and accepted.

"Hey, Matt."

"Hey. Thought I'd give you a ride to work."

"I don't work Tuesdays." But he knew that already.

"So maybe we can grab a burger at Lonnie's?"

"I'm not hungry." Kreo and Maggie were now pretending very hard to watch TV. I motioned for Matt to stand so we could leave the lounge, and then the school.

"I wasn't sure I was ready to see you, after everything," I started as soon as we were outside. "But you don't have to explain anything to me."

"What would I be explaining?" he asked.

"Just about—you and Dave."

"Dave and I aren't—we're both dealing with—"

"Right. That was a gay bar we were in, last month. And the only person who was surprised to be in it was me." I hadn't meant to sound so bitchy, hadn't meant for my pain to come out like that.

"Okay, okay," Matt said quietly. He hated this, maybe even more than I did.

He didn't say anything until we were in the parking lot. I felt like he was giving my words even more time to sour. I wished I hadn't said them.

"I knew about your epilepsy," he said as we turned into the lot. He reached into his blazer pocket for his car keys. "For years, I guess. I can't remember who told me. Maybe some Argyll girl who'd seen it happen. The way I heard about it, they made you sound kind of like a freak. That was also why I didn't call you, freshman year. Too risky. When I was younger, I was obsessed with what other kids thought of me. I'm still scared of what I am. I hate admitting any of that. But it made me feel good to know this thing about you that scared you, too. I even read up on epilepsy. I know a lot about it."

I stopped walking. "You do?"

"In case you ever had a seizure." Matt stopped, too. His eyes on me. "I wanted to be prepared, but I was fine if you never wanted to talk about it. I was okay either way."

I hadn't expected such sweetness. My face burned with shame and maybe gratitude.

"You never let on."

"An epileptic didn't seem like a thing you wanted to be."

"I am, though."

"Yep."

And then he stepped forward, cupped his hands around my face, leaned over, and kissed me. A real kiss, from his heart. Slow, soft, perfect as a shooting star.

As we broke apart, a few girls, heading over to the fields for lacrosse practice, hooted at us and made stupid kissy faces.

"It's so easy to pretend that we're this normal couple," I said as we watched the girls dip across the fields. "But it must have always felt like a lie to you."

"My whole life feels like lies," said Matt. "All these decisions my parents make for me—where I go to school, what I wear, what sports I should play, my haircut, my future. But you never felt like a lie, Lizzy. I really chose you."

"You just liked that your mom would never pick me for her empty wedding frame."

He laughed. "Well, yeah. There's that."

"What *is* your deal with Dave anyway?"

"He's just a friend who knows me. Knows me for real." Matt shrugged. "When I met him, he was pretty up front about who he was. I wasn't ready to be like that, but he made me see myself. Face myself."

"The first time I hung out with Claire," I said, "she did my eyeliner. Then she turned me to the mirror and told me to face the strange. I knew what she meant, that I needed to look at the real me. I never even thought of myself like that. After that, I couldn't see myself any other way."

"You were lucky to meet her."

"I was lucky to meet you, too," I said.

Matt nodded. "Back atcha."

"Let's be something better than we were," I said. "Remember when you asked for that? I didn't understand why you wanted that. Now I think I might."

When Matt looked at me, my heart hurt for all of it—for everything Matt was trying to be, for all that prevented us from being together, and for how ridiculously important he was to me anyway.

"I'm in," he told me. "For whatever we are, Lizzy, I'm in."

# forty-eight

"EIGHTY-EIGHT? CONGRATULATIONS. ESPECIALLY considering it was the creepiest assembly of the year." I flipped the index card onto the dashboard of the Beetle as we pulled out of the school parking lot.

Icy, sleeting rain was falling slantwise. Claire's windshield wipers squeaked back and forth in effort.

"My best grade all semester," said Claire. "So don't knock it."

"I'll give you big points for holding the audience's interest—but your topic?" I shivered. "The Mütter Museum is the worst. Pictures of brains and tumors in jars."

"I could have done my second choice, Ted Bundy."

"Ted Bundy, the serial killer? Ugh."

"My shrink agreed. Too intense."

"A few years ago, Dr. Neumann said I should do my assembly on living with epilepsy. When I realized she wasn't kidding, I almost passed out in her office." I laughed uncomfortably past the dryness in my throat. My first try with Claire on that word. "Can you imagine?"

"As far as advice goes, it's not totally shitty." Claire gave me a sidelong look. "I bet people would have been pretty interested. Me, for example. I don't know anybody else with epilepsy."

"I'll tell you about it one day maybe."

"Deal."

We pulled into the Acme and dashed inside. My idea, Claire's credit card. We filled the shopping cart with bananas and apples, bagels, instant soups, granola bars, price-slashed Valentine's cookies, and sodas.

Down from the paper goods section, I spied a bottom-shelf toaster oven. "Check this out. No box, on sale, half off. Probably because it's dinged on this side." I hauled it up and then, because she wasn't disagreeing with me, I lowered the toaster carefully, like it was a sleeping dog, into the cart.

"It's still a lot of money." Claire looked hesitant.

"Your aunt's kitchen wouldn't pass one single health inspector's code. The way I see it, she *owes* you this toaster oven. It's your health at stake. Seriously, think of all the things you can do, Claire—heat soup, roast a potato—"

"Toast cat tails." She wasn't making a move to put back the toaster oven. "Aunt Jane never comments on the grocery bills if I come back with all the things she needs: tissue boxes, soda pop, cat food . . ." One corner of the cart was piled high with Kleenex boxes, Fancy Feast tins, and Dr Peppers.

"You're doing her a favor, always shopping for her. She can do you a favor."

"Okay." She blew out her lips. "Let's get it."

At the house, we stopped in the kitchen to unload Aunt Jane's items, then we kicked mewling cats out of our path on the way to Claire's bedroom. I cleared out the bookcase, restocking a whole shelf with grocery items. Claire made space for the toaster oven.

"I'm way more excited about this than I thought I'd be."

"It looks cute. And these groceries should keep you till March." I brushed off my hands and stepped back to survey it all. "If you made this corner of the room into a tiny kitchen, you could fit a microwave right there."

"Or a mini fridge." There was a shine in Claire's eyes. "The less time for me in Aunt Jane's kitchen, the better. This will help me stomach Lilac House—literally—till summer, when I head out to California."

"Have you thought about where in California?"

"Nope. That's what I like about it. A new start, maybe with an ocean breeze."

When Claire talked like that, I didn't feel as crazy about the thoughts chasing around in my own head. School for art. Art for school. A new plan had been hatching in my brain: I could stay home, save money for a few months, and then enroll in RISD for January. As cool as this plan seemed one moment, in the next breath RISD seemed like somebody else's lunatic dream. But I'd never reflected on whether I should lift art above my real, practical ambitions. I got good grades in art because I got good grades in everything. And that didn't mean anything.

Except that possibly it did?

"Want to see a secret room?" Claire wriggled her eyebrows. "It's upstairs."

"Show me."

We left the library for the hall. Claire stopped in front of a narrow closet and hauled out a sleeping bag and a couple of thick plaid-backed field blankets, then began climbing the stairs to the second floor.

She pointed out Aunt Jane's closed bedroom door as we hurried past.

Another flight of stairs, and at this landing Claire opened a paneled door, revealing a staircase that led to an empty dome-shaped room, its ceiling crossed with open beams and rafters. On the floor was a double-armed candlestick and Bic lighter.

"I know where we are. Your gargoyles are right outside this tower."

Claire nodded. "But no bats in the rafters, luckily." With a snap, she unrolled and then unzipped the sleeping bag. "Although I'm sure if we *had* bats, Aunt Jane would name them and dress them in doll clothes and feed them milk from a bottle." She sat, her legs crisscrossed on a blanket. "The silence is nice here, right? I'm always searching for the most beautiful kinds of silence."

I dropped down next to her, pulling my own blanket over my shoulders to insulate me from the wall. Leaning back, finding support for my head. My meds could make me feel sleepy. But it also felt so, so good to be friends with Claire again, in this secret room with the ancient sound of pattering rain all around us.

She lit the two candles, and we watched their flames jerk and cast shadows. She pulled her blanket over her lap.

For a while, we were quiet, listening to the rain and the peace, until in a soft voice, Claire spoke. "It started at the beginning of last fall. All the girls loved Jay. He was so good-looking, with that crooked smile and green eyes, his cute laugh you could hear all the way down the hall. He drove a vintage Alfa Romeo Spider and he'd park it right on the field during games—just a little bit of a bad boy thing. But it wasn't until last year that I got him for a class, French Lit. That's when he began paying extra attention to me. That's when I really got to know him.

"Of course I was flattered he'd picked me out. I signed up for his office hours, and he started to bring me morning coffees in to-go paper cups—no big deal. And then at some point we started passing notes, making plans. Tiny little spillover plans, like once we shared a Sunday-afternoon picnic to read a book by Victor Hugo that he'd left off the syllabus. Or a few times we met up on a garden bench in the local cemetery to continue an office-hours chat. Another time we went to see a matinee in the town just one over from Strickland."

"Did it always feel like a secret between you two? A bad secret, I mean?"

"Jay never acted guilty. Maybe that helped fool me? His only rule was 'No joiners,'" Claire said. "At first I thought he meant no other kids—as in tagalongs. But I guess what he was really always on the lookout for were the other Strickland teachers. The other adults."

She told me about their road trips, including the one to Philadelphia when she lost her virginity and got her tarot tattoo—at the last minute, Jay decided not to get a matching one. She told me about their endless searching for "privacy," and their wishful conversations about their being "really together" once she graduated from Strickland.

"I thought it was real. I trusted him. I had no idea what *forever* meant. I mean, not that I understand it much better now. But I had even less idea then."

"He was *married*, Claire. Didn't that feel like an obstacle?"

"I don't know. He gave me Steph's expired driver's license so we could get into bars, which seems kind of psycho. But at the time I was just, like, cool. I didn't want to think about Steph, so I didn't. And believe me, Jay made it pretty easy to forget about that little thing about him being married."

"Weren't you scared of her?" I asked. "You could have been caught anytime."

"I should have been more scared of *all* of it," Claire agreed. "But in the end, see, we *weren't* caught. Jay just . . . ended it. In the beginning, he chased me down so hard, and then a couple of months later, when it all bored him or got too complicated with my feelings, he told me I was clingy. He told me Steph had become suspicious, and that he needed space. It's probably the textbook behavior for this situation, except who owns that text-book? Not me." Claire's grip around her calves had tightened and her chin dropped to rest on her knees. "One afternoon, he told me Steph had found the Rati amulet I'd given him. It was a private gift—Rati is a Hindu goddess, and it was a name Jay had for me. Probably it was his pet name for her, too. I don't know.

"Anyway, when Jay confessed it to Steph, I'm sure he made it sound like I had a schoolgirl crush that he'd let go too far. They both went arm in arm to Strickland Human Resources, like they were this worried couple complaining about me, basically. Painting me as this unstable kid, and if Jay *maybe* had taken *some* advantage, the real problem was how messed up I was. By the time any of this had got back to me, Strickland had called my parents, and all the supposed adults had worked out a decision: Jay'd go to counseling and he'd keep his job, minus teaching French Lit, so that he wouldn't be tempted by female students. But as for me, I'd have to leave the school I loved, the school I'd been going to since seventh grade."

"That's ridiculous." And then, after a pause, I made myself ask it. "At the time, did you think maybe you *were* a little bit unstable?"

Claire seemed to sink into herself, wrapping up in the blanket like it was armor. "I don't know. I thought I was doing fine before Jay, but I was probably lonelier than I knew. After he dropped me, I wasn't sleeping or eating much, my grades were tanking, I was cutting classes and sports. So, sure. Call me unstable." She closed her eyes. "Mostly I couldn't figure out what the hell had happened to me."

"After he confessed it to the school, were you two in touch at all?"

"I phoned him a couple of times at home, right after it all went down. I was in shock. I just wanted Jay to understand how much I needed to stay at Strickland. But that's when he cut me off completely. He reported me, twisting it up so that it looked like my calls to his home proved his point, that I was overly emotional and needed to go."

"What about his letters? Those are pretty incriminating."

"I did show a couple of them to Mr. Steele, the head of Strickland. He said it was all a terrible mistake, and I should get rid of them. He said it would be hard enough that Jay and I'd both have to live with consequences of our 'foolish behavior.' He promised me nothing would be on my permanent record, and I should be thankful for that. My mom saw the whole drama as a sign for a fresh start—she'd been struggling in New York, money-wise. And Aunt Jane convinced her to come here to take care of her while also keeping an eye on me while I finish up at Argyll."

My head was swimming with all of it. "The Mosers got to stay on campus?"

She nodded. "Faculty housing."

"But he's like a fox in the henhouse. Don't you think he'll do it again?" I hadn't counted on that question striking as hard as it did.

"Yes. Yes, I do." Claire sounded as bitter as I'd ever heard her. "And it's so wrong. Strickland was the only happy place for me, after my parents split up. I was vulnerable that way. I wanted to connect with something good and real, and Jay was part of what I loved about a school that had always felt safe." Her voice was shaking a little. "Now someone else will be vulnerable. He destroyed me, and he'll destroy someone else."

I searched for things to say that would combat the rage burning in her. "Except you're not destroyed," I said finally. "You had a terrible, painful experience, and I can't guess how you feel about it, except if I think that maybe what happened to you is like my seizures." I pushed for my courage, knowing Claire needed it. "I've always thought of a grand mal as my fatal flaw. That it was always lurking and waiting to be this humiliating story, the main story about me. It's not till lately that I've been able to understand epilepsy as just another thing about me. A thing on the side, not the center. And it can't turn into the reason behind why I'd hide from everything, or the fear behind every risk I don't take."

Claire was nodding, listening. "I get that."

"So I hope what happened to you last year doesn't become the main thing about you. Neither of us should beat ourselves up with stories that make us feel horrible. Let those old stories crumble, because it's the new ones that matter. The new stories are all we need." I could feel my hand on my heart, but I believed it so much, it felt like a promise to us both.

# forty-nine

I spent another night at Claire's so that we could go into the city. Saturday night, we strolled South Street while devouring slices of brick-oven pizza. I confessed things at random. I told her about the endless tangle of my feelings for Matt, I told her about my confusing meeting with the Custis-Browns, I told her about my decade-long fantasy crush on Theo.

But on the topic of Jay Moser, I sensed that Claire was wiped out, and so I didn't bring him up until the next morning, when she dropped me off for my Sunday shift at Ludington.

"Send those letters to his house," I said as I popped open the car door.

"Wait—what?"

"Jay's letters. Get them out of your room. Stick them all in a giant envelope, address them to Stephanie Moser—or better yet

Mrs. James Harrington Moser, and send them off. He's her problem, not yours. Let her have them."

"Oh my God. Imagine."

"Yep. Imagine."

And I hoped, as I shut the door, that maybe she would. As much as I wanted to help Claire, I really didn't have anything by way of advice. It undid me to picture him strolling around the Strickland campus while Claire's life was a netherworld, living with her batty aunt Jane and with no real plans beyond running west, once she was finished with Argyll.

Claire's thumbs-up for art school was no surprise. The shocker for me was when I mentioned RISD to Mimi and Gage.

"I say go for it. Art is something you never claim," said Gage. "You should. It's something you are just so crazy good at that you never acknowledge."

"Yep. Total claimlessness," agreed Mimi. "I'm so psyched the Custis-Browns called you out. I can just see you in your future studio in SoHo with hairy armpits and a nose ring."

"Eww," I said, though I liked the studio part.

But I still hadn't done anything more about it by later that week, when my mom and I were in my parents' bedroom, folding laundry.

"Strangest thing," Mom began, already sounding so self-conscious that I looked up.

"Strangest thing what?" I asked.

"Just that Phil and Jean Custis-Brown had a bizarre conversation with me today. Jean has some nerve, not even working here this semester. But they cornered me in the faculty lounge and told me that they both passionately believe you should go to art school. Those words exactly. *Passionately believe.* They spoke in a very aggressive way. Honestly, I felt attacked." Mom reached in for a pair of Owen's jeans, bisected them, then squared them into his clean laundry stack. "I told them that it was up to you."

"You did?"

"Of course I did."

"Is it?"

"I mean"—Mom sighed—"of course it is. If you want to make a silly mistake without any sort of adult perspective about how life actually works. Then, yes. That is your youthful mistake to make, with Dad's and my blessing."

The grinding twist of a fight was inside me. I snapped a wash-cloth from the basket. "Jean said in twenty years, she never gave anyone a ninety-six in art before me."

Mom made a sympathetic face. "Lizzy, I get it. You have growing pains. And I'm sure art feels like a wonderful escape and even a rebellion, when you work so hard on your core subjects. But once you get into Princeton, I think you might feel differently."

"I could take some art classes at Princeton. Art feels like a bigger thing than an escape."

"However the muse moves you." Mom rolled her eyes slightly. "But the point is, the odds of becoming some superstar like Keith Fairley—that's a complete lotto ticket. I would caution you not to throw away your future to make a point to Dad and me. Because we'll still love you, no matter what. Even if you fail. But there you are, failed. And where did all that arty rebellion get you, in the end?"

The noise in my head was too loud. Later, when I'd cooled down, I was able to see the fault in her argument. Later, I had a hundred perfect comebacks. But not in the moment. "Keith Haring, you mean," was all I said. "Keith Fairley is one of Owen's friends from Little League."

# fifty

THEO WAS GOING TO Bermuda with the Kims for spring break.

"Sure you can't join, Bliz?" he asked. "Violetta's doing this all-girls trip down to South Beach, but my friend Clark's coming, and it'd be a good-friend foursome with you and Mimi."

"I know, I know. Mimi gave me the rundown. But it's just way too expensive," I told him. "I've still got extra hours at Ludington, and this isn't the best time to run up debt now that I'm pretty much out of it. But I really wish I could go." When the call waiting beeped, I knew it was Matt, and I almost didn't pick up except that Theo had to get off, too.

Theo's calls were so rare, usually just for information—like this one. But my thoughts drifted back to it, even as I flipped on with Matt to hear about how much he was dreading going away with his family to Hilton Head, where he'd been half a dozen times before.

It was exciting to think Theo wanted me along on the family trip—and it didn't feel like he was exactly asking me to round out a *friend foursome.*

"You should hang out with Dave this week," said Matt right before we hung up. "Since you're around all spring break, and Claire's going to be in Florida."

Dave still felt too much like a stranger. "Tell him if he calls, I'll pick up." But I wouldn't be making the first move.

That call came in sooner than I'd thought, on the Friday afternoon that school let out.

"We're spring break's leftovers, Lizzy," he said. His voice was deep and gravelly, unfamiliar enough that I'd snapped to attention. "We should make the most of it."

"Sure," I said. "What's going on?"

"That would be nothing. Want to meet up? Get depressed together that we're not on the beach drinking piña coladas?"

"A misery-loves-company date?"

"Exactly."

"Cool. I hate piña coladas anyway."

I took the train into Suburban Station, walking distance from the patisserie Dave had suggested. He was already there, reading the *New York Times.*

"So what's the news?"

"Not much. This guy's gone." He let me see what he'd been reading, the obituary of a famous photographer, the one who'd sometimes dressed up like a woman or the devil. I thought of the last time when I'd been out with Dave, and how he'd made fun of the skinny guy with HIV, when underneath all the time, he must be so freaked out by this new world order of men dying everywhere we looked, and him hardly allowed to react to it, except to joke it off.

Dave signaled the waitress. We ordered hot coffees and decided to split some fluffy pastry things, a cheese followed by blueberry. Then he folded up the newspaper and gave himself a minute to stare out the window at the gray snow crusted high on the sidewalks.

"Do you think about it? Like it could happen to you?" I asked softly.

"Yeah, sure I do," he answered. "But I also grew up knowing something was going on. Dad's lost too many friends to count. He stopped taking me to funerals because he said no kid should have to attend that many."

"I didn't know your dad was . . ."

"Out? He's not at work. But my mom died when I was in second grade—cancer, and Dad wanted to be honest with me about them. That they'd had this quickie relationship and then agreed to be friends and raise me together, that she would have accepted me for who I was, because she totally supported my dad. All that."

"Do you think Matt will ever do it?" I asked. "Come out, I mean? To anyone besides us? Like, to his parents?"

"No." Dave's face quickly turned scornful. "No time soon. I met the Ashleys last summer, when they picked up Matt from camp. He was even petrified to introduce me to them. As if just by meeting me, they'd know his dark secret."

"Was there anything between you and Matt?" I looked him in the eye. "Ever?"

"We've only held hands. It's a lot to admit, though, holding hands, and I was his first." Dave smiled. "But Matt and me, we're meant to be friends. When I met you at my Halloween party, I really hoped it'd work out with you two. Matt sees you as a soul mate. He wanted it all so badly." Dave's smile was sad.

"Sometimes I think Matt feels guilty that I fell in love with him," I said.

"Sometimes I think you feel guilty that you made Matt know what love feels like," said Dave.

"Either way, love can be a pretty big responsibility." We caught a glance at each other; somehow I knew we both were thinking about Jay.

"That tool." The notch of Dave's jaw tightened as he shook his head.

"And the fact that he's still there. No punishment, nothing."

"When Claire first told me the story, I almost mailed him a bag of dog shit."

I burst out laughing, but later I'd remember this moment as Dave's and my first—though not last—conversation about it.

Over those next days, the idea began to cast its spell.

*We could do it like this*, I'd start. Dave would listen in that way I was coming to know, a slight left-side tip of his head and his face stone still.

"Or . . ." he'd say.

Or or or. There were so many *or*s.

We liked talking about it. We liked finding and dismissing our options. All week, whatever we were doing, going to the movies, browsing the vintage shops, searching racks and barrels for the Clash or Sex Pistols T-shirts, strolling whichever of the city's campuses we'd wandered into, testing this new frozen yogurt or that salad bar, Dave and I were always talking about it.

The plans changed shape a few times, but the idea stuck.

"It's crazy," I said as we stood in the aisle at Blick Art Materials. By now, we'd finalized most everything. We'd even set a date: two weeks' time, April Fools', and that Dave's station wagon (solidly crap) would be our car. When Matt and Claire returned from their spring break trips, all they'd need to do was hear the plan, then get in and go with us.

"It's only kinda crazy." Dave picked up a canister and shook it to hear the ball bearing rattle inside. "More importantly, you're the artist. What color?"

But he knew it already, because he was holding a can of purple.

Purple, the color of poison.

# fifty-one

MATT DIDN'T WANT TO do it.

"This is a problem," I told him.

"If we got caught for this, my parents would cut me off. No questions asked." Not for the first time, it seemed to me that Matt waited for our phone calls to say the things that he had a harder time expressing in person.

"What, you think mine would be cool about it?" It was late, and I'd stolen down to the kitchen. One thin wall separated my parents' bedroom from the upstairs den. I preferred a whole extra level of distance whenever I talked about the plan.

"It would be a sin, in their minds," he answered. "My dad hasn't talked to his sister in fifteen years, over some fight they had—and I couldn't even tell you one thing about it, except that I'm a hundred percent sure Dad thinks God is siding with him.

If I got caught for this, my parents and God would *not* be my cheering section."

Into my silence, he said, "Come on, you know how much I want to be part of this, Stripes. But I can't risk it. You think you three will be cool without me?"

"I guess. But it wouldn't be the same." Our plan without Matt in it didn't even feel right. Whenever Dave and I hashed out our plan, we'd seen ourselves as a foursome.

So when Dave's station wagon crept down my block at the appointed time that Saturday night, and I saw Matt in the front seat, a jolt of joy ran through me.

"You're my hero!"

We grinned stupidly at each other. As I hopped in and slung my overnight bag next to me, I wondered if this was the real magic of the foursome. That nobody was more "with" one person than another?

It also felt okay for me to reach out in that old familiar gesture and let my fingers graze the back of Matt's neck.

He angled back, just as he always had. Caught my fingertips and kissed them.

Claire, our final pickup, was waiting for us outside, probably guarding the guys from entering her house, or keeping Aunt Jane at bay. But they didn't seem curious, and Claire was electric as she leaped the distance to the car. Like the rest of us, she wore a dark hoodie paired with black jeans and soft dark sneakers. Everybody was dressed the same, my idea. My reasoning was that if any-one saw us—not that we anticipated it, at such a late hour—we'd be confusing for eyewitnesses. Privately I'd liked the symbolism, that we were four interchangeable bodies all coming together in this night.

But now I wondered: Were we interchangeable, or was tonight a completely different thing for each of us? I believed in the artistry, Matt saw rebellion, Claire needed vindication, and Dave wanted the dare. In the end, of course, it didn't matter. What we had in common was that we'd all shown up for one another.

The radio was on, and we'd decided that finding stations was the job for shotgun. We'd all memorized the route, too, with a bathroom break once we were ninety minutes in. We stretched our legs at the McDonald's parking lot, and dove into the take-out bags as we started the final stretch north.

"Want to hear something that'll freak you out? I heard apples in McDonald's apple turnovers are actually potatoes cooked in corn syrup," said Dave as he polished off his last bite. "It's cheaper for them, because potatoes don't go rotten. Potatoes can sit around for, like, years."

"That sounds like an urban legend," I said.

"If it is, I'm okay with it," said Claire. "I can totally handle eating old potatoes pretending to be apples."

"Yuck," I said. "Old, sitting-around sweetened potatoes? I'm not sure everyone would."

"You think people would feel betrayed by fake apples?" Claire glanced at me through the rearview. She'd switched seats with Dave at the McDonald's. We were all taking turns driving, even me. In some ways, I was more anxious about this piece of the plan than anything else. Every time I thought about driving for two hours on the highway, my heart started pounding, and I could feel my flushed chest warming up the wispy tin chip of my dog tag that I'd started to wear.

"Well, I know *I'm* definitely grossed out and betrayed by potatoes impersonating apples," I said. "Though it's also hard to gauge people's different freak-out levels."

"I think Walt shot himself because he tested positive," said Matt.

Nobody spoke.

Claire's glance at me in the rearview confirmed that no, she'd had no idea, either. Light-headed, I dropped my chin and closed my eyes, but there didn't seem to be any easy way to absorb what Matt had just said. Even he seemed to know how shocking he'd been. "Sorry," he added. "I guess because we were on the topic of freak-outs. It's something I've thought about for so long. Too long, I guess."

Dave whistled through his teeth. "Damn."

"It's nothing I know for a fact," Matt said. "When he'd first started talking about it, I thought he was being paranoid. He'd caught the flu in September, and his roommate had mono, so for a while, Walt thought he had mono, too. But the last time I saw him, I asked him how he was feeling, and he told me he'd been to Student Health and he'd got tested and he was waiting to hear back.

"He seemed restless, and he was really focused on this photography project. He kept saying there was no way he could ever have gotten sick. He kept repeating that part. It was like he was practicing that sentence to tell his parents. Which made me think—later, not at the time—that he already had the results. I keep rewinding it and replaying it in my mind. I wish I'd had the balls to speak up. It felt impossible to come out and ask him what was going on. But I knew, *I knew* he was more messed up about it than he was giving away."

I was confused. "So his parents never knew if Walt might have killed himself because he was sick?"

"He cut it off at the pass," said Dave.

"I go back to our last conversation a thousand times a day. Maybe I didn't ask because I didn't want to know? I felt so helpless, totally unable to handle it."

"You can't beat yourself up about this, Matt," I said softly.

He shook his head. "Yeah, actually, I can."

"I'm glad you're here with us tonight," said Claire after a moment. "*That* took balls."

We exited old Route 9, the road we'd traveled since we left the interstate, and the passing town was so quiet it seemed abandoned. Dave finally broke the silence by changing the crackling radio to a pop hit by New Kids, one of those songs everyone simultaneously despised yet could sing every line.

It was like we couldn't take on all of it at once—Walt, illness, suicide, injustice, payback. And so instead of thinking of everything, for a couple of minutes we went hard at nothing, filling up on music as the station wagon pulled us through a moonlight spiked by gathering anticipation for all this night might mean.

# fifty-two

As we passed a sign pointing us in the direction of Strickland's ice hockey rink, it all plowed through me. Tonight would be something I'd remember forever. For almost the entire drive, in the casual talking, in balling up fast food bags and listening to Dave's exaggerated burps, in scratching at itches and shifting positions and endlessly searching the radio, I hadn't focused on that.

Now it was real. We were here. We'd come up around back, Claire at the wheel and routing us above the campus so that we could make a shortcut getaway, once the deed was done. As we dipped around the bend, I caught sight of Strickland's shadowed, rolling landscape. The puritan New England saltbox houses, the stylistic modern additions, the clean-cut playing fields. The picturesque sweetness of it all.

"Okay, folks. Tipton Lane, next left." Claire spoke under her breath. Dave, in the passenger seat, spun the volume down to nothing, and I took hold of the plastic Blick Art bag, capturing it tight on my lap. Was Keith Haring an artist or a vandal? Plenty of people thought both. But there wasn't any way better than graffiti to get a message across when you'd been left with no way else to say it.

Claire parked us under a tree about a hundred yards from the street of Victorian gingerbread houses with wraparound porches.

Faculty row.

Our target house, luckily, didn't have the extra obstacle of a porch.

Claire had mapped out three alternative exits. She'd also briefed us on everything beforehand—both of them tended to turn in early, their yippy dog slept in the kitchen; the glow of the television didn't necessarily mean they were awake.

It was a two-story, peaked-roof house with a long lawn, and a front door painted pale as putty. Per the plan, Claire would hit the front and Dave the back, while Matt and I both acted as guards, alert to the unexpected anything. Once Claire cut the engine, I distributed the canisters of paint.

My heart was charging. I'd never been more terrified of something going wrong with the mechanics of me. Seizure. Heart attack. Blacking out.

So far, I appeared as normal as the rest of them.

We crept in all at once, and then the guys vanished around back, leaving Claire to dart up to the front door while I hung in the shadows, gripping my canister, eyeing their fence-post mailbox.

330 • adele griffin

Fifteen seconds, we'd reasoned. How long did it take to tag a door with a seven-letter word? I heard Claire start. The sound of spray paint was like air hissing from a punctured tire.

I couldn't think about it too hard. I shook my can—*Do it!*—and then I pressed the nozzle. The sudden spurt of ink surprised me as much as my ease with these letters, all capitals, a purple jet, dark as blood.

Had I ever written this word before?

But now the Mosers' dog was yipping excitedly. Time was up, the guys appeared, now we were sprinting, my heart pumping as the house took shape from the shadows, a pop of light in multiple windows, our sneakers pounding across the yard, a shove of bodies back into the car, Matt's whispered "Lessgo lessgo lessgo!" as he turned the key in the ignition, doors softly slamming as the engine sprang to life like a startled bear, Claire pointing us toward the shortcut country road that would take us off campus to safety.

We were gripped and silent, all we wanted was more and more distance between the car and our crime. Even after we'd left the grounds, we were still holding on to the shock of it. It was only as we reached the interstate exit that Claire allowed a tentative whistle. And then we all were whooping, laughing, our voices overlapping as we started retelling the story.

We'd done it. We did it. It was done.

"I tagged the mailbox!" I bragged at the same time Dave yelled "I tagged the lawn!" But my gaze also kept straying over to Claire. She hadn't been to Strickland in almost a year. It must have been so strange for her to return in this way, under the cover of night, with these plans of revenge. I couldn't tell what she was thinking. Maybe it wasn't my business to know.

Matt and I switched seats at the Exxon, and I was surprised by how calmly I took over, how assuredly I met road rules, how easily I remembered my brights and my turn signal, how neatly I finished a merge or decided a yellow.

I was a good driver, maybe? At least I could vouch that I was an attentive one, bolt upright in my seat, letting myself exhale a small sigh of victory only once we took the exit onto the Pennsylvania Turnpike.

This was it. The real way to enter the city.

It was almost two in the morning by the time we arrived at Dave's apartment. I wanted to sketch us all as we appeared, identically dressed and totally shot in the mirrored-glass elevator. Inside, we silently stripped the bed and sofa, and then made a nest of pillows and covers for us all to collapse inside. My hand reached out automatically for any hand, and the press of limbs was so comforting, even the act of sleep itself felt so knotted up in our togetherness that I wondered, as I drifted off, if we'd be sharing one another's dreams.

# fifty-three

MONDAY IN HOMEROOM, CLAIRE was all smiles as she bounced over to me, her fingers snapping like rubber bands around my wrists. Seeing that light in her face made any unease I'd had about getting caught and in trouble all worth it.

"I couldn't call you yesterday because it was too late," she whispered. "But another Strickland senior, a friend of mine, phoned last night to tell me about a pretty major April Fools' prank that got played at Mr. Moser's house. Nobody can talk about anything else!"

"Do they have any leads on who did it?"

"Luckily no," Claire said. "It could have been a bunch of kids from the town. But the prank was kind of personal, so they're thinking it was seniors."

I nodded thoughtfully. "Seniors do get up to mischief in the spring. What kind of a prank was it?"

"Just some graffiti, but it was super embarrassing for Mr. Moser and, of course, everyone in the entire school knows. As a matter of fact, a lot of people were shocked to learn that Mr. Moser is a pervert."

"And now even the mailman knows," I added. "Oh, poor Mr. Moser!"

"Poor, poor Mr. Moser!" Claire shook her head in mock dismay. "Also, his wife will be getting a package of letters, to add to his troubles."

"How sad."

"Very sad!" But then Claire's expression turned serious. "If she reads those letters, she'll know that something is wrong with him. That he pretended to be one kind of person, a safe person—when all along he was so dangerous. And if he goes after another girl, he'll do it the same way, with charm and letters and all that phony safety. When I dropped that package in the mailbox, Lizzy, I felt like I was sending her a warning. And I knew it was the right thing to do."

Claire wasn't aware that she'd been squeezing my wrist so tightly as she spoke, and as she released her hold, she laughed self-consciously. But I was happy for her grip, and even for the faint mark that held my skin a while after, because it made me feel so strong and present for her.

Later that day, I zipped over to the upper fields to watch the varsity lacrosse game, where Claire and Gage were bringing the team ever closer to the Inter-Ac League championships.

Jonesy and Kreo had broken up over spring break, so none of the usual Lincoln guys were in the bleachers, but I cheered for Kreo anyway. She'd never be a friend of mine, but she wasn't really just another bitchy Nectarine to me anymore, either. And slowly, over that week, I let myself shake off the last of that unreasonable nagging in the back of my mind that some tipped-off cops might show up at my door, or that I'd be summoned to Mrs. Birmingham's office for an inquisition about my whereabouts on the night of April first.

When nothing like that happened, part of me wished something would. We'd achieved something wild and perfect that night. We'd made a pledge to right a wrong, and we'd executed it with total success. The blight of Claire's year, and the punishment that fell so wrongly on her shoulders, would always leave me feeling upset about Strickland. None of the so-called grown-ups had protected her when they should have.

But I felt deeply satisfied, like we'd restored a tiny purple karmic chip in the universe, whenever I thought about Jay Moser walking out into his perfect spring morning and seeing the truth staring back in his face from his doors, his lawn, his mailbox.

PERVERT

PERVERT

PERVERT

PERVERT

We'd done that.

I would never regret that.

# fifty-four

THE NEXT SATURDAY, MIMI and I drove all the way up to Norwalk Community College, where Gage was competing in a fencing tournament. It was something Mimi and I had been planning for a while. I'd mentioned it briefly on the phone to Theo since Yale wasn't too far, but I was as surprised as his sister when he strolled into the college gym.

"Theo?" Mimi was on her feet. "What are you doing here?"

"Don't get too excited." Theo's expression was perfectly nonchalant as he approached us, but I could feel my every nerve on end as he climbed the bleachers to join us. "I've never seen her compete."

"How did you even know about it?"

"Gage never stops yapping about her fencing. I'm here for proof. Let's find out if this girl's as good as she says she is." Theo put his fingers in his mouth and whistled through his teeth at Gage, who was on the floor practice-jousting with a teammate. When she looked our way, he raised his voice above the din. "I'll take you out for pizza if you don't totally embarrass us."

Gage lifted her mask. "Nobody invited you, Theo!" Her face was suffused with delight. If Mimi suspected anything was slightly weird about the fact that Theo had shown up in Norwalk for Gage's fencing competition, she wasn't speaking up about it now.

What Mimi also didn't know, but I did, was that after spring break, Theo and Violetta had decided to take some time off from each other. He'd called last week and we'd stayed on the phone for over an hour, and even though the conversation was about Violetta, we both knew something between us was changing, or would.

Maybe even today, it was shifting. Even in this pretend-casual way we were sitting next to each other on the bleachers, all this spark in the space that separated us as we watched Gage. Her fencing style was so excellent that when she took fourth foil, I got a little teary.

When we all jumped to our feet to cheer and stomp, Theo's eyes held mine just that second longer, before we glanced away.

After the match, we hit a pizza place in town, where Theo and I sat next to each other again. Theo's forearm, resting on the table, touched mine by a hair. Nothing suspicious, but my own arm felt like a bar of magnets drawn to his. We split a large cheese pizza plus an order of garlic knots and buzzed through an intense discussion of Star Wars trivia that was just as dumb and fun and easy as ever. Mimi, Gage, Theo, me—old friends who knew the old me best. Except that I also felt completely new.

Later I waited with Theo for the check as the other girls headed out for the parking lot. Nobody seemed to think that was unusual, either. I was just keeping Theo company. But after the check came, and he paid and signed, and we ducked out through the side entrance, we both knew exactly what we were looking for—a single stolen private moment. He stepped toward me and quickly bent to brush my lips with his. His kiss lit me up like a flame in the darkness.

"Guess I've been meaning to do that for a while," he said.

I moved forward and kissed him back. "Me, too."

Then we just looked at each other. A little bit shocked. We'd known each other for so long. Was he also thinking how it was impossible to know the shape of this brand-new door we were opening on our story? Except that nothing was supposed to stay the same forever, and the timing felt right, and so did the butter-flies—and right now that was enough for me.

# fifty-five

MATT SWORE HE WASN'T worried about it. "I hardly even think about it," he'd said more than once. But the thing was, he'd brought it up on the phone too many different occasions, and I was starting to get skeptical.

"It was last spring break," he told me over the phone. "It was just casual." On another call, he let slip more details. The guy's name was Ryan and he was older, a college kid. And they'd been safe. "But seriously, I almost never think about it." The third time he brought it up, he said that he didn't know anything much about Ryan—and that they'd been *mostly* safe.

"Can't you get ahold of this guy, Ryan?"

"Nah, that's not gonna happen."

"Never?" I questioned.

"Uh-uh," Matt answered crisply. "But, I mean, I hardly think about it. I don't know why I brought it up."

Brought it up *again*, he meant. Had this thing with Ryan been a brief encounter, or maybe a few? I had more questions. I didn't pry.

But when Matt brought it up for a fourth time, I was ready.

"Listen," I broke in, "you're thinking about this a lot. It's seriously on your mind, and my advice, for what it's worth, is that if you want to be one thousand percent sure that you never have to worry, doubt, or overthink it again, there's a health clinic right on Broad Street that can give you test results in twenty-four hours. It's all privacy protected, too. You don't have to give a social security number or a phone number or anything."

"Really? How do you know?"

"Because I called over," I said. "I was asking for a friend."

I could hear tension in his laugh. "Stripes, you get me better than I get me."

"It won't be a big deal," I told him, though of course I had no idea. I wanted to be brave, but how could I not be a little worried myself? I knew you couldn't get it from a kiss, but what about that night in Valley Forge? Did that qualify as risky behavior? "You're just going to get the test to learn that you don't have it," I said calmly, to assure us both. "But I think you should take a friend along for support. If you want, you can pick me up at school on Friday, and we'll do it together. Then we go back Saturday for results. They don't tell you on the phone, because you need to show ID."

"Huh."

I could feel my advice, unwieldy, a little bit unwelcome in his brain. "It's a solid plan, Matt. Let's do it together."

He let go of a slow breath. "This has been giving me some stress. I mean, I know I'm okay. Mostly I know that. But if I could, yeah, not think about it anymore . . . and you're sure you're cool to come with me?"

"Yes. If not this weekend, next. Whenever you're ready."

Matt was in the senior lounge that Friday. After we went into the city, and he took the test, we attempted to shake off the mood by hanging out for a while, dropping into a Chinese noodle shop for dinner, and then a vintage poster store where we discussed how we'd decorate our dorm rooms next year.

The next day's return trip was different. We were quiet most of the way.

"It sucks to think about Walt doing this all by himself." He sat back and cracked his knuckles down the line. "Although I guess some of the worst things you do are also the loneliest."

"For what it's worth, I'm right here," I reminded.

"For what it's worth, I love you," he answered.

The words were so unexpected we both burst out laughing.

"I love you back," I told him, meaning it.

We found free parking on a street a couple of blocks up from Broad, an easy walk. April was greenly budding in trees whose species names I didn't know, which all seemed to share a living-monument splendor as guardians of the city.

"Funny to think those results are somewhere," Matt said, almost to himself. "In a tube. Marked with a label. As yet unknown by me." He pushed through the reinforced glass door, and then held it open.

tell me no lies • 341

*"I'm* not worried," I told him as I slipped past. "You're only getting it done so you can stop thinking about it, remember?" I knew my chirpy confidence had been helping Matt, easing him along, and since being a worrywart would do no good, I kept my fears to myself, holding back yet again for more about this lost Ryan, who happened to share Walt's middle name.

The waiting room was crowded. We'd be here awhile. After we checked in and settled into our seats, Matt leafing through and tossing one magazine after another, I imagined that tube, too. Marked with his name, all his fate contained within it.

"Next month, Theo's coming home for the summer." I knew I was chatting to distract myself. I'd told Matt a little bit about Theo and me. I really didn't want any more secrets with Matt.

"Oh, yeah?" Matt tossed his magazine on the table. He seemed glad for the distraction of some conversation, too. "Have you broken it to Mimi?"

"Not yet. I'm going to tell Gage first. See how she thinks I should approach."

"Yeah, maybe it'll be easier if she gets good news from Berkeley."

"Ugh, I keep forgetting college acceptances went out this week." I slumped back in my chair. Was I getting in anywhere? Nowhere? I'd finished the RISD application, too, but I hadn't pulled the trigger on mailing it, and I wondered if I ever would.

At my side, Matt had become very still, impassive, yet looking so sweet and soft and young, drawing me back, as he often did, to the first moment of our meeting, all those years ago. That inexplicable spark in me when I'd first caught sight of him at the mixer. The cartwheeling sense that he was about to fall into my life just like that crooked little fire-opal heart, loose and precious and not yet fashioned into any traditional, predictable shape.

I reached up and brushed my fingertips light against the nape of his neck.

"I'm so afraid, Lizzy," he said suddenly, turning to me, his eyes holding all that wildness of his soul. "I'm not ready for the wrong answer."

"Neither am I," I admitted.

"I'm glad you're here with me."

"Me, too." I threaded my fingers through his, and then he closed his eyes, and I closed mine, and we waited together for whatever came next.

# Acknowledgments

IT TAKES MANY PEOPLE to make a book! A big thank-you to:

Elise Howard, brilliant and beloved, for your razor-sharp insights and delightfully unexpected editorial what-ifs. From our thinking-out-loud lunches to the elegant precision of your letters, comments, notes (and notes on the notes)—all the way down to the very last round on the whole kit and caboodle, my heartfelt thanks.

All the wonderful people at Algonquin Young Readers, where I feel so lucky to have landed: Sarah Alpert, Jodie Cohen, Brooke Csuka, Debra Linn, Ashley Mason, Michael McKenzie, Lauren Moseley, Craig Popelars—what an amazing group. With an extra thanks to Robin Cruise and your copy editor's eagle eye. It was so fun homing in on the big eighties together.

Emily van Beek, my agent, and to Folio Jr. It's been such a pleasure to work in partnership-friendship with you, Emily, and I am always so appreciative of your advice and expertise. Thank you!

My writing community—ever-texting with Julia DeVillers, Sarah Mlynowski, and Christina Soontornvat reminds me how lucky I am to be in this business. And big cheers to my YA writing lunch bunch, in no order (but plenty of disorder that keeps the day so bright)—Jen Smith, Micol Ostow, Anna Carey, Lynn Weingarten, Michael Buckley, Morgan Matson, Robin Wasserman, Bennett Madison, Siobhan Vivian, Melissa Walker, and an extra big thanks to Jenny Han, night owl extraordinaire.

My dear friend Courtney Sheinmel. I'm so grateful for your notes on the political and social climate during the AIDS crisis, and our conversations were such a bonus to this book. I know your thoughts came from a deep, personal place—thank you for your wisdom.

Priscilla Sands, my mother, who taught theater at my high school, and who couldn't be more philosophically different from Lizzy's mom. I have friends who hold cherished eighties memories of Mom taking students via minivan into Philadelphia for performances of *The Normal Heart*, facing down all attendant controversies, so firm was her faith that this play deepened our understanding of a plague that devastated and stigmatized too many. While her pre-GPS sense of direction might have made these journeys extra challenging, she was always steadfast in her compassion, empathy, and trust that art sees us through the darkest hours.